THE RETRIBUTION OF EDEN PRUITT

THE RETRIBUTION OF EDEN PRUITT

BOOK 4

K.E. GANSHERT

Cover Design by Courtney Walsh

ALSO BY K.E. GANSHERT

THE CONTEST

THE GIFTING SERIES

The Gifting, book 1

The Awakening, book 2

The Gathering, book 3

Luka, a book 1 companion novel

THE EDEN PRUITT SERIES

The Fabrication of Eden Pruitt, book 1

The Aberration of Eden Pruitt, book 2

The Retribution of Eden Pruitt, book 4

For Mr. Carpenter

If only the world had more people like you! Thanks for making such a positive impact in the lives of your students.

RETRIBUTION

THE ACT OF PUNISHING

FOR WRONGDOING;

VENGEANCE

1

Before the hatch opened, before the giant climbed down the ladder with a girl slung over his shoulder, Tycho—first-born of the Electus—was having a dream. A wonderful, beautiful dream. He wasn't in captivity, being poisoned by the enemy. He was diving off the dock into the harbor on a hot summer day. His powers had just come in. He was the first of his kin to receive them. Intoxicating strength. Thrilling speed. Incomprehensible reflexes. He was showing off, and Aurelia was amazed. Enraptured. Soon, her powers would come, too. The promise made her giddy.

To be interrupted from such bliss set his teeth on edge. Dreams were the only good thing in his life anymore. Increasingly rare. When they slipped away, he was left not only with this unbearable pain, this excruciating weakness, this mind-numbing monotony, but a soul-sucking despair that made him yearn for a more permanent sleep, one from which he could never awaken.

Tycho—beloved child of Pater and leader of his special army—was living the same torturous day over and over again, and there was nothing he could do to make it stop.

Here, suddenly, was a change in that day.

Something new.

Something suspicious.

The giant stomped across the room with a scowl and set the girl in the corner. By now, Tycho knew the giant was named Asher. Tycho also knew the unconscious girl was named Eden. They'd been together—Asher and Eden—right here in this room not too long ago, when bombs fell two and a half miles south of their current location. The betrayer, the snake, the backstabbing demon named Prudence Dvorak had been missing among their ranks. Tycho didn't know where she was, nor did he know the name of their location. Even if he did, he couldn't communicate it with his siblings. The poison had stripped him of this ability. The poison had stripped him of all abilities.

When those bombs fell, his hopes had been rejuvenated. He was positive they belonged to Pater, who'd finally come to save him. But then the bombs stopped and his torture continued. His hopes were crushed. His thoughts grew dark and heretical.

Pater had abandoned him.

Pater didn't care about him.

If he did, he would have come by now.

Tycho's mind was a battlefield.

He had to fight the heresy. This was a test, after all. A trial. He must not fail. He needed to remain faithful. He needed to fight against the contamination. To keep his traitorous thoughts at bay, he took to silently repeating long passages from the sacred book. He clung to their truths. And he stoked the fire of his hatred. He let it crawl through his veins like an army of red ants. He would have his revenge. Somehow, some way, he would escape. He would kill the snake. He would end her life, like he was always meant to do. Then he would rejoin his kin and he would lead them as they carried out their purpose.

Until then, here was something new.

Another break in the monotony.

This girl. Being bound like he was bound. She released a delirious, pain-soaked moan as the giant finished securing her ankles. Her skin was pale, her eyes closed, her hair matted with sweat. As if …

No, that couldn't be. A regular person wouldn't survive the poison they'd been injecting in his veins.

Their death would be immediate. And why would they inject her when she was on their side?

"You're just going to leave her down there?" someone hissed from above, through the opened hatch in the ceiling.

Asher clomped to the ladder. "What else is there to do?"

There was a pause.

And then, "I don't like this. It's not right. She isn't like him."

"She's exactly like him," he replied in a flat tone. "She's just been lying about it all this time."

Tycho narrowed his eyes.

First at the giant.

Then at the girl.

"Set your timer, Nairobi. She'll need another dose in four hours." With his face as grim as his voice, Asher climbed up the ladder and closed the hatch.

Tycho pressed his back against the wall.

Another dose?

What trickery was this?

He shook his head, unwilling to be such a fool. Whatever game they were playing, he would not fall for it.

2

Eden Pruitt awoke in pain. A deep ache throbbed in her bones. Needles ran through her veins. Ice picks split her skull. A groan slid up her parched throat. She fought against the lethargy, convinced something of vital importance was impatiently waiting for her to gain consciousness. With every ounce of strength she could muster, she pried her eyelids open.

Quadruple vision turned into double vision, and finally—double vision came together into one congruent picture. She was inside the underground bunker in the east tower of the IDA, with its pallets of water and boxes of protein bars and hairline fractures running up the walls. She was slumped in one corner. And she wasn't alone.

The asset sat on the other side, watching fastidiously.

Clarity came in a burst.

Panic grabbed her by the throat.

They'd poisoned her. In the boardroom. After tranquilizing Cassian. All because she told them the truth—who she really was. *What* she really was. She'd been stubbornly confident in her decision. So much so, she ignored Cassian's misgivings—just like she'd done before, when she and Cleo decided to follow a tunnel to see where it went. Now he was in trouble all over again.

So was she.

Poisoned by the Resistance. Locked up with an enemy soldier. Oswin Brahm's five-star general. Eden tried to move, to reach into her back pocket to see if the gadget she was using to communicate with her parents—with Barrett and Violet—was still there. But her hands and feet were bound. She attempted to pull her wrists apart—to snap the plastic digging into her skin—but her hands were too heavy to lift from her lap. She couldn't decide what was worse—the unbearable pain or this incapacitating weakness.

How long had she been down here?

What did they do to Cass? Where was Cleo?

And what about her parents? She'd been waiting for them to contact her. Had they tried? Had she missed their call? Were they staying in a safe house that was no longer safe, waiting for her to reach back? The world was on fire. A deadly toxin was attacking the cities on Cleo's map. First Minneapolis. Next Madison. Then Milwaukee. Her parents were out there somewhere. By last count, in Chicago. With Mona the betrayer.

The asset watched her struggle—mentally, physically—with his head slightly cocked. She tried to imagine enduring this repeatedly, like he had for the last month and a half. The Resistance had been torturing him right under her nose while she ignored the maltreatment. And now, it seemed, they were going to do the same to her.

Eden looked at him, dismayed at the amount of energy it required. So much so the effort squeezed her eyeballs. He blurred in and out of focus, but here was what she could grab:

He was eighteen, three months younger than herself. His blonde hair was shaggy with neglect. His scruffy facial hair was a deeper gold, thicker on his chin than anywhere else. Clear blue eyes, high cheekbones, a sculpted jawline. Her attention moved up the length of him, from his leather boots, to his rugged cargo pants, to his waffle-knit henley, past his clavicles, up to his perfectly symmetrical face. He was approximately six feet tall, which made him slightly shorter than Cass, but nowhere close to Asher.

Asher.

Fury coursed through Eden at the thought of him. She ground her teeth. Or at least, she tried. He had the body of a pro-athlete and the mind of a grandmaster. He was the creator of the Amber Highway, Oswin Brahm's biological son, and a perpetual thorn in Cleo Ransom's side. He'd taken part in the ambush. He'd bum-rushed Cassian with a needle.

"What are you doing here?" the asset asked—suspiciously, accusatorially—the tilt of his head deepening. He stared with such unmitigated focus, his next dose had to be soon. "Why have they locked you up with me?"

Eden didn't know what compelled her. Some random grain of information planted by her best friend, Erik Gaviola, who had—once upon a time—taken a keen interest in cults? Because of that interest, Eden knew the steps required to combat extreme indoctrination. Identifying yourself as part of the in-group was one such step. Or maybe it had nothing to do with Erik and his obsessions. Maybe it was a deep-seated belief exposed in the throes of her weakness—that at her core, this *was* her true identity.

"Subject 006," she croaked in a voice so weak it was barely audible.

His eyes rounded. "That's impossible."

Eden huffed.

Impossible.

So many *impossible* things had been happening lately, she stopped believing in the word. Oswin Brahm, the true villain. Violet Winter, somewhere out there without a Queen Bee. Cassian, free and alive. At least he had been before this unexpected turn of events.

"The original six were destroyed," he said.

"Not … all of them."

He studied her like she'd just told him blue wasn't blue or water wasn't wet, his suspicion multiplying by the millisecond. She didn't blame him. Why should he take her word for anything? She was part of a group that had tied him up and tortured him repeatedly. At least, she thought she was part of that group. Now, however? Clearly, she'd thought wrong.

She tried again to pull her arms apart, to break the ties around her wrists, but it was no use. She had zero strength. Her head fell back against the wall, her attention landing on the camera mounted in one corner of the bunker. Someone would be watching—monitoring her like they'd been monitoring the asset. Were they waiting to poison her again? If so, when was the next dose?

"How long does this last?" she rasped.

"How long does *what* last?"

"The effects … of this poison." She took a painful breath and whimpered on the exhale. Whatever cocktail they'd created made oxygen feel like sandpaper in her lungs. But she couldn't very well stop breathing.

He narrowed his eyes. "You are good at this."

"At what?"

"Lying."

"I'm not ... lying."

"That is what a liar would say." He smiled a humorless smile and shook his head. "Whatever information you are trying to get, I will not give it. You can keep me down here for the next ten years, and I won't give you anything that could be used against Pater."

Pater meant father.

Eden pictured her own dad—the way his eyes crinkled when he smiled, his easy laughter, his generous affection, his corny jokes—and a fresh wave of pain seized her. "Is he really ... your father?"

"He's responsible for my existence."

She pulled in another breath, then gritted her teeth and looked at the hatch. "What about ... your mother?" she panted.

He pursed his lips.

Eden considered the pamphlet she and Cassian had found in the Bryson's safe, with a long list of names on the back. All of them women. *Magnes Matres*, they were called. Great Mothers. "Was she .. a martyr ... for the cause?"

"She wasn't a martyr for anything." He delivered his answer like a snap, drumming up curiosity in her, color in him. It rose in his cheeks as he closed his mouth and glanced away. Eden recalled the information Francesca Burnoli had shared when they'd been trapped together in another bunker. A more secure bunker. One that existed beneath the White House.

There were ninety-four soldiers in Oswin Brahm's army. But only ninety-three names on the back of the pamphlet. Prudence Dvorak, leader of the Resistance, was not listed among them, even though she had given birth to a soldier.

Despite her cloudy thinking, the insufferable pain, understanding curled into an icy fist in Eden's stomach. "Is Prudence … Dvorak … your mother?"

His expression soured. It was all the answer Eden needed. She didn't know how it worked—how, exactly, this army had been conceived. A plethora of question marks surrounded the particulars of this sickening cult. But here was one answer—Prudence Dvorak had given birth to this young man. Did she know he was the baby she had delivered? Did she know this was who she was torturing? Nausea rolled through her gut.

There was so much she wanted to tell him. A tirade of truth. A waterfall of facts. Oswin Brahm was an abuser, a mass murderer. He'd killed millions, including the Great Mothers, who never had to be martyrs at all. They died because Brahm tricked them into drinking poison. His dear father was the villain. But how could she convince this boy of that when she'd aligned herself with a group that was torturing him?

She swallowed, her throat sore and tight and painfully dry. "What's your name?"

"Why?" he snapped back.

"I'd like … to call you something … other than 'the asset'."

He seemed to consider this, as though rolling the answer around on his tongue like one of Cleo's candies. In the end, he kept the name to himself. All the while, her head throbbed. Her eyes ached.

Was this going to be her life now? Trapped down here without Cassian, without Cleo, without her parents or Barrett or Violet or any answers. Ever. Just this underground room and this young man and a fresh round of torture every four hours?

Her soul curdled at the prospect.

Above, a bolt unlocked.

The hatch opened with a groan.

A ladder slid through the hatch.

Nairobi climbed down into the bunker. She was a tall, athletically built Black woman. Eden didn't know her well, but she seemed like a nice enough person. And yet, she held a syringe in her hand. She'd been tasked with administering the poison—one so cruel Eden would rather walk through the seventh level of hell than be injected a second time.

"Nairobi," Eden said, a quavering plea in her voice. "Please …"

The young woman refused to make eye contact. But there was a crumple in her brow, a frown on her lips that told Eden her conscience was at war. She knew what she was doing was wrong.

"Where … is Cassian? What did you do to him?"

Nairobi didn't answer. She looked staunchly away as she advanced upon the asset.

Panic rose in Eden's chest. It wrapped its cold fingers around her neck as if Nairobi were advancing upon *her*.

The asset strained. He bucked. But he couldn't get away. His restraints were too strong, his body too weak.

Nairobi held him down and inserted the needle. The sound of his screaming filled every crevice of Eden's mind.

3

Thud.

The sound reached deep into the depths of Cassian Gray's subconscious. He struggled to follow it, to fight toward the surface like he had when he was at the bottom of the Potomac.

Thud.

One eye cracked open.

He was lying on the ground, the left side of his face heavy against a cement floor. The room was dim. His arms were asleep. He tried moving them, but his wrists were bound behind him, and for one terrible moment, he was back in his prison cell, staring down the barrel of execution.

Thud.

He rolled onto his shoulder, trying to locate the noise, and there—beyond dusty shelves and several metal filing cabinets—stood Cleo, pounding on a door. His muscles went weak with relief. This wasn't prison. He searched through the dark abyss that was his memory, trying to figure out where he was and how he'd gotten here. What was his last memory?

Eden.

After weeks of separation—deprivation—he'd been with her. Stubborn, foolhardy, beautiful Eden. But then she'd willingly put herself in harm's way. She had divulged the truth to these people who wanted her dead. There'd been a new development, so he'd walked with her and Cleo to the IDA. And then?

Thud. Thud. Thud.

He bolted upright and quickly discovered his ankles were cuffed like his hands. He kicked his legs like a bucking horse and landed his boots hard against a nearby filing cabinet.

Cleo spun around. "You're awake!"

She hurried toward him on the ground.

"What's going on?" he demanded, his tongue thick from the tranquilizer.

"They're idiots, that's what," Cleo answered. "Complete and utter idiots!" She shook her fist at the door, as if the idiots might be standing on the other side.

"Where is Eden?" he asked.

"They put her with the asset. They injected her with that awful poison after they tranquilized you. Didn't bother to tranquilize me, however. No restraints, either." She held up her fists with a look of maniacal outrage. "I guess I'm not big enough or strong enough or *man* enough for such consideration."

"Cleo." He spoke her name in a low rumble. Now was not the time for one of her tirades. Not when his head was swimming, his heart thudding. Over that word. *Poison*. "What poison did they inject her with?"

"It weakens them somehow." Her eyes narrowed into slits. "It causes pain, too."

Outrage stretched through his muscles until every fiber hummed with fury. He was going to murder them. Every single one. "Get me out of these," he said, jerking against his restraints.

"Trust me, I've tried. Unfortunately, I don't have superhuman strength." She stalked to the door and rattled the knob, kicked the wood. "Asher, if you leave us in here for one more second, I swear to Mother Teresa, I will smother you in your sleep!"

The door swung open.

Despite the bold declaration, Cleo took a startled step back.

Asher took an aggressive step forward, ducking slightly like he might hit his head on the door frame if he didn't. He wore an expression that was equal parts triumphant and grim. "I breached her network."

The monster inside Cassian roared awake. If Asher

had breached Eden's network, how long until he found the self-destruct function? Once he found it, how long before he used it? Cass bucked again, landing another blow against the filing cabinet.

But Asher didn't even look at him. His attention was fastened on Cleo. "It took me two hours and fifteen minutes. How along did it take your pal, Jack?"

"You could have asked her!" Cleo picked up a heavy duty stapler and hurled it at his head.

Asher ducked.

It sailed through the open door and thudded against a wall.

Cleo closed the gap between them. She squared off with the giant—toe to toe, but nowhere near eye to eye. "I cannot believe you're doing this."

Asher glared down at her like his emotions were every bit as hot and snarly. "*You* can't believe? We let her in. She sat in our meetings. We allowed her to join us, and she was lying the whole time."

"She wasn't forthright with her identity. If memory serves, you weren't forthright with yours." Cleo leaned back on her heels and folded her arms. "For someone who despises his father, you sure are acting a lot like him right now."

Her accusation was gasoline to fire. He looked mutinous.

But Cleo didn't even flinch. "I guess it's true when they say the abused often turn into abusers."

Asher's neck corded. His nostrils flared. His fists clenched, like he was two seconds from raising his hand and proving her point. Cass twisted his behind his back, his own anger bubbling beneath the surface. If Asher so much as laid a hand on Cleo, Cass would make him pay.

"Enough!" Dvorak swept into the room, her ink black hair streaked with a few strands of silver. Upon hearing the news of Amir Kashif's death, she had fallen to her knees in anguished lament—a moment of weakness in the back room of an old man's speakeasy. Ever since, she'd covered that grief with focus and enmity. Now here she was, stepping between Cleo and Asher like a referee between rounds. "If you want to be angry at someone, be angry at me. He was following my command."

"Your command was moronic," Cleo spat.

Dvorak's beetle-black eyes flashed. "I don't know your friend from Adam. I only know that when she showed up, I lost nearly everyone. And now, my oldest friend is dead." Her voice broke. She closed her eyes, like she was broken, too. But then she exhaled, lifted her chin, and unfolded a metal chair leaning against the wall. "We did what we did as a precautionary measure. I couldn't have one of Brahm's mutants roaming about."

Cass ground his teeth. Eden wasn't a mutant.

"I had no idea the council would be so divided by such precautions." Dvorak set the chair on the floor with a sharp tap. "Or that we'd get absolute hell from one very irate Editor-in-Chief."

"He's ready to burn the place down," Asher said, his attention flicking to Cleo.

"I hope he does," she retorted.

Dvorak held up her hand. "We don't have time for this. We're here to fight Oswin Brahm. Not one another." She turned to Cass and motioned toward the chair. "We have some questions."

When he made no move to get to his feet, Asher clomped across the room. He heaved Cass up by the armpits. Cass reared back, prepared to head-butt Asher like he'd head-butted the guard, but Dvorak issued a warning. "Unless you want Eden to be on the receiving end of another dose, we're going to need your full cooperation."

Asher shoved him into the chair.

Cassian seethed.

"If not for you, I'd still be at the bottom of the Potomac," Dvorak said, a sharp hint of annoyance in her voice, like she didn't want to owe him anything. "You must have been very convincing to get Amanda Hawkins on our side, which means you would be a credit to the Resistance. If only you weren't such a liar."

He glared.

"I told you my story. It's time you tell me yours. The true version."

"What do you want to know?"

"Everything about Eden Pruitt."

"So you can use it against her?"

"So we can have a better sense of what we've gotten ourselves into." Dvorak crouched in front of him. She set her elbows on her knees and folded her hands. "How are you two connected?"

"I was hired to find her."

"By Nicholas Marks?"

"By a bookie named Yukio at the request of Nicholas Marks. Apparently, her network came online, which meant she wasn't dead. Marks wanted to present her to the Monarch."

"Along with Subjects 003 and 004?"

Cass nodded. "I didn't know anything about Swarm or Oswin Brahm. I was just trying to pay off a debt."

And thus, earn his freedom. That was what he'd cared about back then. Before his life collided with Eden's. Before she turned everything inside out and upside down. Bringing color when there was none. Tenderness and passion, too—the kind that reached deep inside his stone-cold heart and forced it to feel things he hadn't in years.

"You found her."

He nodded again.

"Why didn't you hand her over?"

The heat in his chest intensified. He pictured Eden in San Diego, standing on the edge of a cliff at night—her arms spread wide, her chin lifted as though daring the wind while it tousled her hair. He pictured her smiling with Erik, laughing with her father, playing board games with residents at an assisted living home. "Because she was innocent."

And good.

Meanwhile, he was rotten fruit from his father's tree.

Dvorak cocked her head. "She said she attacked her parents."

"Only because I gave Marks her location." A selfish decision that nearly destroyed her. After she watched the footage—after she realized she had harmed her parents—she'd all but come undone. Cass could still feel the weight of her file as she set it in his hand, exposing herself even then. Trusting him—a complete stranger—with such classified information. All because she didn't want to put *him* in danger. When it was *he* who had put *her* in danger. Bile burned the back of his throat. "Believe me when I say she would have rather chosen death."

He pictured her in his apartment, sitting on his bed—pale and resolved. She invited him back into her life because she needed someone to take her out of the ring. They'd found a way to do it. A self-destruct command. It didn't scare her. On the contrary, it had come as a relief. Because she would rather die than hurt anyone.

The ache in his chest sharpened into an unbearable point. His love for Eden had become an invisible hand that punched through his sternum and grabbed him by the heart. Was this how his father felt about his mother? The intrusive question slithered through his mind. It wrapped itself around his neck and squeezed.

Dvorak was talking, but he couldn't hear. Not over the ringing in his ears. She was asking a question, waiting for him to answer. But he couldn't answer. He could hardly breathe. His collar was too tight, but he couldn't loosen it. His arms were trapped behind his back, and there wasn't enough oxygen in this box of a room. It was too small. Like his prison cell. Like that closet.

Cleo set her hand on Cassian's shoulder—a gentle touch that loosened the chokehold around his neck. He inhaled while she answered on his behalf. "Eden wants to destroy Oswin Brahm as much, if not more, than anyone here. She has more ability to do so in her left pinky than you and Asher combined."

There was a moment of consideration—a face-off between Dvorak and Cleo, wherein Dvorak seemed to measure Cleo's words. "Even if that is true, we remain at an impasse. So long as she can be controlled, she remains a threat."

"We could use the magnet," Asher suggested.

The magnet.

Strong enough to put Barrett Barr and Violet Winter to sleep for three whole months. Strong enough to do the same to Eden. Asleep, she'd no longer be able to put herself in danger. She'd no longer be able to do anything. Like help her parents. Or fight against Oswin Brahm. She would never forgive him if he didn't do everything in his power to prevent such a fate. But then, what did it matter if she forgave him? Should this war end and they both survive, he could conceive of no possible scenario in which he belonged in her world. He was a washed up fighter with no legal identity, and a mountain of rage rotting him from the inside out. If his goal was to keep her alive, the magnet would do the trick.

But Dvorak shook her head. "We already talked about this. We need her system online. It's the only way you can study her network."

"There is another option," Cleo said. "A way for you to have your precautionary measures with access to her network, and her cooperation, too."

Dvorak crooked her eyebrow. "What is this magical option?"

"Go fetch one of the nurses at Kaiser, and I'll be happy to tell you about it."

4

The asset roused with a name on his tongue. He muttered it over and over like a verbal talisman with the power to save. Eden was so intrigued, he had barely opened his eyes when she pounced with the question.

"Who is Aurelia?"

His face paled. His pupils dilated. His chest labored to breathe. Eden grimaced on his behalf. Oxygen no longer felt like an enemy in her lungs, but she remembered the pain well, and she never wanted to feel it again.

"How ... do you ... know that name?" he asked between labored breaths.

"You were calling for her."

He closed his eyes.

Eden shifted, more alert now that the worst of the

pain had subsided. She was still too weak to break the ties around her wrists or ankles. But she could hold her head upright for extended intervals without feeling sheer and utter exhaustion. "Is she a member of the Electus?"

Eden could hear the elevation of his heart rate. It only solidified her intrigue.

Aurelia.

So they did have names.

She hadn't been sure. Maybe they were all assigned numbers. She'd been eighteen months old when Dad found her. There'd been no name in her file. And when Mom begged for her life on the rooftop of The Sapphire, calling Eden by name, Mordecai had responded angrily.

She has no name until she is given a name!

The soldiers had been given names.

At least, this Aurelia had.

Eden studied him. His skin was pale and clammy. His lips, dry and colorless. Even so, he was still handsome. Still a picture of perfection, if not a struggling one. In any other setting, he'd be the guy she would take pains to avoid. He was too pretty. Probably too popular. But this wasn't any other setting. He was a soldier, like her. A super freak, as Cleo would say. Their nature was the same, but their nurture couldn't have been further apart. How had he been raised?

She tried to imagine it. Ninety-four superhuman

soldiers brought up together. Indoctrinated together. And yet, of all those soldiers, the asset had called out for only one. Oswin Brahm had murdered the Great Mothers to keep his soldiers from forming attachments to anyone but himself. Call her crazy, but she didn't think he would approve of his general's attachment to Aurelia.

"Are your feelings for her romantic?"

A blush crept into his cheeks.

Eden worked hard to keep her expression clear of distaste. If she wanted to gain this boy's trust, she couldn't express judgment. She didn't know how he'd been raised, or whom she might develop romantic feelings for if she'd been raised like him. She only knew how she, herself, had been conceived. Via in vitro fertilization. She'd existed in a state of limbo as a frozen embryo. Oswin Brahm had stolen her and—by the sound of it—hundreds of others from IVF clinics.

Ever since learning this truth, she'd pictured her preself growing in a test tube. Not until she learned about the Great Mothers and the Electus did she consider the possibility of a surrogate. Was this what the mothers were—surrogates? Or were they biological mothers? If so, was Oswin Brahm their biological father?

Bile rolled up her throat.

She swallowed it down. "Are all of you biologically related?"

He glared at her—suspicious, skeptical. He wouldn't give her any useful information. He had declared as much, and wouldn't even divulge his own name. Eden didn't expect an answer. When he gave one, she sat up a little straighter.

"No," he said.

Eden wet her lips. "So, Oswin Brahm isn't actually your father?"

"He is in every way that matters."

Despite his weakness, despite his obvious pain, the asset's voice rang with conviction. Eden understood his conviction. Her dad wasn't her biological father, either. But that didn't make him any less her dad.

"I'm surprised," she said.

"Why?"

Because Oswin Brahm was a narcissist, among other things. She would think he'd want to spread his seed far and wide. She swallowed the accusatory words. They would get her nowhere. "You say he's a father in every way that matters. Why not make himself a father in every way, period?"

"His mother was an addict."

Eden blinked. She knew this, thanks to the thick tome that was Oswin Brahm's biography. Brahm would have the world believe his son was an addict, too—a dead one. A tragedy that made Oswin all the easier to root for.

But his son wasn't dead. He was alive, and currently holding Eden hostage.

"Addiction can be hereditary," the asset continued, his voice weak. "He didn't want us to inherit the predisposition."

"So … no defects?"

"Not a single one."

The hatch above them opened.

Eden's blood ran cold. Was it time for another dose already, when she was only now feeling somewhat human? She pressed her back against the wall as the ladder descended.

Asher climbed down.

A scream ballooned in her chest.

No.

They couldn't do this.

She couldn't endure it.

Her body broke into a cold sweat as another person climbed down into the bunker after him. Cleo's nurse from Kaiser. He held something in his hand.

She sucked in a breath and tried to press further away, but the wall would not allow her. She cursed it. She cursed her restraints. She cursed her weakness. She cursed *them*.

"We aren't going to hurt you," Asher said, holding up his meaty paws. "No needle. See?"

"What is that?" she asked, her wild eyes on the contraption in the nurse's palm.

"It used to be an insulin pump."

For diabetics.

"It contains a lethal dose of tranquilizer."

Eden's careening heartbeat slowed. The sharp, panicked pain in her chest abated.

"It was Cleo's idea," Asher said.

"Cleo," Eden replied with a fast, loud exhale. "Is she okay?"

"She's fine."

"And Cassian?"

"He's fine, too."

"My parents. Did they—have they called?"

"Not to my knowledge."

The fountain of relief pouring through her stopped. *Not to his knowledge*? What reason could there be for such a delay?

Asher nodded at the nurse. "He's going to attach this to you, and we're all going to move on from this debacle together."

Eden glanced at the nurse under discussion. He stood by the ladder like he didn't want to get any closer. Like she was a contagion. A leper. Or a cold-blooded killer waiting to pounce on her next victim.

"She won't hurt you," Asher said.

The nurse looked at her as though waiting for verification.

Eden confirmed with a shake of her head. It was a ridiculous thing to confirm. Her hands and feet were tied. She had no weapon. She was too weak to lift anything, let alone her own arms. But even if she had her full strength, she wouldn't hurt him. She would never hurt any of them. They were the ones who had hurt her.

The nurse took several tentative steps forward. Then he dove in, making quick work of connecting the pump —this one attached to the back of her upper arm. The one she'd worn while staying with Dr. Norton had been attached to her abdomen. As soon as it was in place, he scuttled away and scurried up the ladder, leaving Asher alone with her and the asset.

"We didn't want to do what we did," he said, removing a switchblade from his boot. He flipped it open. "But there didn't seem to be another choice. You were keeping a pretty huge secret that put all of us at risk."

"If I told you, you wouldn't have let me help."

He grimaced, like he knew it was true, and cut Eden's ties.

She rubbed her wrists.

She could feel the asset's stare boring into them. He thought this was a charade. He thought they were lying to get information from him. Now that they were releasing her, did he still think so?

Asher cut the ties around her ankles and pulled Eden to her feet.

The world spun.

She felt weak and woozy.

He offered his support by grasping her elbow. "Most of the effects should wear off by the twenty-four-hour mark."

She cupped her forehead, which had gone clammy all over again. "If that's true, why do you inject every four hours?"

"Precaution."

More like cruelty.

Eden took a shaky breath.

The asset continued watching them. A boy who loved a girl named Aurelia. "What about him?" she asked.

"What about him?"

"Can we get him a pump?"

Asher scoffed.

Eden bristled. She had been complicit in his torture. She had looked the other way. Ignored the brutal treatment, as if doing so would make it untrue. All the while, he had been enduring hell. At the hands of a woman who had carried him in her womb. Eden felt sick.

She pulled her elbow from Asher's hand and showed the asset the pump. She explained how it worked. It was filled with a single dose of tranquilizer, strong enough to incapacitate the wearer should the need arise. It didn't hurt. It didn't impact her abilities at all. But it did come with a remote—possibly several—that could activate the pump from a safe distance. Surely, after months of torture, he'd be inclined to take the peace offering. But he only glared from her, to Asher, then back again. "If you try attaching that to me, I will use the first chance I get to kill every single one of you."

5

Eden could barely make it up the ladder. Her arms and legs felt like lead. According to Asher, she had several more hours of this weakness in front of her. Thankfully, a good chunk of those hours would be spent sleeping. She'd never been so enticed by a bed in all her life.

But first, she needed to get to Cassian. And Cleo. According to Asher, they hadn't yet been released. Apparently, he was too volatile; he had murder in his eyes. Asher seemed to think Eden might be able to tame him.

Eden wasn't sure.

She pictured him in the boardroom, looking through the windows into the courtyard. At her. His cheekbones, pronounced. Chiseled from weeks of prison food. He had cuts and scrapes and dark circles under haunted eyes. Her chest had pinched tight—with need, with desire. She wanted to erase those dark circles. She wanted to take away his pain. When they came together —his body pressed against hers—her heart felt like it might explode. The memory of it made her skin flush. But he'd stopped too quickly. He'd stepped away. He created distance. In her frustration, she made her declaration and their blissful reunion came to an end. She needed to stop hiding who she was. She needed to tell the Resistance the truth. So she had, and now here they were.

Eden wasn't a fool. She knew his brooding aloofness was a front, behind which lay anger. Hot and seething, the bulk of which wasn't directed at her, but his father. And Mona.

She braced herself on a hand rest inside the elevator as it crawled up the shaft, bringing them from the basement to the ground floor. She felt woozy. Off-kilter. Nauseous. Like her mother had when she'd been struck with pneumonia three Christmases ago. As someone who had never been sick in her life, the sensation was a very vulnerable, unwelcome feeling.

Asher kept eying Eden warily, like she was going to barf on his feet at any moment. When the elevator lurched to a stop, she thought maybe she might.

The doors slid open.

Prudence Dvorak waited for them outside, flanked

by Nairobi and Dayne. The former looked contrite; the latter nearly collapsed with relief. He stepped around Dvorak and took Eden by the elbow in an offer of support.

"See," Dvorak said, her tone thick with aggravation. "She's going to be just fine."

"She doesn't look fine," Dayne said.

"It'll wear off."

Eden wobbled. Dvorak coming in and out of focus. She forced her eyes to focus and asked her question in a tumble of accusatory words. "Are you his mother?"

Dayne went still beside her.

Dvorak's expression remained stalwart. Outwardly, nothing changed. But inwardly? Her heart rate doubled. Her breath quickened.

Eden's mouth hung open. Dvorak knew exactly who she was torturing. Eden shot a look at Asher and Nairobi, wondering if they knew, too. Judging by their lack of confusion or surprise, she deduced they did. "I can't believe you are doing this to your own son."

Dayne made a choking sound. Apparently, he hadn't received the memo.

"He is no such thing," Dvorak said.

"You gave birth to him."

Dvorak pinned Eden beneath a contemptuous stare. "He is nothing more to me than the leader of an army designed to do unfathomable harm. You can be appalled.

You can give him your sympathy. Just know that I have none. He is a means to an end. That is all."

The hatred within her was astounding.

So over the top, Eden couldn't help but think of the famous Shakespearean quote from Hamlet. *The lady doth protest too much.* Perhaps it was easier for her to feel angry and hateful than address whatever lay beneath.

Dvorak pulled a remote from her pocket. She handed it to Nairobi. "Nairobi has agreed to stand guard outside your door for the night. Come morning, we will have to establish a rotation."

Dayne scoffed. "This is so over the top."

Dvorak turned on him. "Do you not understand what she is capable of?"

He took a breath and opened his mouth, ready to issue his retort.

Eden set her hand on his forearm. "It's fine," she said. She wasn't offended. She wasn't even upset. Unlike Dayne, she knew very well what she was capable of. They could take all the safety precautions they needed if it made them feel better. Truth was, it made her feel better.

"If you wouldn't mind communicating how fine you are to Cassian and Cleo, that would be most appreciated. We really don't have the time or the energy for a riot."

Another scoff from Dayne.

But Eden nodded.

"Tomorrow, after I meet with the council, Asher and I would like to conduct a thorough examination."

"Of what?"

"You."

Eden shrugged in compliance, too spent to respond in any other way.

Dvorak nodded curtly and excused herself. With Dayne's support, Eden followed Asher and Nairobi, struggling to keep her eyes open, each step labored as she trudged down a hallway.

Finally, Asher opened the door to a storage room and Cleo was upon her, bombarding her with a hug so fierce, she nearly bowled Eden over. She held on to keep from collapsing, then spotted Cassian over her friend's shoulder. Her breath caught at the sight of him, sitting on a chair with his hands cuffed behind his back.

Asher wasn't lying. There *was* murder in his eyes. Hunger, too. When Cleo let go, Eden had to brace herself against a cabinet. Weak from the poison. Lightheaded from Cassian's ravenous stare.

Asher held up a key. "Let's make this a truce, shall we?"

Cleo glared.

"Letting you walk free, even with that pump on your arm, requires an immense amount of trust on our part. Don't make us regret it." He handed Eden the key. "You're going to unlock him. The three of you will go to your apartment. All of us will get some shuteye, except Nairobi, who has volunteered to stand guard, and we'll start fresh in the morning. Does that sound good?"

Cleo continued glaring.

Eden gave a weak nod.

With the key in hand, she limped forward—toward the young man who refused to look away. Toward the young man who was devouring her with his eyes. She could read every one of his emotions—anger, exasperation, relief. She unlocked his ankles first. Then his hands. As soon as he was free, he lurched to his feet, the legs of the chair scraping the floor. He pulled Eden to him with such strength, she let herself collapse. Finally, she gave in to the weakness, the cloying lethargy.

Cass didn't miss a beat.

He swept her into his arms.

She relished the feeling of being swept.

"I've got you," he said, his voice a deep rumble in her ear as her eyes sank closed.

6

Violet Winter released the handhold she'd been gripping like a vise for the past twelve hours. Beside her, Barrett did the same. They dropped to the cement in the center of the road, flat on their backs, under the cover of darkness as the truck they'd been riding beneath ambled away. The pain in her fingers lasted only a moment. By the time she and Barrett rolled onto their sides and army-crawled behind a patch of bushes, the stiffness had disappeared too.

They crept forward to look down the embankment in front of them and beheld the scene below, bathed in moonlight. Tall fencing topped with barbed wire ran around a giant warehouse of a building. The fencing hummed with electricity. She watched the gates buzz and open. She watched the vehicle drive into the yard. She watched a team of officers in RRA uniforms drag

Eden's parents and Ellery's parents and Dr. Norton into the night.

But not Ellery.

She wasn't inside that vehicle.

She'd been shoved inside a different truck after being shot with a tranquilizer dart when they'd attempted to run from the Damen Silos. Cassian Gray and Eden Pruitt told them to run. The silos weren't safe. Mona wasn't trustworthy. But the warning came too late. They had been ambushed. Violet and Barrett got away. And now here they were, watching as Ellery's mom cried and Eden's mom cried and Jack Forrester demanded to know where they had taken his daughter. His nose was crooked and his face, covered in blood.

Another truck rolled through the gate.

More guards descended, dragging a second load of people into the giant, stark warehouse. Upon registering the sheer number of heartbeats inside, Violet gasped.

"Where did they take Ellery?" Barrett whispered, more to himself than to her. Like it was a puzzle he might actually solve, when in fact, they had no clue other than the single word an officer had said. *Command*. That could be anywhere. Just like Father could be anywhere.

He'd been taken, too.

Not by an officer of America's Resident Registration Agency, but by three superhuman soldiers who'd come looking for Violet and Barrett. Father had finally come home. He'd been drunk and irate. Violet hid in the garage, frozen solid with fear. Barrett had knocked him unconscious. The soldiers had taken him away. To the *Blockhouse,* which was as mysterious as *Command.*

Violet fisted the cold grass while her breaths escaped in puffs of white. What were they supposed to do now? They couldn't fight all those guards, no matter how special they might be. Even if they incapacitated them, what would they do with all the people? There had to be a thousand, at least, and they were in the middle of nowhere.

As if realizing the hopelessness of the situation, Barrett turned away from the scene. He sat on his bottom and draped his arms over his knees, and released a long, defeated sigh.

Violet mimicked his posture.

"I froze." He shook his head and tugged a weed up by its root. "There were only ten guards in Chicago. Regular guards. There was nothing super about them. And I just … I hid."

The guards had tranquilizer guns. That's how they'd gotten Ellery. If Barrett would have done something, they would have gotten him, too. That would have been an awful, awful thing.

"You were ready to help." Barrett's eyes welled with tears. "But I just stood there while that officer threatened to shoot Eden's dad."

Her insides twisted. Seeing Barrett so sad reminded her of Kitty, kicked by Father. And eventually, *killed* by Father. Violet rested her head on his shoulder, wishing she had some comforting words to give. She reached for her voice, but it had retreated again.

"I guess that's what I do," Barrett continued. "I freeze."

Violet frowned.

It wasn't true. Barrett didn't freeze when Father came back. He'd clobbered him on the head with a frying pan. She wanted to say so. But her words were trapped again. Pinned beneath a mountain of fear.

"Here I am, a real-life superhuman. Heck, we just clung to the bottom of a traveling vehicle for twelve hours straight. It wasn't any harder than strapping on a seat belt. But when it comes to a moment of actual heroism …" He dropped the weed and massaged one of his palms. "I hide in the dark and listen to an officer cock his gun."

Violet took his hand and gave it a squeeze. So what? He froze. She did the same when faced with Father. She didn't think she was capable of not freezing when faced with Father. It didn't make Barrett a bad person. It just made him … scared. Violet understood being scared.

He twisted around to look down the embankment. There were twenty guards outside, at least. Each one strapped with a gun that was menacing in size. Who knew how many more were inside.

Barrett took a deep, cleansing breath. Or maybe a resigned one. "I kept an eye on the signs as we traveled. *Fred* is short for Fredericksburg. According to Mona's map, there's a safe house nearby. Hopefully, they'll have a backpack I can borrow."

He gestured to his bulky coat, inside of which he'd stuffed half of Father's journals. He'd left the other half —the half he'd memorized—back at the Silos, inside the rucksack he'd been carrying them in. He was hoping to find answers in the journals. Namely, how had Father eliminated Violet's Queen Bee?

"Hey," Barrett said, as if just remembering something. He let go of Violet's hand and reached inside his coat. "I've been meaning to give this to you. But with all the running and hiding and holding on to the underside of a truck, I keep forgetting." He removed something from one of the pockets. It wasn't a journal, but a small booklet. Barrett opened it and Violet gasped, her hand fluttering to her mouth.

Because there she was.

Mother.

Not gone or lost.

She was right there, in Barrett's hand.

"I made it before we left Dr. Norton's," he said. "He didn't know how to fix the camera either, but he got the chip out from inside and he was able to transfer the pictures to his computer so we could print them."

Tears welled in her eyes. She blinked at Barrett, wishing she could say thank you. But her voice was too far gone. The moment Father's truck ambled up her old driveway, it retreated somewhere very, very deep. She took the gift—this precious, priceless gift—and tucked it inside her pocket. Right next to her heart.

7

Cass put himself through a rigorous workout. He moved from the treadmill to the pull-up bar to the rowing machine to the dip station until sweat poured down his body and the muscles in his arms and legs and back and chest howled. He pushed himself to exhaustion, like a man desperate to outrun his demons.

If only he were fast enough to outrun them.

The memory of his father, sitting in that interrogation room, would strike without warning—a sudden flash of lightning illuminating the disaster zone that was his mind. Ever since his father's visit, all the things Cass had spent the last decade repressing had rushed to the surface. No matter how hard he tried, he couldn't shove them back down again. They were there, simmering right beneath his skin, ready to boil at the slightest provocation.

He increased the treadmill's speed, his legs pumping. His arms, too. But his latest nightmare stuck to him like epoxy. He couldn't stop seeing it. Eden in a pool of crimson. Standing over her with a bat in hand, its metal barrel dripping with blood. Her blank, unseeing eyes as the bat clattered to the floor and he begged her to wake up.

He'd jolted from sleep drenched in a cold sweat with the sky still dark outside. The microwave clock had read 5:42 am. He'd lain there on the couch, trying to calm his breathing, reminding himself of the truth. He was no longer locked inside a prison cell. He never had to see his father again. He was free and Eden was alive, sleeping down the hall. He'd carried her there himself—filled with equal parts relief and madness. He thought that madness would vanish once they were together again. Only here they were—*together*. And the ominous storm just kept brewing.

Everywhere he turned felt perilous. The government knew about her. The Monarch knew about her. Now, the Resistance knew about her, too. All three entities saw her as a threat, which put him in the ring again. On high alert. Opponents closing in on all sides. He wanted to keep her safe, but how could he when she kept putting herself in danger?

He increased the speed once more with two high-pitched beeps. The incline, too. His ears pounded with blood. Dread crawled through his body like an army of millipedes wiggling under a rock as the memory flashed for a second time.

The monster in a business suit with his face buried in his hands, his shoulders heaving as he begged for forgiveness. *I loved her so much,* he had sobbed. *I didn't mean to kill her. I lost my mind.* Cass had lost his mind, too. During a fight, he killed an innocent man. A husband, a father. Cleo said the abused often turned into abusers. Was this his future, his inescapable fate?

With a sharp jab, Cass turned off the treadmill. He used a towel to wipe his sweaty face. He found athletic tape on the shelf and wrapped his hands. He moved to the punching bag, hoping the familiar movement might silence the condemnation in his head.

Several minutes later, the door swept open. Cass paused only long enough to glance over his shoulder.

Cleo walked inside. She was dressed in oversized sweats, her braids in a messy bun on top of her head. "You know," she said, taking a seat on a stationary bike nearby. "This would be a lot more fun with some loud, angry music. I can give you recommendations."

Cass kept punching. His breath came in hisses and grunts. The chains suspending the bag rattled.

"You're up early."

Jab, cross, hook.

Shuffle-shuffle.

"Was the couch not to your liking?"

Jab, cross, hook.

Shuffle-shuffle.

Cleo twisted her lips to the side. She twisted her ring, too, spinning the silver skull until it made a complete revolution. "Mona's a real piece of work, huh?"

Jab, body rip, hook.

Shuffle-shuffle.

Mona.

The sellout.

The betrayer.

The reason his mother was somewhere out there in an unmarked grave. At least, he hoped she'd been buried. He didn't actually know what happened to her body. He hadn't thought to ask when he was twelve and beaten to a pulp. Back then, he'd done his best to forget.

Cleo picked at the black nail polish on her pinky. "I spent, like, an hour thinking about it last night in bed. Wondering if I should be worried about my mom. The two of them are as thick as thieves."

Jab, uppercut, hook.

Shuffle-shuffle.

"I think she should be fine. Mona has zero financial incentive to turn her into the authorities. And as sick and twisted as this might sound, I think Mona actually cares about the kids at the silos."

Cass punched harder.

Jab, uppercut, hook, hook.

"She's not gonna find anyone else willing to provide healthcare for free."

Jab, uppercut, hook, hook.

"So, I think she should be okay. I just wish I could tell her *I'm* okay."

Jab, hook, uppercut.

"Speaking of *okay*..." Cleo dipped her chin. "Are you?"

He kept going. No more shuffling in between—punching harder and faster—until he struck with such force, the bag tore at the seam.

Shredded black foam flew into the air and landed on the floor.

Cleo blinked. "Whoa."

Cass turned away and strode to the garbage can, where he removed the tape. Despite the protection, his knuckles were bleeding.

Cleo extricated herself from the exercise bike. She came to stand in front of him and leaned against the wall. "Seriously, Cass. What's going on in your head?"

"Let's see," he said, tearing off more tape. "My scumbag of a father shows up out of nowhere acting remorseful. He cries about how sorry he is. How he didn't mean for any of it to happen. I don't know how you show up with a baseball bat in that scenario, but you know. He loved her, I guess. I land at the bottom of the Potomac. Nearly drown. Now here I am, with a bunch of people who want to destroy my reason for living. But she seems fine with it, so why shouldn't I be?"

Cleo bit her bottom lip.

He had just strung together more words than he had in a long, long time. It didn't make him feel any better.

Cleo folded her arms behind her back. "For whatever it's worth, I don't think they want to destroy her."

He huffed.

"Don't get me wrong. They handled this whole thing horribly. They panicked. They had what we might call an overreaction. But we have to move past it. I mean, we're kind of stopping a world takeover, here."

Cass dropped the ball of tape into the trash. "*We*?"

"Yes. *We*."

"How am I supposed to contribute?" Other than lurk about, feeling angry with Eden. In love with Eden. Worried about Eden. Jacked up in the head about Eden.

Cleo studied him, her eyes slowly narrowing before jerking her head over her shoulder. "Come with me."

"Why?"

"Just c'mon." She backpedaled toward the door. "I'm going to show you your contribution."

Cleo spread her arms wide. "Ta-daaaa!"

They were standing in the newsroom, which was just as busy as yesterday. A commotion of moving parts—each traversing with a sense of purpose and urgency.

Cleo took it all in with eyes that sparkled. "Here is the nucleus of a resistance that came before Prudence Dvorak. A resistance that didn't even realize they were resisting. They were just living their lives." She stepped aside as a middle-aged woman bustled past with an opened laptop balanced in one hand. "Off-the-gridders. Non-conformists. People who flip the proverbial bird at a government that has seriously crossed a line."

Cass scratched his temple. "You want me to write for them?"

"I want you to lead their patrons to freedom." At his look of confusion, Cleo dropped the theatrics. "Dayne thinks I should take charge of the Secret Passage, and I think you should do it with me."

"What's the Secret Passage?"

"The name we've given our very own Underground Railroad. Together, we're going to create a route that will get these non-conformists here before they are completely eradicated."

Cass looked around, then quirked his eyebrow. "Is

this a pity ask?"

"This is a strategic ask."

His quirked eyebrow arched higher.

"You know your way around technology better than most people here. Thanks to your tracking endeavors, you are well acquainted with the Amber Highway. You've always been a fast learner. And it's in your blood."

"What's in his blood?" Dayne had stopped beside them in the center of the bustling newsroom. He asked the question over the rim of his coffee mug before taking a sip. His hair was tousled. There were bags under his eyes. He was clearly sleep-deprived, but in an energetic sort of way, like a man who thrived off the work keeping him from slumber.

"America Underground," Cleo said. "Cass's mom used to work for you."

"Really?" Dayne perked. "What's her name?"

"Sarah Gray," Cleo answered.

Cassian's muscles had gone tight. He didn't like when Cleo sprang his past upon him without warning. He didn't want to talk about his mom, or see the blank look on Dayne's face when he failed to remember her. Which was what Cassian expected. His mother had an ordinary name. She'd never worked full time for *America Underground*. And the work she had done was a long, long time ago.

Except, Dayne's bleary eyes didn't go blank; they brightened with recognition. "Sarah Gray," he repeated, looking closer at Cassian than he had before. His attention wandered from Cassian's sweat-soaked clothes to his bleeding knuckles. "No kidding."

"You remember her?" Cass asked.

"How could I forget her? She was one of the best writers I've ever had the pleasure of working with. This girl here has a similar style." He hitched his thumb at Cleo. "Brutally honest with a keen sense of irony, wrapped up in evocative language that just *mmm,*" he moved his hand into a chef's kiss, "makes a person *feel.* You don't come across that kind of talent very often. When you do, you remember it. Any chance she'd come back and write for me?"

"She's dead."

"Oh." Dayne's cheeks went pink. Then he frowned. "I'm really sorry to hear that."

"It was a long time ago."

"Still." He released a long sigh, then lifted his coffee mug. "I'm sure she'd be happy knowing her son is here, contributing to the cause."

Cass felt doubtful.

But he also felt touched.

It was an odd sensation. Usually, talk of his mother dredged up anger. Rage. Regret. His memories of her too often boiled down to the way in which she died. But here, in this hectic, humming newsroom, he was reminded of the way she lived. She really did love to write. She'd found the work invigorating. Meaningful. Even after a long day of cleaning houses, then feeding Cass dinner and tucking him into bed, he would fall asleep in their small apartment to the sound of clacking computer keys.

Dayne tipped his chin in an encouraging, paternal sort of way, then continued onward.

Cleo took Cass by the arm and pulled him toward a cubicle in the far corner. She grabbed an extra chair and set it inside so the two were crammed next to one another, then she gave her hands a clap. "You can be my Finn. Remember Finn? You met him once."

The scruffy-faced, quirky kid in Cleo's dormitory. They'd ridden an elevator together. "He rambled about meet-cutes. Then he told me he wasn't gay."

Cleo laughed—a loud bark of a sound. "That sounds like Finn. Man, I miss that guy." She motioned for Cass to take a seat in a chair.

He looked down at his attire. "I should probably shower first."

"Right! You get yourself cleaned up, then meet me back here." She plopped down in the other seat and shot him a wink. "This is gonna be good, Cass. It'll keep us both sane."

8

Eden crept out of her room, wincing when a floorboard creaked underfoot. She'd never had a hangover before. How could she? She'd never consumed a drop of alcohol. But she had to imagine it was similar to how she was feeling now. Her body ached. Her head pounded. Given her genetic makeup, she wasn't accustomed to either.

She peeked through Cleo's half-opened door and saw a rumpled comforter, but no Cleo. She crept down the hall and spotted the corner of a blanket curled over the back of the couch.

Her stomach swooped.

Her memory of last night was spotty at best. As soon as she was released, her adrenaline crashed and the ensuing exhaustion had been indescribable. She did remember one thing. Cassian carrying her in his arms.

His strength—his steadiness—had lulled her to sleep. He must have carried her to bed, then made himself comfortable on the couch.

With a frown, she opened the bathroom door and nearly jumped out of her skin.

Cass wasn't asleep in the living room. He was right here, in the bathroom, wearing nothing but a towel around his waist. With a yelp of apology, she shut the door. Then stood there in the hallway, her cheeks flooding with heat. She scrunched her face, curled her hand into a fist, and tapped the center of her forehead. She blamed her discombobulation on the poison. It was obviously still in her system. Otherwise, she would have heard him inside.

The door opened.

Cass stood framed in the bathroom entryway amidst a backdrop of steam, his waist still wrapped in a towel. She tried not to gawk at his bare upper half, but it was hard to resist. His physique had always been chiseled, but even more so now after three weeks in prison. And that tattoo …

She remembered well the warmth of his skin as she traced it with her finger back in Dr. Beverly Randall-Ransom's kitchen. Another wave of heat rolled up her neck at the recollection.

"It's all yours," he said, avoiding eye contact. "I'll get

dressed in Cleo's room." He moved like he was going to walk right past her.

She said his name.

He stopped.

Not more than two days ago, she thought he was dead. She thought she had lost him. Then she discovered the truth—Cassian had survived. Yesterday, they were reunited. Now, she was standing here in this hallway not more than two feet from him, and yet, he'd never felt so far away. It made her chest tight. Her lungs, hot and scratchy. There were so many things she wanted to say to him, so many questions she wanted to ask. But what came out was this: "Did you sleep okay?"

"I slept fine." His attention dipped to the gadget in her hand. "Have your parents called?"

"Not yet." The answer stole the air from her scratchy lungs. What was taking them so long? Where were they? She hated waiting, and she hated this awkwardness, too. This blasted formality. She felt certain that if she reached out to touch him, he would move away. Where was the warmth, the familiarity, the intimacy they had established at the Miller's? "Do you want to grab breakfast?" she asked, tilting her head, trying to get him to meet her eye.

"I'm headed to the newsroom to help Cleo with a project."

"What's the project?"

"A way to get illegal residents to safety."

"Oh. Right." This had been discussed last night in the newsroom. Right before Eden dropped her truth bomb. "That's amazing."

He shrugged, like it wasn't a big deal. Then he shifted his weight and dipped his chin—a clear, nonverbal request for her to move so he could get by. Apparently, he was done with this conversation, and she wouldn't be receiving an invitation to join them. Her heart sank as she stepped to the side.

He let himself into Cleo's bedroom.

The door closed with a soft click.

Eden stood in the hallway, bereft. By the time she stepped into the bathroom, a lump had risen in her throat. She set the gadget on the vanity, demanding it to ping, while outside, she listened as Cass finished getting dressed and left the apartment. Without even a goodbye.

Eden swept into the open area of the IDA's basement with Nairobi on her tail. She eyed the portable freezer where the vials of poison were kept, then unsheathed the steak knife she'd taken from her kitchenette.

"Wh-what are you doing?" With a look of jarring alarm, Nairobi reached for the walkie-talkie clipped to her waist, or maybe she was reaching for the remote in her pocket. With one push of a button, Eden could be rendered unconscious.

"Relax." She lifted her hands unthreateningly. "I just want to speak with him."

"What do you need the knife for?"

"I told him who I was and he didn't believe me. I'm going to prove I wasn't lying."

Nairobi looked confused. And wary. Obviously unsure how a knife could prove anything.

"How long until his next dose?"

After a moment's hesitation, Nairobi opened the door to the enclosed booth nearby, where she and a team of others supervised the asset via surveillance monitor. She checked a hanging clipboard near the booth's entrance. "One hour."

"You can watch me the whole time. If I do anything you don't like, all you have to do is push the button on your remote." Eden lifted her eyebrows, giving Nairobi an opportunity to object. To unclip her stupid walkie-talkie and call for backup. When she didn't, Eden waited a moment longer, then pulled open the hatch and climbed down.

The asset was slumped in the corner like he'd been last night. His half-opened eyes tracked her sluggishly. She sat on the ground across from him, not more than an arm's length away. When he saw the knife, he shifted.

Eden didn't say a word. She held up her hand. She placed the blade against her skin. Making sure he had a clear view, she swished the knife downward in one decisive stroke, creating a deep slice through the middle of her palm. The pain was hot and sharp and not nearly as brief as she expected. Blood seeped from the wound and dripped onto the floor. For one unsettling second, Eden wondered if the poison had stolen her body's ability to heal at warp speed. But then, before a second drop could fall, the wound closed itself.

The asset gaped—shocked amazement slowly morphing into disbelieving horror. "How is this possible?"

Eden told him.

By the time she finished, his horror had only intensified. "How can you be on *their* side?"

It was *their* side, or the Monarch's side. Seeing as Brahm was a manipulative, narcissistic madman who wouldn't stop until he'd whittled the world into a swarm of people who worshipped him, her choice was them. But she couldn't say this. Not if she wanted to sway him to the truth. "They are trying to stop really awful things from happening."

"Pater created us. We owe him our existence."

You give him too much power.

The words belonged to her father, weakly spoken in the aftermath of two nearly fatal gunshot wounds. At the time, he'd been talking about the world's most infamous terrorist, Karik Volkova. At the time, they both thought he was the one who had given Eden her superhuman abilities. At the time, neither of them had the slightest clue there was an even more malevolent mastermind at play. Nevertheless, his words still applied.

He couldn't create human life. He could only alter it. You existed before him.

Perhaps this was true for Eden, but what of this young man in front of her? Had they begun as frozen embryos or had Oswin Brahm really willed the Electus into existence? He'd recruited the women. He'd induced labor so the children would be born on his favorite day of the year. Had he also arranged for their conception?

"And he does not want awful things to happen," the asset continued. "He wants a new world. A better world."

"*Caelum In Terra*?"

The young man's eyes sparkled at the phrase.

Heaven on earth.

Utopia.

It had to sound pretty amazing to him right about now, given his current condition. Eden folded her hands in her lap and tried to keep her tone benign. "How does he plan to create this better world?"

The asset recoiled. "You're trying to get information from me."

"No, I'm not," Eden said. "I'm trying to get you to see—or at least consider—that maybe Oswin Brahm isn't the good guy." Her tone was too sharp, her patience on the verge of snapping. She blamed Cassian and the stone wall he'd erected between them. If she couldn't tear that one down, she'd do her best to tear at this one. "He's raised you to believe in certain things your whole life, but they're lies."

The young man shook his head.

"He's killed millions." She expected him to deny this, too. Instead, his expression crumpled into one of deepest sorrow. He knew. He knew what Brahm had done, and yet he excused it. "You still think he's good?"

"You're incapable of understanding."

"Try me."

The asset drew in a long breath. "It was a necessity. A burden only he could bear. One that has taken its toll."

She stared incredulously.

"See?" he huffed. "Incapable."

"You're justifying the slaughter of millions."

"Their lives were contaminated. Just as yours is contaminated."

"With what?"

"Poison. Not as painful as the kind these monsters inject into my veins, but that only makes it more insidious. Everything Pater does—everything he will have us do—is to eliminate that poison."

Eden blinked at him. Flabbergasted. Dumbfounded. Not only by what he was saying, but *how* he was saying it—with complete and utter conviction, as if nothing else could be true.

Oswin Brahm had turned the world into a battlefield. People in the Resistance—anyone at all who wasn't part of Swarm—were poison. According to the asset, Brahm was attempting to eradicate that poison. In so doing, he promised his soldiers and his followers a better future. This current hellscape wasn't their home, so to hell with it. They were fighting for a new home, where some were included and most were expendable. That kind of thinking excused all manner of atrocities. The ends would always justify the means when utopia was at stake.

Eden lifted her chin. "What about the Great Mothers?"

"What about them?"

"Were their lives contaminated, too?"

"Of course not."

"Then why did he kill them?"

"He didn't."

"He did."

The asset shook his head. "They sacrificed their lives in order to bring forth ours."

"They didn't have to sacrifice their lives at all. They

survived labor. They only died because Oswin Brahm tricked them into drinking poison."

He stared back at her, unimpressed.

Eden grappled for proof. Something that might convince him she wasn't spinning a web of deceit. "If you really think they died in childbirth, then why did Prudence Dvorak survive?"

"She was physically stronger than the others. But mentally weak. Morally corrupt."

Eden studied him—this young man so sure he was right. She glanced at the camera mounted in the corner of the room. Then she nodded at the hatch in the ceiling. "Those people up there call you his five-star general."

His mouth flattened into a grim line.

"What does that mean?" she asked.

"I'm the leader," he replied.

"Why you?"

"Because I am the most like him."

She frowned.

"Pater does not have a mother, and I do not have a mother. At least, not one either of us can be proud of. He killed his, and some day, I hope to kill mine."

Eden recalled Brahm's biography. His father was killed in a riot. His mother turned into an addict. She was unfit. So much so, Oswin had been removed from his home and placed into foster care at a young, impressionable age. According to his biography, his mother died of addiction. According to this young man, she died because Oswin killed her.

"He could have made me a pariah. An outcast. Instead, he chose me. He placed me in a position of honor. One day, when he is no longer able, I will step in and take his place as ruler of the new world."

Eden narrowed her eyes. There was more at play. She was sure of it. A conniver like Oswin Brahm wouldn't make someone a five-star general because of sentiment. And yet, judging by the asset's pupils, by the rate of his breathing, the steadiness of his heartbeat, he believed his own words.

"Prudence Dvorak didn't survive because she was physically stronger," Eden said. "She survived because she didn't drink the poison."

"What reason would he have for poisoning them?"

"To eliminate attachments."

"We are allowed attachments."

"Like Aurelia?"

He blushed.

"Does he know the depths of your feelings for her?"

A muscle ticked in his jaw.

She had definitely struck a nerve. "Will he permit you to be together?"

"Once we've fulfilled our purpose. So long as my love for him remains primary—"

"Is your love for Aurelia secondary?"

He blanched.

"You didn't call for Oswin Brahm when you were sleeping. You only called for her." Eden continued. She pressed harder on the insecurity, determined to find a chink in the armor. "I don't think there is anything wrong with loving someone. I do think there's something wrong with making a person feel ashamed about it."

The muscle in his jaw worked harder. He was avoiding eye contact now, just as Cassian avoided eye contact. They had reached an impasse. Eden didn't know what else to say, and the asset was no longer engaging. She wished Erik were here. Maybe he would know how to do this.

Her hand tightened around the knife's hilt. She glanced at the mounted camera again and hoped what she was about to say wouldn't set off alarms. "Even if I wanted to join you, he wouldn't let me."

"Of course he would."

She eyed him skeptically.

"The loss of his original six still grieves him greatly. He would be overjoyed to have you return."

"If I returned, he would control me."

"There would be no need. Join us. Submit to cleansing and you will see. It is our delight to obey him. He's given us everything."

"Except free will."

"I have free will. At least, I did." He leaned against the wall, his bound hands limp in his lap.

"We were designed to be controlled." A memory intruded. Pointing a gun at Cassian, then her mother on The Sapphire's rooftop. A shudder rippled up her spine. "And if that doesn't work, he'll dispose of us."

"He would never."

"Then why the self-destruct command?"

The asset's brow furrowed.

"Three buttons and your life is done. That's how easily he could end it. That doesn't strike me as something a caring father would build into his *beloved* children."

He studied her shrewdly. "You're lying," he finally said.

She held up the knife. "You accused me of that yesterday. I wasn't lying then."

His lips pressed tight.

She wondered if she could show him proof. If there was a way Asher could pull up her network and locate the command in question. Doing so would require her to tell Asher about such a command. Something told her Cassian would be infuriated.

The hatch above them opened.

Nairobi let herself down.

The asset shrank into the corner.

Eden's lip curled. She hated this. They were trying to

defeat evil by carrying out evil. Surely there was another way to keep the asset from going on a rampage. She got to her feet. "This is wrong, what you're doing to him."

Nairobi refused to make eye contact. "Jericho called for an assembly. Everyone is to meet in the auditorium in fifteen minutes."

With the shake of her head and an expression of disgust, Eden retrieved one of the bedrolls and a pillow from the opposite side of the bunker, next to the pallets of water. She lay out the bedroll in front of him and set the pillow on top. "The next time I come, I'll bring you food."

She could feel his suspicious stare on her back as she walked to the ladder.

"My name is Tycho," he said.

She looked over her shoulder.

The asset peered at her from his spot in the corner. "As a fellow soldier, I thought you should know."

9

When the worst of the pain subsided, when he could finally form a coherent thought, Tycho marveled at this newfound discovery. This wild impossibility.

Subject 006.

Alive!

It couldn't be, and yet he'd seen the proof with his own eyes. He'd watched her hand heal. There was no other explanation. She really was one of the originals.

She hadn't been brutally murdered as a baby, like he and his siblings had been led to believe. She was alive, and the poisonous world had led her grievously astray.

Did Pater know?

He didn't think it possible that Pater *could* know. If he did, he would have shared. He would have enlisted Tycho's help to get her back.

He loved his children, no matter what the girl said or thought. Tycho didn't blame her for the heresy. Pater wouldn't blame her either. It wasn't her fault she'd been raised in such depravity. Once she passed through cleansing, her eyes would be opened and Pater would rejoice.

They all would.

He would have to go through cleansing, too. After being stuck with these people for so long, this was to be expected. His entire body ached for it. He missed his family so much, at times it felt more unbearable than the poison.

He missed Pater the most.

Of course he did.

Pater.

Pater.

Aurelia.

Eden's question taunted him.

Is your love for Aurelia secondary?

Tycho shook his head. He couldn't control who he called for when he slept. Who he pictured when the pain was most severe. Who he longed for when he couldn't breathe.

He closed his eyes in despair.

His love for Pater *should* be primary. But deep down, in his heart of hearts, he knew it wasn't. So long in this place with nothing but loneliness and torture had finally robbed him of all pretense.

It was Aurelia he missed most.

In all her life, Eden had been examined by precisely two doctors. A competent, grandfatherly gentleman named Dr. Benjamin Norton, and a brilliant, impeccable neurosurgeon named Dr. Beverly Randall-Ransom. Now, a third doctor was examining her, and he was nothing like the other two.

Dr. Carl Millard was a twitchy man with stooped shoulders and a skittish bedside manner. The crown of his head was shiny and bald, but he didn't lack hair. It fell past his ears in curly, dark tufts. His eyes drooped. The corners of his mouth, too. He smelled like sweat and antiseptic and he mumbled to himself throughout the examination, as though one half of his brain needed reassurance from the other.

Meanwhile, Asher and Dvorak stood in front of a holographic interface on the other side of the room, conferring in hushed tones. Dr. Millard had already conducted several scans, which had been uploaded to Asher's laptop and transferred to the interface, which was slowly morphing into a three-dimensional rendering of Eden's system.

It reminded her of the device in her father's possession, which made her stomach twist into knots. Throughout Jericho's assembly, she'd begged the gadget in her hand to ping. Now, here she was, staring straight ahead as Dr. Millard shone a light into each of her pupils. The gadget had yet to make a peep.

The doctor mumbled under his breath as he took some final measurements. He checked the tranquilizer pump attached to the back of Eden's arm, then put away his medical equipment and shuffled across the room to give his final report. When he finished, he made a hasty exit without bidding any of them farewell.

Dvorak pointed to a tiny blotch on the interface located inside Eden's left ear.

"It's a scrambling device," Eden said, sliding off the examination table. Her ability to answer a question that had been whispered on the other side of the room seemed to catch them both off guard.

"This is a waste of time," she said, gesturing to the rendering. It was slowly and painstakingly loading one node at a time. She had thousands.

"Mapping your network will give us insight into his," Asher said, the condescension in his voice on full throttle.

He was referring to Tycho.

Dvorak's son.

She joined them on their side of the room. "A map of my network already exists."

Asher scratched the top of his head, momentarily flattening his stack of curls, his mouth quirked in annoyance.

"My father is in possession of a device. It contains a map of my entire system. Along with a map of Oswin Brahm's army." She raised her eyebrows, daring him to maintain his disinterest.

Beside him, Dvorak rubbed her jaw, which was ever so slightly pockmarked with acne scars. "What kind of map?"

"One that tracks their location."

Asher's hazel eyes lit from within. The Resistance had been working hard to find Brahm's headquarters. It stood to reason the soldiers would *be* at Brahm's headquarters.

A tiny trio of wrinkles formed a triangle between Dvorak's eyebrows. Instead of excitement over this potential discovery, she looked uneasy, like Eden was playing a trick. Dvorak didn't trust her. That much was abundantly clear. Eden was free because Dayne raised hell, and the council was divided. If it were up to Dvorak, Eden would still be in the bunker with Tycho.

She slid her hands into her pockets and nodded at the blotch that was her scrambling device. "My parents had that inserted when I was four. Rumors started circulating about weaponized humans. They wanted to protect me in case the bad guys were still out there."

She could feel Dvorak's attention on the side of her face. Those rumors had originated from Dvorak in an attempt to grow the Resistance.

"If not for that insertion, I would have been found and taken to Oswin Brahm as soon as my network came online."

Dvorak's attention grew hotter, more pointed. "Your friend, Cleo, seems to think you want him dead more than the rest of us. Given what I've gone through, what Asher has gone through, I find this hard to believe."

Eden considered her next words. What could she say that might make Dvorak understand? Eden wasn't the enemy. She wasn't a threat to their cause. She turned the silent gadget over in her hand. "I had a brother named Christopher. I never met him. But I grew up watching my parents grieve him. He died because of The Attack. Because of Oswin Brahm."

According to Tycho, Christopher was nothing more than contamination to be disposed of. Eden watched another dot load on the interface. She turned from it and stared straight at Dvorak. "Because of him, I attacked my parents. I almost shot and killed my own mother. Do you have any idea what that feels like—to lose all control of your mind, your body? To be at the mercy of someone so sadistic?"

Dvorak stared back at her like a woman mesmerized. "I do, in fact," she replied. "When I was forced to carry life against my will." Her hands curled into fists. "It felt like I had an enemy growing inside me. I wanted to rip it from my womb."

"I understand the feeling."

"How could you possibly?"

"I've wanted to rip these nanobots from my veins ever since I learned of their existence."

Dvorak blinked—several times—like one being hit with a sudden, unexpected truth. Here was someone who *could* relate, who had to live that reality day after day after day.

"If you think for one second I don't want him as dead as you do, then you are a fool." Eden locked eyes with the woman. A spark of respect, a glimmer of camaraderie glowed like a candle flame. "I will use what he did to me, and if it's the last thing I do, I will make him pay."

10

Cleo unwrapped a Tootsie Pop and stuck it in her mouth. She sat with one leg crossed over the other, her foot propped on the coffee table, which she'd scooted closer to the armchair. Her other foot bobbed as the glow from the television illuminated her profile. About twice every ten seconds, she cast a furtive glance at Eden.

Whose chest was tight.

Her insides, crawling.

Her nerves, frayed.

She finally felt physically normal. But emotionally? She was a mess. If Cassian had built a wall before Eden was poisoned, he'd erected a fortress after. She tried not to feel so hurt by that fortress. She tried not to take his request for his own suite so personally. It was normal to want his own space. Still, it would have been nice to hear it from him instead of Cleo.

All of it was made worse by the mysterious disappearance of her parents. She finally had confirmation. They never arrived at the safe house in Beecher. The gentleman there hadn't seen them or the Forresters or Dr. Norton or Violet and Barrett. Dayne sent two of his Chicago correspondents to the Damen Silos to see if they were there, only to discover that the silos were empty. Just like the illegal residential communities in Minneapolis, Madison, and now Milwaukee.

Worry parked itself in her gut, turning into a hungry rodent that gnawed incessantly. She crossed her arms tighter and glowered at chief anchorman, Chuck Perez, as he reported bold-faced lies to the public.

Cleo removed the sucker from her mouth. "I can't believe his audacity."

Nor could Eden.

Concordia News was finally addressing the six prisoners who *hadn't* made a Houdini-like escape from the back of a prison van. But none of the address was true. According to Chuck, the prisoners weren't dead; they had escaped, adding a hot, dry wind to the wildfire of fear and panic that was spreading just fine on its own.

Cleo shot another glance in Eden's direction.

It was the proverbial straw.

"What?" she barked, then flushed immediately. Her

tone was unwarranted. Cleo had done nothing wrong. She was simply the messenger. She'd also spent the entire day with Cassian, a fact that had Eden feeling more jealous than a hormonal girl crushing on her bestie's boyfriend. She apologized.

Cleo shooed it away. "I'm just wondering when you're going to swear or yell or ask me some questions."

"About what?"

"Cass. Being such a bonehead." She chomped on her sucker and chewed the Tootsie Roll filling. "You do know he cares about you, right?"

Eden shrugged.

"Seriously, Six. In his very own words, you are his *reason for living*."

Her brow furrowed skeptically.

"That's an exact quote."

"Then why is he ignoring me?"

"Because he's freaking out about you. And he's mixed up about his dad. And he's super pissed off about Mona."

"He talked to you about his dad?"

Cleo squeezed a small space of air between her thumb and forefinger. "Un poco."

Eden shook her head, aggravation flaring.

"He hardly said anything. The little he did say, I had to drag out of him. You know how he is."

Did she?

Eden wasn't sure anymore.

Her attention returned to the screen, where Concordia Nightly cut to a commercial break. An advertisement for CogniFuse—one of Brahm's more recent acquisitions—filled the airspace.

Eden picked up a throw pillow and hugged it to her chest, watching as an actress tore off a bulky VR headset and tossed it in the garbage. Another actress screwed up her face in frustration while replacing the battery in a newer model. A third dug through her handbag as she waited in her car for grocery pickup.

All the while, a male voice-over spoke about the inconvenience of clunky headsets, inferior battery life, and the inaccessibility of the metaverse. Then the footage changed. The frustrated female actresses were replaced by a gray-haired woman answering her door to a drone hovering above her doorstep. She stepped forward with a bright smile and held her hair back as the drone pricked the spot behind her ear with something like a needle.

The male voice-over continued. "In this time of national crisis, when we must sacrifice for our safety, let's not sacrifice love."

The footage changed once again to the same older woman with the same excited smile, opening her door to sunshine and two small, bright-eyed children who exclaimed, "Grandma!" as they wrapped their arms around each of her legs.

Cleo's feet hit the carpet.

Eden sat up straight, her mind racing.

CogniFuse had created a microchip.

One that offered superior, anytime access to the metaverse with drone insertion upon request. The male voice-over informed viewers that the company was partnering with healthcare providers to make this available and affordable for one and all.

The commercial came to an end with the older woman beaming at the camera as she cradled a sleeping baby. "Stay connected with the ones you love via CogniFuse."

"He's going to put chips in our brains," Cleo said, her eyes as round as saucers, her half-eaten Tootsie Pop standing straight between her fingers.

A chill burrowed inside Eden's bones.

Now more than ever—holed away in their homes because of a deadly toxin—people would want that chip. Once they were inserted, what would Oswin Brahm have access to? Thoughts? If that was the case, how long until he policed those thoughts? How long until he controlled them?

It seemed like an impossibility. A farfetched nightmare. But so had Eden's nanobots when she first learned about them. Oswin Brahm had created advanced nanotech long before its time. Advanced nanotech not even Dr. Beverly Randall-Ransom could comprehend, and she was one of the world's most renowned neurosurgeons. The man was an undeniable genius who had a knack for making the impossible possible.

Eden's horror expanded.

Was CogniFuse part of his end game? He'd acquired the company after the bombing of his hotel. A bombing he had orchestrated. CogniFuse's founder and CEO died in the tragedy. So here came Oswin—the proverbial hero—scooping the company up so its five hundred employees wouldn't face the threat of unemployment. Was he going to use this chip to carry out his plans? If so, might this recent development provide insight into what those plans could be?

The Resistance knew in part, thanks to Amir, who was now dead, Lark, who had—once upon a time—been a member of Swarm, and of course, Asher, who was Oswin Brahm's son. His end game was *Caelum In Terra*. His final move, the Great Winnowing. But what exactly this Great Winnowing entailed and how extensive it would be remained a mystery.

A buzzing broke through the chaos in Eden's mind.

With a shriek, Cleo pointed.

It was the gadget.

The communication device was buzzing!

Eden snatched it up and jabbed the button.

A holographic projection of Barrett appeared, his dark hair sticking up in all directions, like he'd run his fingers through it a thousand times.

"Barrett!" She gripped the device with both hands, her knuckles white as Cleo joined her on the couch. "What's going on? Where have you been?"

"We were ambushed outside the Damen Silos. By RRA officers. Violet and I are okay, but they got everyone else."

Eden's heart stopped.

They got everyone else.

"They had tranquilizer guns. One of them shot Ellery. They loaded her into a truck and everyone else into another. Violet and I climbed underneath it and hitched a ride. All the way to freaking Fredericksburg."

"*Virginia*?" Cleo squawked.

Barrett nodded.

Cleo looked at Eden, but Eden had no reaction. She couldn't speak. She couldn't even move. Her mind was blank. Her ears, ringing. Cleo scooted closer and took the device for herself. "What's in Fredericksburg?"

"Some sort of facility. There are loads of people there. I mean, hundreds if not thousands. They took Eden's parents inside. Same with Ellery's parents and Dr. Norton."

They took them inside.

"It's a detainment facility," Cleo said, more to herself

than Barrett. "For illegal residents. Dayne knows of one in Utah. A correspondent is writing an article about it. What happened to Ellery?"

"We don't know. They took her somewhere else. Somewhere called *Command*."

Eden's stomach rolled. RRA officers had taken Ellery with tranquilizers, which meant they knew what she was.

"Where are you now?" Cleo asked.

"In a safe house in the city, if you can call it a city."

"Can you get Eden's parents out of there?"

"The place is more heavily guarded than a high security prison. With no knowledge of the layout, there's just no way."

Eden bit her lip. She wanted to tell Barrett to suck it up. Be the superhuman he was and get in there. Rescue her parents. But then, who was to say her parents wouldn't be killed in the process? Who was to say Barrett and Violet wouldn't be captured and taken to *Command* like Ellery?

"Okay, look," Cleo said. "Fredericksburg is only an hour away from us."

Barrett's eyes widened.

"You and Violet need to make your way to the Reagan National Airport. Get there as quickly as possible. But be discreet. You cannot be followed, do you understand?"

Barrett nodded.

"We'll make sure someone's waiting for you when you arrive."

With one more nod of confirmation, Cleo ended the call.

11

Cleo pounded on Cassian's door.

A few seconds later, it swung open.

Cass stood on the other side with a five o'clock shadow and hair more tousled than Barrett's, his heather gray undershirt half-tucked into his joggers. His attention flicked briefly to Eden before rigidly adhering to Cleo, who didn't wait for an invitation, but marched inside his apartment.

"The RRA has Eden's parents."

"*What*?" he exclaimed.

"They have Ellery, too."

Eden wrapped her arms around her midsection and followed Cleo inside.

Cassian shut the door.

The place was like theirs, with a kitchenette and a

living room. White walls and beige carpet. By the looks of his coffee table, Cass had been sitting on the couch, working. There was a large map stuck with several post-it notes, along with an opened laptop computer he must have borrowed from Dayne.

"How do you know this?" he asked Cleo.

"Barrett called. Jericho's on his way to the airport to meet him and Violet right now."

When they'd knocked on Jericho's door, he'd immediately asked Eden about her father, who was in possession of the coveted device. Eden relayed the same information Barrett had given her. Her father was taken by RRA officers. Her mother, too. Barrett and Violet got away.

For a moment, Eden worried he might not go. It was the device they wanted, not more superhuman soldiers. He looked incredibly uncomfortable, like the risk of having them in their midst was his tipping point. Eden imagined Barrett and Violet waiting at the Reagan National Airport. She imagined nobody coming. What would they do?

In the end, her worry was for naught. After alerting Dvorak and collecting two more tranquilizer pumps from Kaiser—which had been prepared earlier in the day for this exact purpose—Jericho had gone. Any further decisions would have to be made in the morning. The words felt less like a statement and more like an ominous threat. What *decisions* was he talking about?

Eden glanced at the clock above Cassian's microwave.

It was 10:58 pm.

Her attention caught on the screen of his laptop—a photograph of a middle-aged man with a pretty wife and two kids. She had seen the man before, on one of the intel boards in the war room. This was Atticus Belby.

Cassian's father.

The laptop snapped shut.

Cass stood by with his large hand perched on the closed computer, his long, strong fingers tented. She followed two large veins running up his forearm, sinewy muscles disappearing beneath the sleeve of his under-shirt. Her attention continued climbing, to the bob of his Adam's apple, to the heightened color on his face. Cass had been researching his father.

Her heart twisted as his golden eyes met hers. "They have your parents?"

Eden nodded.

Fear swirled in his golden eyes as he turned to Cleo and stated the obvious. "That's a problem."

"You think?"

His swirling fear darkened like storm clouds. Eden knew what he was thinking. She was thinking it, too. If the government had her parents, they would use them as bait. Just like Mordecai had. And if their lives were threatened, Eden would go. She knew it, and Cass knew it, too.

"They're being held in a detainment facility in Fredericksburg," Cleo said.

"Is there a way to get them out?"

"Barrett said it's heavily patrolled. We would need access to the facility's layout, at the very least."

"Maybe we can find something online." Cass collected the sticky notes and folded them inside his map. He sat down, re-opened the laptop, and quickly brought up a new browser. He searched a myriad of phrases, but no layout was found. He dragged his hand along his jaw.

Eden sat beside him, relishing the warmth of his body. The scent of The Landing's bar soap. The way it mixed with his natural chemistry turned the basic scent into something very appealing. She set her hands on her knees. "Can you pull up surveillance footage of the facility?"

He tried first with drones. When that failed, he tried again with satellite. It took a moment to find what they were searching for. When they did, Eden couldn't look away. She stared, taking in a bird's eye view of the warehouse-like complex with high-security fencing around the perimeter and a squad of RRA vehicles dotted along the grounds. She wanted to zoom in, as if doing so might bring her parents closer.

Without thinking, she moved her hand to the touchpad. Her finger brushed his. He pulled away like her touch was fire. Her heart thudded. She could hear his heart thudding, too. She could feel his tension. His longing. But then he stood abruptly and made his way into the kitchen to pour himself a glass of water.

Cleo looked between them with raised eyebrows.

Cass drank, then set the glass down with a sharp tap. "I assume Ellery is dead."

His matter-of-fact tone was jolting. "Why?" Eden asked.

"The RRA is part of the government, and the government wants you destroyed."

"According to the Resistance, the government is in Oswin Brahm's pocket," Eden replied. "I don't think he would destroy Ellery. I think he would ..." She couldn't bring herself to say the rest. Just thinking it had a sharp bout of nausea rising up her throat.

"You think he would what?" Cleo prompted.

"Add her to his army."

Cleo blanched.

Cass's mouth went grim.

According to Tycho, Ellery would be cleansed. Then —Eden knew—she would be controlled. Because Ellery Forrester had a Queen Bee. So did Barrett, and so did

Eden. But not Violet. She was Queen Bee free. Eden might be jealous, if not for the horrible abuse Barrett had alluded to. She'd paid a severe price for her freedom.

"Personally," Eden said with an acerbic bite in each syllable, "I'd rather be dead."

12

Two and a half hours later, Jericho stood in the hallway with Barrett and Violet in tow, along with three Alexandrians. One had already been standing out in the hallway with Eden's remote, an older man who agreed to be on watch for the night. The other two were new, and by the looks of it, half awake. Eden didn't care about them. She cared about Barrett and Violet. She didn't know either particularly well, but they were cut from the same cloth and she was so relieved to see Barrett's friendly face, she threw her arms around his neck.

He returned the embrace—a nice big bear hug of a squeeze.

When they came apart, Eden smiled at Violet, who stood beside him looking twitchier than ever as she peeked out from behind a familiar curtain of dark, choppy hair. Eden would hug her, too, if she didn't suspect it would scare the girl more than make her feel welcome.

Meanwhile, Jericho looked at the three of them with obvious apprehension. Like they were a group of unwieldy children playing with guns that may or may not be loaded. He scratched his salt and pepper goatee. "Prudence has called for a meeting first thing tomorrow morning."

To make *decisions*.

Eden swallowed.

"She wants all five of you in attendance," he said. "Until then, I can get our two newest guests settled in a suite, if they'd like."

"No need, Jer." Cleo stepped forward with a smile too sweet to be genuine. "Violet will stay with us. Barrett can crash with Cass."

Behind her, Cass did a double take.

Jericho conferred with the three Alexandrians. Only two were needed. One would stand guard outside Cassian's apartment with Barrett's remote. The one already on Eden duty would now be on Eden and Violet duty. He felt confident he could handle two remotes. Eden felt confident two remotes weren't necessary. Violet couldn't be controlled. But they would not take her word for it. Asher and Dr. Millard would conduct their own examination after tomorrow's meeting.

As soon as everything was settled, Cleo shut the door in Jericho's face.

"I really wish someone would have warned us about these," Barrett said, shrugging off a backpack and coat to touch the tranquilizer pump attached to his arm. He slid a concerned look at Violet, who was—Eden noticed—visibly shaking.

She considered everything she knew about the girl—the abuse she endured, the terror she exhibited when surrounded by medical equipment in Dr. Norton's basement—and mentally kicked herself for not being more considerate.

"It's okay, though. Right, Vi?" Barrett said encouragingly. "They don't hurt at all."

Violet nodded. Or at least, gave her best effort at a nod.

Cleo held up the backpack. It was bubblegum pink and covered in hearts. "What's this?"

"The family at the safe house had a daughter. She gave me her bag so I wouldn't have to keep lugging these around in my coat." He unzipped the backpack to unveil several leather-bound journals. "They belonged to Violet's dad."

Cleo removed one from inside.

"I was hoping they might lend some insight into how he eliminated her Queen Bee."

"Have you had any luck?" Eden asked.

"Unfortunately, no." Barrett walked to the couch and plopped down on one end. He peered at the door where Jericho had stood. "So, they're assigning us bodyguards?"

"It's just a safety precaution," Eden said. "To make everyone feel better." But one look at Violet, and another at Cass, made the words ring hollow. *Everyone* very obviously did not feel better. To Cass, the guards were probably a reminder of the boardroom ambush. The tranquilizer they'd forced upon him, and the poison they'd forced upon her.

Eden needed to shoot straight. Barrett and Violet deserved full disclosure. She probably should have given it before they came. The situation she'd invited them into was precarious. With a resigned sigh, she told them about the poison, about being injected against her will and locked up with the asset, who was named Tycho. Then she dropped the bombshell.

"He's Dvorak's son."

"*What*?" Cleo exclaimed.

Beside her, Cass reacted, too. Just not with words.

She didn't blame them. It *was* big news. The kind she probably should have divulged earlier. The thing was, Eden had been too out of sorts last night to say anything. By the time she woke up, Cleo was already gone and Cass didn't want to talk. Eden spent most of her day being poked and prodded, fighting the urge to tell Asher about the self-destruct function so she could show it to Tycho—more proof that she wasn't a liar.

By the time they were done, her mind had been completely focused on Cassian. Surely a full day apart would have given his anger ample time to cool. Surely they would finally be able to connect in the way she longed to connect. Only instead of seeing Cassian, she learned from Cleo that he'd moved into his own suite. All thoughts of Prudence Dvorak and her five-star general of a son had fallen by the wayside.

Cleo made herself comfortable in the armchair, tucking one leg beneath her and pulling the other toward her chest. She clasped her hands over her knee and looked at Eden as though expecting a story.

Eden shared what she knew.

By the time she finished, Cass was sitting backward on one of the kitchen chairs. Violet hadn't moved at all. She remained by the door, as if venturing too far might be dangerous.

Cleo turned to Barrett. "Your turn."

He launched into his own story, which was decidedly longer than Eden's, filled with plenty of exciting detail. The way he spun it made the whole thing sound much less like a horror story, and much more like a grand adventure. One that enticed Violet to take a few steps closer.

"The RRA officer said something about there being two more. He had to be referring to us."

Eden's stomach rolled at the thought of Ellery. Taken. Activated. *Cleansed*. Brainwashed. The whole thing made her feel sick.

Barrett folded his hands on top of his head and leaned back against the cushion. "I can't believe we're here. I can't believe what's been happening. My brain is just ..."

"Spinning?" Cleo offered.

"Failing." He held up his hand, where four names had been scrawled in ink. Eden, Cleo, Graham, and Dr. Norton. Her heart twinged on his behalf. She'd take her bursts of pain over a glitchy form of dementia any day.

"Oh, I almost forgot." He leaned forward and pulled something from his back pocket.

Eden gaped.

She'd assumed the device was with her father in Fredericksburg and had told Jericho as much. But here it was, in Barrett's possession. This thing that contained a detailed map of her network, along with another detailed map that just might shed light on the elusive whereabouts of Brahm's headquarters.

"I had it with me when the RRA showed up." Barrett handed it to her.

Eden turned it on.

A three-dimensional butterfly spun into a map. There

were no longer only five erratic dots jumping about, but nearly a hundred. And the new ones weren't erratic at all, but steady. Concentrated in four different locations.

Eden captured the holographic map and zoomed out, then zoomed out again, until an outline came into view. "It's the United States."

Cass came out of his chair. He sat in the center of the couch, between Eden and Barrett, and began mapping the coordinates. He plugged them into his laptop, which spit back specific locations, the last of which Eden recognized.

"Fredonia," she said out loud. Her brow furrowed as the memory slid into place. Just like Atticus Belby, she'd seen this before in the war room, on a list of recon missions Lark had conducted. "It's in Arizona. But they've already checked Fredonia. There's nothing there."

It was so remote, there wasn't any drone footage. Like Fredericksburg, they had to use satellite imaging. Cass pulled up the location on the off chance something had changed since Lark's reconnaissance. On the off chance some sort of super soldier society had settled in the ghost town. Unless that settlement existed underground, which was always a possibility, the location was wrong. It was a desert wasteland. He searched the other locations as well. They were no different from Fredonia.

The letdown was intense.

Eden could feel her hope crashing as Cleo's mouth split with a yawn. According to the microwave, it was three in the morning.

Cass leaned back against the couch, his eyes bloodshot. "We should get some sleep."

Nobody objected, even though Eden doubted she'd get any. At least not while her parents were locked up in a detainment facility. Still, she and Cleo and a hesitant Violet bid the boys goodnight. As they walked down the hallway, Violet peeked longingly over her shoulder, past their security detail, toward the sound of Barrett's jabbering.

"Cass is going to kill you," Eden muttered.

"The company will be good for him," Cleo said.

Eden wasn't sure she could say the same for Barrett. If he didn't shut up, Cass might kill *him*, too.

Back in their apartment, Eden led Violet to her bedroom. "You can sleep here," she said, standing on the threshold. "I'm more than happy to take the couch."

The girl wrapped her arms around her midsection like a little kid with a stomachache. According to Barrett, she was talking now. Eden had a hard time imagining it.

"I'm glad you're here," Eden said, injecting as much warmth as she could into the statement.

Tentatively, Violet removed something from her pocket and set it on the vanity. It wasn't a journal, but a small sort of book. Violet opened it to the first page.

Eden rose on tiptoe to get a better look. It was a photograph of a woman who shared Violet's likeness. She blinked. "Is that your mom?"

With a nod, Violet traced the shape of the woman's mouth.

"She's beautiful," Eden said.

Violet's eyes went glossy.

Eden wanted to say more. Offer the girl a comforting word. But what comfort was there to give with such a tragic tale? Besides, it was late. Tomorrow was going to be a big day. An *important* day. A tide-turning day. At least, Eden hoped so. She touched the device in her pocket—one that might help her get what she wanted. She wasn't satisfied with simply being part of the Resistance. She wanted to be one of the decision makers. The council had welcomed Nairobi to their ranks earlier this morning. Eden heard Asher and Dvorak talking about it during her examination. Perhaps, if Eden played her cards perfectly, they might add her, too.

She gave Violet's elbow a squeeze and bid her goodnight. Eden made herself a bed on the couch. The pillow smelled like Cassian. The blanket, too. She wrapped it around herself and beckoned sleep to come. But it danced out of reach. She kept seeing her parents locked up in a cell, and Atticus Belby, smiling at her from a screen.

13

Cass twisted his Styrofoam cup on the table, his mood as black as the coffee. His irritability was exacerbated by another sleepless night and his chatty new roommate. If Cass couldn't have Eden, he wanted privacy. His own space. Instead, he got Barrett.

He took a drink of his coffee and watched as Eden passed a plate of bagels to Violet with a look of kind encouragement. She was like this with oddballs, with outcasts. He'd noticed this about her from the beginning, as soon as he saw her laughing with a rail-thin, acne-faced kid named Erik Gaviola. Girls who looked like Eden didn't typically hang out with boys who looked like Erik. Now, she seemed to be taking Violet in like a bird with a broken wing.

She passed the plate along and ran her fingers

beneath her hair—a windswept tumble over her left shoulder. Cass was well-acquainted with the silky feel of that hair. If he let himself, he could relive all the times he'd run his own fingers through it back at the Miller's, when Eden's parents were safe and he was in denial. Operating under the delusion that they might actually have a future together.

She lifted her gaze and caught him staring. He didn't look away. He didn't want to. If he couldn't have her, he could at least look at her. For one torturous, blissful moment, she stared back—color rising in her cheeks—before severing eye contact. Maybe this was what alcoholics felt like, staring down a bottle of the finest brandy. Resisting the thing that was bad for them. Craving the thing that was bad for them. Only Eden wasn't the bad thing.

He was.

The plate of bagels reached him. He leaned back, allowing Barrett to pass the food to Cleo, as another council member arrived—an Asian woman named Lark. She looked every bit as uneasy as Jericho had before her. Something about seeing Eden, Violet, and Barrett sitting all in a row turned them wary. Dayne Johnson was the only one pleased to see them. Or at least, intrigued. He'd introduced himself with a handshake—not at all taken aback by the oddity that was Violet—before snagging a seat next to Cleo.

Cass took another sip of his coffee and kept his eye on the door until Nairobi, Dvorak, and Asher entered. According to Cleo, the guy was Brahm's biological son. He was also the creator of the Amber Highway.

Dvorak shut the door behind her. She took the seat at the head of the table and set two familiar contraptions side by side. Not remotes, but gadgets like the one Eden carried with her. Dvorak used them to patch in a holographic projection of a white-haired man named Harlan Wallace and the owner of the speakeasy in Bethesda, an Irishman named Emmett.

She cleared her throat and pulled at the hem of her blazer. Cass wondered where she got it. The same place Jericho had gotten his clothes, by the looks of it. Everyone else was relegated to sweatpants, crewneck sweatshirts, and Henley's. "Jericho tells me your parents are in a detainment facility in Fredericksburg."

Eden nodded.

"With the device that might help us pinpoint Brahm's headquarters."

It wasn't true. The device was in Eden's possession. Cass watched to see what Eden would do. If it were up to him, he wouldn't be so quick to divulge it. He didn't trust any of these people. Should the need for a bargaining chip arise, the device would provide one.

But of course, this wasn't Eden's way. She removed it from her pocket and set it on the table. "I could have kept this to myself. But I'm determined to be transparent."

Dvorak looked taken aback, her intentions for this meeting obviously derailed.

"Oswin Brahm has murdered millions, including my brother. My entire life has been upended and my parents are in trouble. He is playing God. I want to stop him. You want to stop him. I think we need to work together in order to do so. And if that's the case, you have to stop treating us like second-class citizens."

Glances were exchanged by everyone but Dvorak and Eden. Their attention remained fixed on one another, until finally, Dvorak asked, "What are you suggesting?"

"Get rid of the security detail," Cleo muttered.

"That's not an option."

"I don't care about the security detail," Eden said. "If you want to assign people to follow us around, fine."

"What are you talking about, then?"

"The council." Eden lifted her chin. "I'd like to be part of it."

Dvorak scoffed.

Surprisingly, she was the only one.

Everyone else exchanged more glances, like the idea wasn't so outlandish.

Dvorak scoffed louder. "She's a child."

"I'm eighteen."

"Exactly."

Eden gestured to Asher. "He's only twenty-two."

"A very smart twenty-two," Asher said.

"Not as smart as me," Eden replied.

"She's better at poker, too," Cleo quipped.

"If you can trust Oswin Brahm's son to be part of your council, then surely there's room for me."

Nobody said anything.

It was so quiet Cass could hear Barrett chewing his bagel.

Finally, Dvorak folded her hands. "So what is this—extortion? We let you be a council member or you refuse to share the information on that device?"

Asher snagged her remote and gave it a lazy spin. "We could just take it."

A growl rumbled in Cass's chest.

Beside him, Cleo glared.

"That would be treating me like a second-class citizen now, wouldn't it?" Her words were cool and composed. Asher's threat didn't rattle her. "I'm simply asking you to give me the same courtesy you gave Nairobi. Call for a vote."

Dvorak quirked her eyebrow. "And if the vote is no?"

"I will share the information on this device, regardless."

More glances were exchanged. By the looks of it, a nonverbal agreement was being reached.

"Hold on a minute," Dayne said, setting his palms

flat on the table. "If we're adding council members, I'd like to toss my name in the hat. I should have been invited in a decade ago."

This was another thing Cleo had filled Cass in on yesterday. Dayne had been completely in the dark about the Resistance and was apparently still bitter about it.

"Fine," Dvorak said with a clear note of impatience. "Let's call for a vote. Yes or no, Dayne and Eden as part of the council. I will start on Francesca's behalf."

Francesca was the girl with the glass eye. The one who had brought Cass and Eden on this wild goose chase to begin with. According to Cleo, she was sedated in Kaiser—their medical facility—battling infection from second-degree burns sustained the night of the prison break.

"She would vote yes to Dayne," Dvorak said. "No to Eden."

Cass came forward in his seat.

If Francesca wasn't there, then Francesca didn't get to vote. But Eden only dipped her chin in acquiescence, like she agreed with Dvorak's assessment.

"My vote is the same," Dvorak added before turning to Nairobi on her left, who looked flustered by the attention.

Her cheeks turned a rosy brown. "This is my first vote. I don't want to mess anything up. But I guess ..."

She smiled apologetically at Dvorak, then said, "Yes to both."

Unfazed, Dvorak turned to Jericho.

"Yes to Dayne. No to Eden," he said in his deep baritone. "I'm sorry, but we don't need two more council members."

Lark was next. She agreed with Jericho and voted accordingly.

Harlan and Emmett agreed with Nairobi.

But it didn't matter. There was only one vote left—Asher's. Given the fact that he'd threatened to tranquilize Eden not more than a ten minutes ago, Cass assumed Eden was out. Eden must have assumed, too, because her face fell. Cass's heart fell with it. In a vacuum, he didn't care if Eden was on the council. But this wasn't a vacuum. This was life, and in this life he cared about Eden, even if he couldn't have Eden. And since Eden cared about being on the council, Cass cared, too.

But Asher surprised them both.

"As far as I'm concerned, you've more than proven yourself," he said with a flippant shrug. "My vote's yes to both."

Cleo let loose a bark of laughter.

They had themselves a tie.

Four yeses.

Four nos.

Everyone looked around like … *now what*? Until Dayne cleared his voice and lifted his pointer finger. "I'm part of the council now, correct?"

Nobody argued. His yeses had been unanimous.

"Which means I get a vote." He leaned back in his chair and crossed his ankle over his knee. "I say yes to Eden."

Barrett stopped chewing his bagel.

The room went deathly silent.

Eden had just finagled her way into the council. The question was, would their leader allow it to stand? Or would she assert her authority and squash this unexpected turn of events?

She stared at Eden with dark, stormy eyes, and nostrils that were slightly flared. "Amir and I were the first council members. We started all of this together. Now he's dead because of a prison break that wouldn't have been necessary apart from you."

Eden stared back, as still as a doe caught in the crosshairs. Only she didn't look afraid. She certainly didn't cower.

"It's hard to let go of that," Dvorak said.

"I understand," Eden replied.

"But I know what he would say. I can hear his voice in my head. 'Get over it, Pru. We have a monster to kill.'" Dvorak stuck out her hand. "Welcome to the council."

14

She'd done it.

Eden was part of the council, which meant she would be included in all the planning. In every decision, too. She wasn't just part of the Resistance; she was one of its leaders. The moment she let go of Dvorak's hand, she made her first request. "I want to get my parents out of the detainment facility in Fredericksburg."

"Another rescue mission," Asher said dryly.

"They will bring value to the Resistance. My father, especially. He was a CIA agent. He has a very particular skill set that could—"

"No," Dvorak said.

"We have to call for a vote at least," Eden shot back.

"Fine. Let's vote. Yes or no to breaking Eden's parents out of Fredericksburg."

Eden voted yes. Emphatically.

Everyone else voted no, even Dayne.

"I'm sorry," he said. "But the last rescue mission was a disaster. I don't think we can survive another."

She could feel her hope slipping away. She needed to rescue them. She couldn't leave them there. "The government will use my parents to get to me."

"Then you must refuse to be used," Dvorak said—her voice sharp. Her expression, too. "This is war. The outcome is bigger than your parents."

Eden swore she could hear a low rumble in Cassian's chest. Her own felt like it was being cleaved in two. Mostly because what Dvorak said was true. They were in the middle of a war, and Eden had decided—the night she thought Cassian was dead—that she couldn't let emotions make her decisions. She was part of the council, which meant she must fall in line. If only doing so didn't make her feel like she was coming undone.

Dvorak pinched the bridge of her nose. "Look, the best thing any of us can do for your parents at this point is win. Defeat Oswin Brahm. To do that, we need to know the specifics of his plan. Which means we need to find his headquarters. Now, if you please, let's have a look at that device."

Dejectedly, Eden moved it into the center of the table and turned it on. She swiped through each of its projections before settling on the one with the blinking dots.

She filled them in on what they'd discovered last night. Those dots didn't lead to actual locations.

Asher rolled a ring in the palm of his hand. It belonged to a guard who'd lost the lower half of his body. Eden had pried it from his finger after he died. "Imagine a beam of light," Asher said.

Everyone looked at him.

"It travels from Point A to Point B in a straight line. But if someone were to take a mirror and put it in the light's path ..." He modeled this using the ring. He held it in the path of the holographic projection. The light caught on the silver butterfly and changed trajectory.

"The light bends," Cleo said.

Asher nodded.

"You think this is what's happening?" Dayne asked.

"I don't *think*, I *know*." He set the ring down. "It's a tactic my father has used before. The deflection provides an added layer of security. Only those who know how the 'mirror' is positioned would know where Brahm's soldiers are located."

"Then it's like an equation," Barrett said, pushing up the sleeves of his navy crewneck sweatshirt. "One variable would be the positioning of the 'mirror' and the other would be the real location."

"You can't solve an equation with two variables," Eden replied. "Not unless you have two equations."

Cleo rubbed her temples. "I'm having high school algebra flashbacks."

Barrett and Nairobi laughed.

Jericho gestured toward the hologram with an upturned palm. "The only way this is useful is if we correctly guess one variable."

"He will not send his army some place random," Dvorak said.

"Nothing Oswin does is random," Lark agreed. "He is meticulously planned and manipulative to the highest degree."

Lark was right.

Eden was living proof. Barrett and Violet were living proof. He'd created an army and sat on that army for eighteen years. The Monarch didn't fly by the seat of his pants. Every move he made was well rehearsed.

Eden came to the edge of her seat. "His soldiers will be somewhere significant."

"Like the cities that've been attacked?" Dayne suggested.

"Or the cities *yet* to be attacked." Cleo scribbled each one on a pad of paper. Detroit. Fresno. St. Louis. Seattle. "Who better to release this toxin than super freaks who can't be killed?"

It felt like a promising place to start.

Asher added the cities, along with lines of longitude and latitude. They began creating equations, using one constant and one of the potential variables until they had worked through all possible outcomes. Nothing viable emerged. No consistent patterns. They tried again with the three cities that had already been attacked. But those rendered no more insight than the others.

"What about the detainment facility," Cass said. It was the first contribution he'd made. He lifted his gaze from the map—now filled with a multitude of criss-crossing lines—and looked at Barrett. "You said the place was well-guarded. Did the guards look young?"

Eden perked. "Like … eighteen years young?"

"Possibly. It was dark and I didn't think to look too close." Barrett peeked at Violet like she might also contribute to the conversation, but she was very obviously not taking part. His face twisted like he was pulling up the memory in his mind. After a beat, he nodded. "The guards were definitely young."

Asher wiped the map clean so there was nothing but the original false locations and the lines of longitude and latitude. He plotted the coordinates for Fredericksburg. They worked with one constant at a time. Creating an algorithm, then applying that same algorithm to the three constants that remained. It took a while, but they finally hit something substantial.

"Wendover," Eden said.

Cleo came out of her chair. According to Dayne, there was another detainment facility in Wendover.

Asher charted the exact coordinates. He plugged them into satellite footage, and sure enough, a bird's-eye view much like the one Cass pulled up last night filled his computer screen. A detainment facility not in Fredericksburg. But in Wendover.

Everyone started talking at once. All the while, Eden stared at the map—at the trajectory of lines. They formed a pattern. It was like seeing a constellation. A clear picture in the sky that had moments earlier looked like nothing more than a random cluster of stars. Eden gasped. She was *seeing* the math.

"Shenandoah, Iowa," she said over the din of animated conversation.

Everyone went quiet.

She reached over Asher and plugged in the coordinates.

A third detainment facility loaded on the screen.

A few seconds later, Barrett slapped his palms on the table, because he was seeing it, too. "It's the Big Apple!" he exclaimed.

This was the fourth location.

New York City, New York.

Specifically, on the eastern shore of Staten Island, where the harbor bottlenecked.

Asher pulled up the area.

"What is that?" Dvorak asked, setting her elbow on the table as she came to the edge of her seat.

Asher zoomed in.

"Fort Wadsworth," Jericho said. "It was closed all the way back in the twentieth century."

A pregnant pause followed.

New York was a nuclear wasteland, the same as Washington, DC. At least on the surface. But Washington, DC, hadn't been radioactive or desolate. The Resistance had been there, building their numbers. Was Oswin Brahm using New York to do the same?

Dvorak's dark eyes gleamed as they locked onto Lark. "I think it's time for another recon mission."

15

When Prudence Dvorak concluded the meeting, Cassian stood so abruptly, Violet startled. He strode from the boardroom, stopping briefly in the doorway to ask Cleo if she was coming. Cleo cast Eden a look of apology before departing. Eden and a very tall boy named Asher watched them go—the former looking hurt, the latter annoyed—as the rest of the room cleared.

Violet snatched the leftover bagel halves from the plate in the center of the table and stuffed them inside the pocket opposite her photo book. Her hunger seemed to correlate with sleep deprivation, which meant it was at an all-time high, for she hadn't slept last night at all.

She'd lain awake, trying not to hear the screams that came like contractions every four hours. Her superhuman hearing seemed to be ultra sensitive, as though

Father's experimentation not only eliminated her Queen Bee, but set her volume dial to max. No matter how hard she pressed the pillow over her ears, the tortured cries squeezed through.

They belonged to a boy who'd been locked up in an underground room like the one Father had used to conduct his research. The distant, excruciating sound gave Alexandria a wrong feeling. An ominous feeling. One that sank like a rock into the pit of her ravenous stomach and there remained.

"What now?" Barrett asked. The room had emptied. It was just him and Violet and Eden and the very tall boy named Asher.

"Pru asked me to conduct examinations," the boy said.

Violet had just swallowed a big bite of bagel. It turned into stone as it slid down her throat. Eden had warned them of this last night. These people would want to conduct an examination. Chart her network. Violet didn't know what charting a network entailed. She only knew that if she cooperated, they might let her take the device off her arm. And Eden looked eager. Eden was nice. Too nice to look eager for anything that could be bad. So Violet drummed up every ounce of courage she could muster and followed the others out of the glass building, into the bright sunshine of a fall day.

The trees were in various states of undress. Some still

donned leaves of bright orange and yellow, others had stripped naked, their branches gnarled and bare. Violet finished one bagel half and pulled out another, as if cramming enough starch in her belly might combat her nerves.

"I'll have to get you one of these," Asher was saying to Eden, holding up a piece from a chess set.

"What is it?" Barrett asked.

"A ticket to the war room," Asher replied.

At Barrett's look of confusion, Eden explained. "It's some sort of nanotech that allows council members to meet at a moment's notice. Asher designed a room in the Amber Highway where we can gather in one space."

"Are they all chess pieces?"

"Everyone's is different," Asher said. "Amir had a monarch pin. Dvorak has a switchblade. Lark's is a bullet. Harlan's is a domino. Emmett uses a shot glass. Francesca has a locket. Nairobi wants to use a penny."

"So, they're all trinkets," Barrett said as they reached a building called Kaiser Medical Center.

Asher opened the door. "A word of advice? I wouldn't let Pru hear you calling her switchblade a *trinket*."

Violet stuffed another bite of bagel into her mouth, her jaw working, her stomach churning, her underarms sweating as she followed Asher down a hallway past scary room after scary room. The fourth hour was approaching.

"I appreciate your vote," Eden said to him.

"It was the right thing to do," he replied, as though aggravated by the gratitude. He stopped in front of an elevator and jabbed a button. "Fran's gonna be pissed, though. Once her sedation wears off, she'll probably hire Lark to assassinate me."

"Fran," Barrett said, rocking back on his heels. "That's the girl with the glass eye, right?"

"Another word of advice?" Asher tipped his mouth toward Barrett's ear. "I wouldn't let her hear you saying that either."

The elevator doors dinged and slid open.

The four of them stepped inside.

Violet tore off another hunk of bagel with her teeth. Her heart was racing. Seconds ticked into minutes and those minutes were inching closer to another contraction.

The lift stopped.

The doors opened.

Asher led them down a long, clean, windowed corridor and entered a lab with white floors and white walls and sterile-looking equipment. Eden followed him inside. Barrett followed Eden. Violet lurched to a stop. Her heart was pounding now. A *boom-boom-boom* that thumped against her eardrums and pounded in her stomach.

Her palms were sweaty.

Her mouth, dry.

She brought her hands to her ears, wishing she could shut them off. Mute her hearing. But she was standing on the threshold of a very scary room and the screams were coming like a race car down a track, increasing in amplitude, inverting her wish into something cruel. The volume went up, not down—all the way to full blast. It wasn't just the screams, but every other noise pounced upon her ear drums. So overwhelming, her knees buckled. Violet crouched into a ball on the floor with her arms curled over her head.

Make it stop.

Make it stop.

Make it stop!

When it finally did, Barrett's face swam in front of her.

"What's wrong with her?" Asher asked, his voice distorted as sound returned to normal.

"Nothing," Barrett said. But his expression said otherwise, like there was something wrong indeed.

Violet clambered to her feet and raced down the hall. She could feel Barrett's gaze on her back as she let herself into a nearby ladies' room and retched into a toilet. When the bagels were gone and her stomach was empty, she shuffled to the sink and turned on the water. She rinsed her mouth, scrubbed her hands, and splashed her face. She stared at her reflection. Water dripped from the end of her nose. Dark tendrils of hair clung to wet skin, hiding one eye. She wiped herself dry with the sleeve of her coat and crept out into the hall.

In the lab, Asher had raised his voice. "How many more secrets are you keeping?"

"It wasn't a secret," Eden replied. "The glitching is a nonissue."

"That episode she just had didn't look like a nonissue."

"That episode she just had is the reason you're able to get into our networks. We need updates. That's all."

"I have to report this to Pru."

"Go ahead."

A long pause ensued. An extended silence fraught with tension. Maybe at the end of it, Asher would kick them out. Maybe they would leave this place and Violet wouldn't have to be examined or hear that screaming ever again. She slid down the wall and pulled the photo book from her pocket. She wished there was a way to make the glitching stop. She hated the bursts of noise as much as Barrett hated forgetting names.

Inside the lab, computer keys clacked. A backpack unzipped. Journal pages flipped.

"There's really nothing in these about her Queen Bee?" Eden asked, her voice tinged with exasperation. "No clue how he did it?"

"I think there is a clue, actually," Barrett replied.

Violet's brow puckered. This was news.

"Her father wrote everything down. In vivid detail. There's nothing in any of the journals about a master node, which means ..."

"He didn't know about it?"

"I don't think he did."

"Then how did he get rid of it?"

"By accident?"

There was another bout of silence.

"Do you have any idea how unlikely it would be to pull off something like that by accident?"

"I do, actually," Barrett said. "I've computed the odds several times, in fact. It's a really chilling testimony to how much experimentation he did on her."

Heat crawled up Violet's neck.

"No wonder she ran away," Eden mumbled. More journal pages flipped. "This is really disturbing stuff."

"Tell me about it," Barrett replied.

Violet brought her knees to her chest, set Mother on top of them, and rested her cheek against the cool smoothness of the first photograph. If she closed her eyes, she could recall her scent and the silky softness of her touch.

The legs of a chair scooted against the linoleum. "She was talking before her dad showed up. Not a lot, but a few words here and there. She hasn't said anything since."

"Sounds like she needs to see a shrink." The statement belonged to Asher. "We have one here, you know."

"Really?" Eden replied.

"A certified trauma therapist. One floor up and down the hallway, with a framed degree hanging in her office and everything."

"Are you seeing her?"

Asher scoffed like the idea was absurd.

"Then how do you know she has a framed degree hanging in her office?"

"I walk by on my way to visit Fran. Her door's usually open. If Violet is suffering from selective mutism and PTSD, a shrink would probably help." There were more clacking computer keys. "Speaking of your freaky little friend, how long is she going to stay in the bathroom?"

"I'll check on her," Barrett said.

The door whooshed open. Barrett walked outside. His stride hitched when he saw her, sitting there against the wall with her cheek pressed against Mother. But then he got going again and sat down beside her.

He nodded at her photo book. "Can I show you which one's my favorite?"

Violet nodded back.

He flipped over three photographs and stopped on a

picture of the woods and Mother's hand, visible only in the bottom right corner as she lifted her walking stick. Violet was four or five years old, pointing in the same direction as the stick, when Mother accidentally released the shutter on her camera. She'd caught Violet mid stride in front of a large fern, its fronds stretching out behind her.

"I call this one Violet the Green Bird and her Magical Mother. That's her magical staff, right there, see. And those are your wings." He set his finger over the green fronds reaching over her tiny shoulders and indeed, they looked like wings.

"Right after this picture was taken, your mother used her staff to sprinkle those wings with fairy dust and the both of you shot up into the sky, straight into the clouds." He zoomed his hand like a rocket.

Violet's stomach swooped in the imagining.

"You landed on the first rainbow you could find and spent the rest of the day slipping down it like a slide." He smiled a lopsided smile.

She smiled back. It was a good story. The best story. But it wasn't a true story. In reality, Violet had no wings and Mother had no staff. The woods were as far as they could escape. In the end, they always had to go back to *him*.

As if sensing her encroaching sadness, Barrett shifted. "Did I ever tell you the story about Rowdy Boxer?"

She shook her head.

"That was his actual name. *Rowdy Boxer*. We had class together in second grade and he was a giant bully. Jameson decided to give Rowdy a good scare after he gave my best friend, Banner, a black eye. It became this whole thing where my parents and Banner's parents and Rowdy's parents were called into the principal's office.

"Afterward, my dad came home, and he said to me and Jameson, 'Boys, we're all living a story. You want to understand a person, understand their story.' Then he gave us a hug and I didn't know what he was talking about until Rowdy showed up the next day with a black eye of his own. He told the teacher he fell, but I'm pretty sure his dad did it."

Barrett flipped another page to a different photograph.

This one, Violet had taken.

Mother in the kitchen.

She looked sad.

"I'm really sorry about your mom, Violet," he said. "Her story shouldn't have ended the way it did, and your story shouldn't have started the way it did."

With a heavy sigh, he leaned against the wall. "One thing that can help when we're trying to process parts of our story is something called therapy." He pulled his earlobe. "Have you heard of therapy?"

Violet brushed her thumb over Mother's hair.

"It's kinda fun. I went for a while after our dog got hit by a car when I was ten. It helped. A lot, actually. Anyway, I guess there's a therapist here you could see if you wanted. I could go with you if you think it would help. Or not. I just ... I think you deserve to feel less afraid."

Less afraid.

Violet tried to imagine, but she had no idea what it might feel like. Before she could try harder, Eden and Asher stepped out into the hall.

"We just received word from Dayne," Eden said, her face pale. "Detroit was hit with the toxin."

16

The toxin hit another city on Cleo's map, making it the fourth attack in fifteen days. Thousands more were sick, which meant thousands more would die. For death—it seemed—was the inevitable conclusion once symptoms set in. Lockdown was no longer optional or recommended, but mandatory and immediate. Until further notice, the entire country was being sent to its proverbial room.

America was livid.

How could these attacks keep happening? Why weren't they being stopped? For the first time in twenty-one years, the public's anger wasn't directed at make-believe terrorists or illegal residents. It was directed at its leaders. The Board was mishandling the crisis, so the people wanted a new Board.

With Oswin Brahm at the helm.

The man had an uncanny ability to anticipate every need. The wealthy thanked him for their luxurious, subterranean homes, which weren't merely bomb proof, but toxin proof, too. Everyone else gushed over his new microchip. Oswin Brahm had given them an affordable, convenient way to stay connected with loved ones while they were trapped inside their homes. Between SafePad Elite and CogniFuse, it was almost like he could see into the future.

If that weren't enough, he gathered a team of top-notch scientists from the private sector to undertake the creation of an antidote. He was paying them from his own coffers to work around the clock until they succeeded.

The man had risen to godlike status. All-knowing, and omnipresent, too. For he was everywhere. #BrahmforChairman trended on Perk, a social media platform that had never before allowed divisive content. He was the headliner of every conversation. On every screen and in every newspaper. Composed, clear-headed, and confident as he stood by Chairwoman Cruz, offering his support. Encouraging the public to do the same.

"Why isn't he giving the people what they want?" Eden had asked during a council meeting several days ago. Why was he playing coy? Surely, he wanted to be the leader of the country. Surely, standing at the helm would enable him to carry out his plans all the more efficiently.

"If he steps in as chairman now," Lark had said, "he'll be responsible for what happens next."

"What happens next?" Eden had replied, her forehead puckered like maybe Lark knew something she didn't.

The woman had only to quirk an eyebrow for the answer to come with bone-chilling clarity.

More attacks.

Asher had released a bitter huff. "My dear old dad won't take over until he can do so heroically."

Brahm's ability to deceive and beguile was truly astounding. He was a master manipulator—the very face of evil—duping an entire nation, perhaps even the entire world, with charm and aplomb. It was terrifying to watch.

With every passing day, Eden's worry for her parents grew. What was to stop this evil man from using them to get to her? She felt like a cancer patient, waiting on a prognosis from her oncologist. Any moment the phone would ring with news that the prognosis was grim. Her malignancy, fatal.

Eden would be exceedingly stronger if her parents were safe, but on this matter Prudence Dvorak refused to budge, and Eden couldn't drum up anger at her refusal. For past her heart, deep down in her gut, she knew it was the right call. Attempting another breakout would be a suicide mission. Which left her with the next best thing—doing everything in her power to win this war.

As a newly minted leader of the Resistance, there was plenty to do. Eager to distract herself from the fate of her parents and the torment that was Cassian's continued rejection, she dove in headfirst. Eden attended every council meeting. She cast her votes with care. She used her voice. She contributed to the reconnaissance planning. She helped organize Alexandria into a proper rebellion. She and Dvorak worked side-by-side, splitting the community into teams. Recruitment, counter-propaganda, and surveillance were the big three.

They needed eyes on Brahm's soldiers, on key members of Swarm, on the four cities that had been attacked, on the three cities yet to be attacked. On the detainment facilities, too, which grew more crowded by the day. Every morning and every evening, pixelated RRA vehicles would arrive with more people, and not a whiff of it reached the news. At least not on Concordia, anyway.

America Underground, however?

This war was being fought on the battlefield of truth. Exposure was the name of the game. *America Underground* led the charge. Dayne's eyes grew bloodshot with sleep deprivation, but his aura glowed with purpose. He was expanding their distribution, brainstorming headlines, and editing articles to ensure they told the truth irresistibly and unflinchingly. Cleo even got the go-ahead to run her incriminating op-ed on Oswin Brahm.

Meanwhile, recruitment teams capitalized on every contact they had, from the highly prominent, like Dr. Beverly Randall-Ransom, to the completely obscure, like Finn and Erik Gaviola. Cleo was thrilled to be in touch with her mother again; Eden appreciated hearing Erik's familiar voice. They enlisted anyone and everyone who might help them plant seeds of truth. The lotus leaf was no longer a simple symbol of the Amber Highway, but a secret sign of the Resistance, one that helped them navigate treacherous waters.

Amir was dead, so they no longer had a mole. But they did have a ring. It belonged to a prison guard, who had used the ring to communicate with fellow members of Swarm. But the man was listed as deceased in Swarm's database, which meant they couldn't waltz into a virtual meeting wearing his avatar. Not without raising giant red flags.

Thanks to Asher, they didn't need to. He knew things about his father nobody else knew, like how to infiltrate various methods of communication. He was able to use the ring to tune in to these meetings from afar, like a virtual peephole with spotty reception. Individuals were assigned to ring duty in three-hour increments. Barrett and Violet were happy to take this duty whenever they weren't being inspected in Asher's lab.

Cleo and Cassian took charge of a team all their own —one that worked to bring people to safety. They fashioned escape routes south to Mexico for illegal residents in Fresno, north to Canada for illegal residents in Seattle, and east to Alexandria for those in St. Louis. A task made nearly impossible in light of the lockdown. Leaving home was no longer permissible for anyone without an essential worker's permit. Drone surveillance had doubled. Law enforcement had tripled. RRA patrol officers were as prevalent as CogniFuse commercials. And only citizens with the highest level of clearance could cross state lines.

The first group of St. Louis refugees was set to arrive in Alexandria tomorrow. The recon mission was happening the day after. A meeting was scheduled to take place in the IDA boardroom in one hour to solidify the details.

Which left Eden with a rare, unwelcome moment of downtime. She spent it on the couch, restlessly thumbing through journals like she might find something new, despite having read and memorized each one. As always, they were depressing and troubling and frustratingly uninformative. She tossed the journal on the coffee table with an aggravated sigh. It landed atop the latest edition of *America Underground.*

The image on the front page staring back at her was as disturbing as the journals. Amanda Hawkins had provided it, a government employee who'd rescued Cassian and Dvorak from the bottom of the Potomac. She'd gained access into Fredericksburg and had snapped the photograph discreetly. Now here it was, telling a powerful story. So long as people were willing to look at it.

The paper crinkled as Eden picked it up. A similar one had appeared on her doorstep once, when she was a little girl. She'd carried it inside with a sense of innocent curiosity before Mom snatched it from her hands and fed it to the shredder. Would that same story unfold across America? Or might some of those mothers unroll the paper and look at the image within? And if they did, would they question what was going on?

It was a gripping photograph. Dayne called it a money shot. An arthritic old man, a painfully thin woman, and two frightened children locked behind black iron bars in an overcrowded prison cell. Not vermin, like Concordia wanted the public to believe, but four human beings forced into deplorable conditions. Eden's parents were among them.

She bit her thumbnail, her stomach twisting with desperation, with helplessness, and noted the time. When she wasn't planning recon or organizing teams or analyzing data or exploring and charting networks, Eden had her own personal side project.

Tycho.

She visited him at least once every day, sometimes twice. Carefully planning each visit so he was strong enough to talk (he usually didn't) and well enough to eat (he always did). She rolled up the paper and exited her apartment, making a pit stop at the commissary before climbing down the ladder for her fifteenth visit.

This far in, Tycho no longer looked surprised to see her. She handed him the tray and sat against the wall with the rolled-up newspaper in hand. When he was finished eating, she showed him the photograph, looking —hoping—for signs of sympathy. Tycho showed none. Not even for Dayne's *money* shot.

"What if this was Aurelia?" Eden asked.

"A prison cell couldn't hold Aurelia. It couldn't hold any of us."

Us.

This was the only progress Eden had made. In their lopsided conversations, Tycho had recently begun to use the inclusive pronoun, like they were on the same side. It roused a sense of unease among certain council members. Why was Subject 006 meeting with the asset and why was Pru allowing it?

Eden maintained her position. Tycho had information. A lot of information. Maybe she could wheedle some out of him. And maybe, while she did, she could make his existence a little more tolerable. He had a bedroll, a pillow, and a blanket now, at least.

With her legs extended in front of her, she crossed one ankle over the other. "I'm going to visit your home in a few days."

Tycho narrowed his eyes.

"Fort Wadsworth. That's where you grew up, right?"

The castle-like structure sat on the northeastern shore of Staten Island, on the Narrows of the New York Harbor. If their calculations were correct, this was where Tycho had been raised. A few days ago, she'd gotten him to share just a little about his upbringing. He made it sound idyllic. Without a single flaw. Like she'd missed out on not being raised with him.

"Is this where Sanctus Liber is kept?" she asked, carefully observing him. It had become a sort of game, trying to read his thoughts by studying his face. The imperceptible tightening of lips. The slightest expansion of pupils. The tiniest movement of muscle. Not to mention her ability to measure heart rate and breathing rate. She could even smell nervousness if she focused hard enough.

"What do you know of Sanctus Liber?" he replied.

"I know it was written by Oswin. I know you used to read from it on Thursdays inside the catacombs. I know it holds valuable information about what will happen next."

Tycho's face had gone pale and drawn. He was both surprised and disturbed by her knowledge of such things.

"Will I find Ellery at Fort Wadsworth?"

His temporomandibular joint gave the teeniest of ticks.

It usually did when they talked about Ellery, which they had at length. The topic was one he actually engaged in—Subject 005, and whether she was alive. Whether the government would have finished the job her father had failed to do seventeen years ago.

"Pater would never allow it," he'd said. "He would rescue her from such a fate."

Rescue.

His choice of word had curdled the food in Eden's stomach. If Ellery wasn't dead, she was in Oswin Brahm's possession, and if that was the case, Eden had no doubt he would control her. It was more bearable to imagine the girl dead.

"If she's alive, will she be properly cleansed by now?"

"That depends on her," Tycho said. "And whether she cooperates with the process."

"What if she doesn't cooperate?"

Tycho frowned.

Eden didn't know Ellery. The first time she'd heard the name was inside a police station in Eagle Bend. Ellery Forrester, a disturbed teenage runaway. Her next encounter had come via an age-progression photograph, which had been given to Cassian, who'd been hired by Yukio to find two girls. Eden could still remember the shock of this discovery.

Cass had been so remorseful. So desperate to make amends, he'd agreed to use the self-destruct command. Now? He didn't seem to care about her at all. Cleo kept insisting he did, but how could he? If he cared even half as much as Eden cared for him, he wouldn't be able to avoid her like he was. But avoid her, he did. So successfully, it carved a crater in her chest. Time hadn't soothed his wounds; whatever he endured in prison had irrevocably altered their relationship, and now she existed as though a permanent weight were pressing down upon her heart. After weeks of fearing she would never see him again, he was back in her life. She saw him every day, in fact. But in the cruelest of ironies, he was more lost to her than ever.

Tycho scratched the blonde whiskers on his cheek. He didn't seem to have an answer to her latest question—what if Ellery doesn't cooperate?

Eden pursed her lips. "I guess that's what the self-destruct function is for."

This elicited a reaction bigger than a ticking temporomandibular joint. He still didn't believe they had a self-destruct function. In his mind, Eden made it up to plant seeds of doubt.

She sank back against the wall. These visits were turning out to be an epic failure. She wasn't getting any information. A blanket and a bedroll could hardly make his stay more humane. And she was nowhere close to convincing him of the truth.

If only Cass would share how he'd done it with Amanda Hawkins. How had he persuaded an employee of the United States government to consider the truth when he was a presumed terrorist locked up in a prison cell? Eden would ask him if he'd give her one second of his time.

Her watch beeped.

The recon meeting was in ten minutes.

Feeling worse than she had before she'd come, she grabbed the empty tray and the newspaper and climbed back up the ladder.

Just as she was shutting the hatch, Barrett appeared, bright-eyed and excited. Violet stood behind him, fidgeting as she eyed the portable freezer where the vials of poison were kept. According to Barrett, Violet was going to therapy. She'd had two sessions so far, and while he couldn't totally tell, he thought it might be helping.

Eden had her doubts. Violet hardly slept. And while

Barrett's list of forgotten names and Eden's searing bouts of head pain seemed to have plateaued, Violet's glitching was on the rise.

"We intercepted a message," Barrett said.

"From the rings?"

He nodded, a cowlick of dark hair bouncing on top of his head. "The reception was staticky, but we definitely heard a very specific phrase."

"What was it?" she asked.

Barrett glanced at Violet, who couldn't look away from the portable freezer. "'Sharks are messing with the weapon again.'"

Eden pulled her chin back. "Sharks?"

"Sharks," Barrett confirmed.

"What does that mean?"

He shook his head. "I have no idea."

17

As soon as Eden arrived at the meeting, she played the message Barrett had recorded—staticky, but unmistakable. When it was finished, Nairobi asked the same question Eden had.

"What does it mean?"

Nobody had an answer.

Not Dvorak. Not Jericho. Not Lark, Dayne, Asher, or Francesca, who had been released from Kaiser two days ago. Barrett called her the mummy of the Potomac Yard thanks to the white gauze wrapped around her face and hands.

"Play it again," Dvorak said.

Eden did.

The phrase was no different the second time. *Sharks are messing with the weapon again.*

Dayne pulled at his cheeks, then tapped the side of

his face. "Do we think they're talking about actual sharks?"

"That would require them to have a weapon in the ocean," Jericho said.

"I bet you anything it's code." Asher spun his queen. "The sharks represent people."

Everyone sat with narrowed eyes. If the sharks represented people, then *what* people? Was there another group out there, fighting against Brahm? Did this group know about some weapon the rest of them didn't?

Francesca curled her gauze-wrapped fingers around her armrests, her chair creaking as she shifted. "The weapon could be the asset."

"Which would make … *us* the sharks?" Nairobi looked doubtful when she said it.

Eden felt the same. "It can't be. Tycho is secure. How could they possibly know if we were messing with him or not?"

"Maybe he has some secret method of communication," Francesca offered.

Eden shook her head. "Doubtful."

Francesca's gauze moved in a manner that suggested lifted eyebrows. If she was disapproving of Eden's presence before getting roasted, she was even more so now. Pre-injury, Francesca was leery. Post-injury, Francesca was downright paranoid. She took everything Eden said to court. It was growing tiresome.

"He's barely able to lift his own head. You have him locked up in a bomb shelter getting poisoned every four hours. In what conceivable way can he communicate?" As Eden spoke, her words grew increasingly heated. She hated how they were handling Tycho.

Hated, hated, hated.

"I guess you would know better than us," Francesca said. "Since you spend so much time with him every day."

"To get information." Asher delivered the statement with a sigh. Apparently he was growing weary of Francesca's suspicion, too.

"I think we're being foolish. What are they even talking about down there? For all we know, they could be organizing a coup."

"Then turn on the sound and listen in," Eden said.

Francesca's hand moved toward her face like she wanted to scratch. She stopped before doing so. Dr. Millard probably instructed her not to touch. "You're treating him like he's some kind of victim."

"You're treating him like he's some kind of animal." Eden turned to Dvorak. "*Worse* than an animal. He didn't choose to be who he is anymore than you chose to be impregnated."

"I chose to leave."

"You left *him*."

Dvorak straightened. "If you think I could have escaped any other—"

"I don't mean to accuse you. I'm just saying, you left when he was an infant, and he's been brainwashed ever since. How is he supposed to know any better?"

"I knew better," Asher said. He sat slouched in the chair with his elbows on the armrests, his fingers tented. "You act like he had no other choice than to *be* brainwashed. But here I sit, proof that he had options. Tycho bought in. I got out."

"It's not the same," Eden replied. "You weren't born with ninety-three other babies. Raised with ninety-three other babies. Force-fed an entire narrative about ushering in some utopia."

"You are determined to defend him," Francesca sneered.

"And you are determined to hate him."

Dayne brought his fingers to his temples and spoke in a cool tone that brought some much needed relief to the heated conversation. "What are you proposing, Eden?"

Everyone looked at her.

"I don't know." She shoved a lock of hair behind her ear. She hated how they were handling Tycho, but even more, she hated that there didn't seem to be a viable alternative. "I just wish we could come up with something more humane."

Asher came forward in his seat. He moved his elbows

to the table and re-tented his fingers. "You told him about the tranquilizer pump. I was there when you showed it to him. If I recall, he wasn't interested."

Eden flushed. And deflated. Asher was right. He'd heard Tycho's words for himself. If they stopped injecting him, he would kill as many people as possible.

What was there to do with that?

Dvorak waved her hand, as though to shoo away the conversation. "We've gotten off track," she said. "Unless anyone has any further thoughts on what this intercepted message might mean, we need to move on."

She waited.

When nobody had anything to add, Dvorak turned their attention to the task at hand. Recon. Lark had done nine missions already. Her job was always the same. Get in, use black-market drones to create a three-dimensional copy of the location, then get out. Once she returned, Asher would create a virtual replica of this location, which they could explore to their heart's content from the safety of home base. This time, though, getting in would be incredibly dangerous.

Ten of Brahm's soldiers remained in Fort Wadsworth. A better number than ninety-three, certainly. But ten was still ten. While Lark typically went on her recon missions alone, Dvorak wasn't sending her in solo this time.

They'd put together a special ops team of six. There was Lark, of course. A talented martial artist and a self-trained sniper who could put a bullet in the dead center of a bullseye twenty-five hundred yards away. Consistently with no nanotechnology to assist her.

"I've been practicing for thirty years," she liked to say with a determined gleam in her eye. She was eager to pay penance for the damage she'd caused when she was young and impressionable and taken in by a charismatic classmate who'd played her like a fiddle. If anyone was going to put a bullet through Oswin Brahm's head, it was her.

The other members of the team were Jericho and Nairobi, who would provide a diversion, and Alexandria's very own super freaks, their aim flawless. One session with the self-made sniper and Violet was hitting bullseyes that had taken Lark decades to master.

Eden passed on her knowledge of hand-to-hand combat. Barrett was exceptionally strong. Violet, wicked fast. Other than the glitching that came and went without warning, they were shaping up to make quite the trio.

And yet, as they reviewed the plans, Dvorak began shaking her head. "There are four points on a compass. We only have three covered. I want Lark guarded on all sides."

"So, we need a fourth," Jericho said.

"I think a fourth would be wise."

"Do you have someone in mind?"

She tapped the table with her finger. "How about Cassian?"

Eden flushed.

"He's strong. Competent. Good with a gun. Quick with his fists."

Quick with his fists was an insult. Cassian Gray was a highly trained fighter as lethal as Lark's aim. He'd be an asset on any team.

"Do you think he'd be willing to join?" Dvorak asked—not Eden, but Dayne.

It hurt. A lot.

But why would Dvorak ask anyone else? Dayne saw Cassian way more than Eden did. The editor was just opening his mouth to respond when Eden beat him to the punch. "I can ask him," she blurted.

With a nod, Dvorak brought their meeting to a close. Asher quickly gathered his stuff and followed Eden into the courtyard.

Frozen grass crunched underfoot.

"Hold up," he said, tucking his laptop beneath his muscular arm.

She slowed only slightly.

"I found something this morning in Violet's network."

Eden stopped, breath bottling in her chest. "About the Queen Bee?"

"A possible access point that might provide some insight into Tycho."

Her hope crashed. Between the dead end that was the journals, the cold shoulder from Cassian, her lack of progress with Tycho, Eden needed something to give. Asher gaining access into Tycho's network wasn't it.

"I need to cross check it with yours and Barrett's to see if I'm on to something." He looked at his watch. "I'm meeting with Dvorak and Lark to trouble shoot the drones right now. Are you free in an hour?"

"Sure." She lifted her shoulder listlessly and started walking again.

Asher walked with her. "Can I ask you a question?"

"You just did," she said.

"What's up with Cass and Cleo?"

"What do you mean?"

"Before he showed up, she was always making it sound like you two were a thing. But obviously, if anyone's a thing ..."

Eden raised her eyebrows.

"It's them." He said it like it was as obvious as two plus two.

"They aren't a *thing*." Eden opened the door to the IDA's west tower. "They're just ... working together."

"*Just* working?"

"Yes, *just* working. Trust me. Cleo and Cass are very, very platonic."

He looked skeptical. Bothered. *Jealous*.

Truth be told, Eden was jealous, too. Not because she thought anything romantic was going on between Cleo and Cassian, but because Cleo got to be with him. They worked together, spent time together. Meanwhile, Cass could hardly be bothered to meet Eden's eye.

The muscles across her chest pulled tight. She would do anything to go back to the way things were, before they followed that stupid tunnel and he was imprisoned. She wanted to feel his warmth, his strength. The steady rhythm of his heartbeat against her ear—a heavenly sound she'd experienced on multiple occasions in Eloise and Elmer's basement, where they would lie together on the couch. He would play with her hair. Tiptoe his fingers up her spine. Trace circles around her shoulder blade. The longing this stirred in her soul was nearly unbearable.

Cassian had grounded her, bolstered her, aroused her. Then ditched her.

With her lips pressed tight, she left Asher in the lobby and made her way to the newsroom. She found them in a cubicle with their heads bent together as they studied photographs tacked to a bulletin board—a group of ten people Cass would meet at the Reagan National Airport tomorrow morning.

Cleo said something under her breath. Cassian

laughed. Actually laughed. Jealousy coiled in Eden's gut as she knocked on the wall.

Cleo turned. When she saw Eden, her expression brightened. When Cass saw Eden, he turned back around and resumed working on whatever it was they'd been working on.

Eden wanted to scream. She wanted to march across the short distance, grab the back of his chair, and spin him around until he was forced to acknowledge her. She'd been so certain this would pass. Positive Cass just needed some space. Eventually, he would work through whatever it was he needed to work through, and he would let her back in. But as he sat there with his strong, well-defined back completely to her, she no longer felt even a modicum of hope.

Cleo half-smiled, half-grimaced. "What's up, Six?"

"Dvorak wants Cass to join the recon mission."

"When is it?" he asked in a low, grumbly voice that exacerbated her aggravation.

When was it? Was he so busy now, so completely over her that he had to check his schedule before he decided whether he would join an important, dangerous mission in which she was involved?

"Wednesday." Which gave him plenty of time to finish *his* mission and join theirs. She waited until her frustration grew too hot to handle. With a shake of her head, she turned on her heel. She would go find Dvorak and tell her sorry, Cassian Gray would not be gracing them with his presence.

"I'll go," he said in the same tone as before.

Eden bit back a fawning thank you and left, trying her best to forget that she and Cassian had ever been anything more than two people forced into proximity.

18

Violet stared at the portable freezer, listening to the conversation unfolding inside the enclosed booth, where a person could observe the young man stuck underground via video surveillance.

When she decided to come, she didn't think she would have to be so sneaky. As it turned out, Barrett was here. Along with Eden and Asher. They were supposed to be in the lab. That's where Barrett said she could find him once she finished her session with her new therapist.

Dr. Lydia Kane was a plump woman with big dimples, brown skin, and rectangle glasses. When they first met, she'd introduced herself with a firm handshake and told Violet to call her Lydia. Barrett had come with. He'd brought the bubblegum pink backpack full of journals. Lydia asked Violet's permission to read them.

The second time, Lydia talked about the journals and the things Father had written. According to her, those things were inexcusable, and none of them were Violet's fault.

This last time, Violet went by herself. Lydia used words like 'chronic abuse' and 'chronic powerlessness'. She gave Violet homework. She was to identify a need, then take steps to meet that need. Which was how Violet ended up here. She *needed* the screaming to stop.

She licked her bottom lip, her gaze boring a hole in the freezer. The vials were in there, filled with a poisonous compound responsible for the screaming.

Footsteps sounded in the stairwell behind her. With her pulse skittering, she ducked into a patch of shadow as Cleo walked by, past the deep freeze, into the booth.

She left the door ajar.

"Well, well, well," Asher said. "If it isn't Cleo Ransom, gracing us with her presence."

"I came to check on Eden," Cleo replied. "How are you doing?"

"I'm fine," Eden answered. But there was a stiffness to her voice that made the words a lie.

"I'm sorry he's being such a jackwagon," Cleo said.

"You don't have to apologize for him."

"I know I don't. But still … he's being a giant turd. I told him so to his face."

He must be Cassian.

Violet didn't like Cassian. He wasn't kind. Not to Eden. Not to Barrett, either.

"How's Operation Secret Passage?" Barrett asked.

"Good, I think. Cass has coordinated everything like a boss, anyway." Chair legs scraped against the concrete floor. "What about you guys? I ran into Dvorak on my way here. She looked ... on edge."

"Can you blame her?" Asher asked amidst fast-paced typing and clicking. "She already lost Amir. Now she's sending Lark on a highly dangerous recon mission with three of Brahm's mutants."

"We're not mutants," Eden said.

Violet crept closer.

Someone inside the booth yawned.

"What if we used radiation?" Eden asked, returning to the conversation she'd been having with Asher before Cleo arrived. They'd been discussing the Queen Bee, and how they might go about removing it.

"How do you radiate a moving target?" Asher replied.

"I don't know. I guess you'd have to isolate it. Figure out a way to track its path."

"That would require access to equipment we don't have."

"Violet's dad used a particle accelerator," Barrett said. "He built one in his basement."

There was a pause.

And then, "Do you know how to build a particle accelerator?"

"Sure, I'll get right on that." Asher's sarcastic words were followed by the aggressive tapping of computer keys. He huffed. "His network is un-hackable."

Violet could hear a hand scrubbing a face. A frustrated sigh exhaled into a palm.

"Is the great and mighty *Gollum* admitting defeat?" Cleo teased.

"Pointing out an impossibility isn't the same as admitting defeat."

Violet was right there. Standing over the freezer, heart pounding in her ears. She lifted the lid. A cloud of dry ice rose from within. Beneath the fog, glass containers were stacked, a hundred vials per tray.

She bit her bottom lip.

Here they were. Hers for the destroying. The question was, how did one destroy them? Carefully, she picked up a vial and turned it over in her fingers.

"What are you doing?"

Asher filled the door frame, his question so loud and accusatory, Violet jumped. The freezer door fell shut. The vial dropped from her hand and burst open on the concrete with a sizzling hiss.

Asher started coughing.

Behind him, Cleo clutched her throat.

Poisonous vapors.

The basement had to be filling with poisonous vapors.

Violet took a lurching step back as Barrett came into view. With terror zipping through her veins, she fled. She raced down the corridor and up the stairwell, out into the night. She sprinted through the dark grounds until she was safely inside the suite she shared with Eden and Cleo.

She pressed her back against the door and slid to the floor, waiting for her breath and her heartbeat to normalize. Waiting and waiting and waiting until a gentle knock sounded behind her.

"Violet?"

It was Barrett.

She got off the floor and opened the door. He stood on the other side with his hands in his pockets, smiling reassuringly. "They're okay—Asher and Cleo. Eden took them to Kaiser just to be on the safe side, but the second they got some fresh air in their lungs they seemed totally fine."

Relief.

Anger.

Sadness.

They marched in a single file line, one by one. She was relieved she hadn't hurt them. She was angry about failing at her homework assignment. She was sad she hadn't helped Tycho, who was due to scream again in one hour and sixteen minutes.

"You were trying to get rid of the poison, weren't you?" His question wasn't accusatory. His questions never were. "I don't blame you. I hate what they're doing to him. So does Eden. I don't think Cleo's a fan either."

She waited for him to say the rest. The excuse. None of them liked it, *but* it was a necessary evil. She was really starting to loathe those two words together. Evil was evil. Did it ever have to be necessary? Thankfully, Barrett didn't excuse it. He didn't add any caveats.

He didn't like it.

Cleo and Eden didn't like it.

Full stop.

Violet went into the kitchen, filled a glass of water, and drank it empty.

Barrett pulled a deck of cards from his pocket. "Gin Rummy?"

She grabbed a pen and the pad of paper they used to keep score. Barrett took a seat at the table and began shuffling the cards.

Violet noticed another name written on the back of his hand. He'd been holding steady at four for a while. Now, there was a fifth. *Francesca.* Somewhere between this morning's breakfast and now, Barrett had lost her name.

She joined him at the table and brushed her fingertip over the letters.

"I'm gonna run out of space soon," he said with a frown. He started dealing—seven cards for him, seven for her. "Will you help me remember when I do?"

The question pinched her heart.

With a deep breath and an even deeper reach, she answered his question with an audible *yes*. Her voice was scratchy and soft. And maybe not buried so deep, after all.

His entire face lit up, the same way it did whenever he talked to his family. This had been a recent development—the recruitment of the Barr family. Barrett had been thrilled. Finally, he could fill them in on everything that had been going on, including a deep fake that made him out to be a murderer. They could only talk in four-minute increments, which were tracked on an egg timer. The second it dinged, he had to hang up. But Barrett could fit a lot of words into four minutes.

He scooped up his cards and fanned them in his hand. "Did I ever tell you about the time I used a card trick to scam Jameson out of his lawn mowing money?"

Violet scooped up her cards, too, and settled in for another one of his stories.

19

Eden sat in the dark on the couch Barrett used for a bed. His blanket lay in a puddle on the floor. Potato chip crumbs decorated the cushion. When she pulled a throw pillow onto her lap, she found a cookie wrapper crumpled underneath.

Apparently, Barrett was a slob. And she was trespassing. Nobody had invited her inside. She'd let herself into his apartment just like she had once before, when she'd needed him to carry out a command nobody else had been willing to carry out. Barrett was in her apartment, playing Gin Rummy with Violet, and Cassian wasn't here. He was probably still in his cubicle, working and preparing for tomorrow.

Eden couldn't stop thinking about him. The harder she tried, the more space he took up in her head. Something had to be done. So here she was, waiting. She didn't care how long or how late. She wasn't budging until he came through that door and talked to her. It was the only way she was going to sleep tonight.

He was leaving for the airport tomorrow on a mission that could go terribly wrong. What if she never saw him again? Anger fed her worry. Worry watered her anger. A self-perpetuating cycle that made her want to crawl out of her skin.

She never thought she would be one of these girls, pining for a guy who wasn't giving her the time of day. She definitely didn't think she would be one in the middle of an apocalypse while her parents were locked up in a detainment facility. She thought she had more self-respect than that. Certainly more sense.

Apparently not.

She couldn't get the imagery of his well-defined back out of her head. Not when she went to the lab to meet Asher and Barrett. Not when they went to the IDA to see if Asher had discovered a breakthrough with Tycho's network. Not when Violet dropped the poisonous vial and not when she escorted Asher and Cleo to Kaiser. Eden had stewed through it all—her anger growing, her worry gorging.

He couldn't even muster the decency to turn around and face her when she asked him a question. It was the final straw. She was the camel with the broken back, no longer willing to let this slide, to give him space, to be ignored.

She was going to make him acknowledge her. She was going to ask him if he no longer cared. If his answer was yes, he could look her in the face when he said it. If he had the courage to do that, she would move on. Put this behind her and focus her energy where it ought to be focused—on the recon mission, on her parents, on taking Brahm down.

The door opened.

Cass stepped inside and kicked it shut behind him. His hair was sweaty. His shirt, too. Which meant he hadn't been working in his cubicle. He'd been working out in the fitness room. He pulled off his shirt and walked to the refrigerator.

Eden's breath caught.

His chiseled physique was an art form.

Despite her scratchy emotions, she was hopelessly mesmerized. She admired every defined muscle—able to name them thanks to the diagram she'd glanced at in an anatomy book back in August. His trapezius. His deltoids. His obliques. The latissimus dorsi tapering to the small of his back in a delectable V.

She watched the ripple of each one as he drank from a jug of water, then set his hands on the counter and leaned forward in a posture so defeated, her anger melted into goo.

His shoulders rose and fell with a heavy sigh, then he pushed himself up and turned around, startling at the sight of her. She could hear the jump of his heart. See the flex of his abdomen as he leaned away, staring warily. "What are you doing here?"

"I had to take Cleo to Kaiser."

"*What*?"

"Along with Asher. They were observing Tycho when Violet dropped one of the vials. They inhaled some of the vapors."

He blinked at her. He looked left, then right, like she wasn't speaking English. Maybe she should try French.

"She's going to be fine, but I wanted you to know in case you were expecting to do more planning with her tonight."

"Okay." He drawled the word slowly, his wariness morphing into visible discomfort.

Eden could feel her blood pressure rising. She uncrossed her legs and stood from the couch. His gaze rolled down her body, then back up again. It heated her from head to toe. "I also figured that if I didn't come tonight, we might never talk again."

His face went impassive. Bored. Blank. Like an erased slate. Like a person who didn't care. But biology didn't lie. His pupils were dilated. His heart rate remained elevated. She could feel the rising heat of his body.

She folded her arms, squared her shoulders, and joined him in the kitchen.

He moved away until his backside met the counter behind him.

Her gaze traveled along the tattoo covering his deltoid and bicep. She'd traced it once before, in Dr. Beverly Randall-Ransom's kitchen. Everything inside her wanted to trace it again. She took a step closer.

"Eden," he said, her name a gruff rumble in his throat. His face was visibly strained. Like he was holding himself back. Keeping himself in check. But only just.

She took another step.

"What are you doing?" he asked. His skin was flushed. His breath, quick. Whatever his emotions were doing, however his feelings for her had changed, this remained an undeniable truth, one he couldn't hide. Cassian Gray wanted her.

She took a third step.

He had nowhere to go, so he held his ground—his jaw tight, a damp tendril of hair touching his brow.

Her finger ached to brush it aside. And why not? She'd gone this far. Why not go a little further? The second she reached, he grabbed her wrist, his golden eyes flashing. "You need to go."

She lifted her chin. "Why?"

A muscle in his jaw ticked.

She stared up at him in defiance, her rebellion on full display. "If you want me to leave, tell me why."

"It's late."

"It's late?" she repeated.

"Yes."

She shook her head. His heart was still racing, his skin as flushed as her own. "That's not good enough."

"What else do you want me to say?"

"The truth."

He let go of her wrist and took a step sideways, scrubbing his hand down his face.

"Why won't you talk to me?" she asked.

His mouth tightened.

"Are you angry? Did I do something to repulse you?"

He huffed like that was a joke.

But she pressed onward. "It didn't seem like you were repulsed at the Miller's, but obviously something changed. Whatever it is, just tell me. Say the words and put me out of my misery."

His chest rose and fell. With his palms on the counter behind him, he was looking anywhere but her.

"Why are you confiding in Cleo, but not in me?"

"Because I don't love Cleo!" The words exploded. They burst forth—loud, and raw, and broken. He pulled at his bare chest, his perfect, gorgeous face no longer closed shutters but pain on full display. "My heart doesn't feel like it's being ripped to shreds whenever I'm in her presence."

Eden stopped breathing.

"And what is it you want me to confide? What exactly do you want me to say? That I feel rage ninety percent of the time? That if Mona was here right now, I would kill her with my bare hands and relish the light leaving her eyes? That every night I'm back in that closet, pounding on the doors while my father beats my mother with a baseball bat? That I spend every minute of every day terrified I'll lose the strength to stay away from you?"

Eden's heart shattered—broke into a million pieces. She shook her head, tears welling in her eyes.

"You don't need a guy like me in your life, Eden. I will not ruin you like he ruined her. So please, just go." He turned to leave, like that was it. This was it.

She grabbed his forearm, right where it rose to meet the inside of his elbow. His skin was like a fever.

He stared down at her fingers as the words he'd given her once before came to her now. After the Prosperity Ball. After her worst nightmare had come true. Words that had stopped her from unraveling. Words that had put her back together again.

You don't think we all have the same struggle—a battle inside that has us doing things we don't want to do? If you're good, you fight it. You starve it. I'm telling you right now, I'm looking at one of the best.

So was she. And she would not let him continue on for one more second believing in lies. "You aren't him," she said in a fierce, insistent whisper. "You're not even close."

Something broke in him, like he wanted so desperately to believe her. She could see the struggle—a battlefield in his mind where truth and deceit waged war. He closed his eyes and shook his head, a man on the brink. Trying—trying so hard—to maintain control.

She grappled for the magic words that would help truth win. "Your anger is a part of you because you want the world to be a better place. You want to protect the people you care about and set things to right, which makes you *nothing* like him." She gave his arm the smallest squeeze. "And I'm telling you right now, the only way you're going to ruin me is by shutting me out."

His eyes opened—twin pools of golden flame that could light the universe on fire. He stood on the brink for half a second longer. Then he dove.

His hands tangled in her hair and his mouth took hers. With every nerve igniting, she wrapped her arms around his neck. He lifted her. Set her on the table, pressed closer as his lips moved to her throat and his stubble scratched against her skin.

She curled her fingers into his hair and leaned her

head back, wanting more of him. All of him. He braced one hand on the tabletop, spread his other up the length of her ribcage, and kissed her collarbone. Her breath caught. She dug her fingers into his broad upper back just as the door swung open.

Barrett stepped inside, whistling a ditty.

Cass wrenched himself away.

Barrett stopped mid-step, his ditty falling into an awkward silence. His cheeks flamed cherry red at the sight before him.

A shirtless Cassian with disheveled hair.

A flushed Eden, sitting on the table.

And for the first time in maybe forever, Barrett Barr was completely lost for words.

Cass stood beneath the frigid spray, his hands splayed against the tiled wall, his heart pounding in his chest. His back rising and falling with breath that needed to slow down.

That kiss.

It had been oxygen after severe deprivation. Sensory overload after solitary confinement. He'd been living in a hole robbed of all senses. No light, no sound, no touch. Then suddenly there was an onslaught. The velvety softness of Eden's hair between his fingers. The irresistible warmth of her lips. The heady scent of her skin. The ravishing taste of her neck. The tiniest catch of her breath.

He turned the water all the way to cold.

As determined as he'd been not to lose control, he'd lost *all* control. He would have kept losing it, too, had Barrett not interrupted. Cass had given in, which highlighted a very real truth—he was a fool for thinking he'd be able to resist her. On this side of their encounter, it certainly felt like an impossibility. He didn't even want to try. It was a terrifying conclusion, for being in her presence felt like standing on the edge of restraint.

I loved her so much, I couldn't think straight.

You aren't him. You aren't even close.

Eden's words and his father's words went to war inside him, tangling and brawling in a battle that left his emotions in a pile of wreckage. As much as he wanted her words to be true, his father's were a more accurate reflection of reality. For Cassian *felt* like his father. In the ring when he killed a man. In that kitchen, just now. Need and desire had pounded through his veins, consuming all reason.

With a groan, he scrubbed his hand down his face. If resisting Eden was no longer a possibility, then there was only one acceptable option—deserving her. But how was that anymore viable than resisting? Nothing he said tonight was a lie. He felt angry ninety percent of the time. Nightmares plagued his sleep. If Mona showed up right now, he would kill her with his bare hands. How could he possibly deserve Eden with feelings such as these? He was a broken man. Terribly and irrevocably broken. He couldn't put that brokenness on her and live with himself.

Cass shut off the water. He opened the shower door and grabbed a towel.

He'd scoffed at Cleo and her hypnotherapy. Allowing another person inside his head, letting them put him in a state of high suggestibility, felt like the opposite of control. But hypnotherapy was not the only therapy. There were other forms. Less bizarre forms. As a matter of fact, there was a trained professional right here in Alexandria. He knew because Barrett wouldn't shut up about it.

He imagined himself laying on a couch, opening up to a stranger, and his muscles clenched. His abdomen tightened into rock. He dried himself off and wrapped the towel around his waist. He stepped out into the living room, where Barrett watched the nightly news, holding a bag of potato chips like a football.

Cass cleared his throat.

Barrett looked over his shoulder, then sat up straight like he'd been caught doing something wrong.

"How is therapy going for Violet?"

Barrett's mouth dropped open as though Cass had

just asked him something unhinged. The kid scratched the back of his head. "She's only had three appointments."

"Is it helping?" Cass asked.

"It's ... not hurting." Barrett shifted. The bag of potato chips crinkled. "Actually, she talked tonight. Which was the first time she's talked since her dad showed up back in Minneapolis."

Cass nodded.

Maybe he would see this therapist, too.

Maybe Dr. Lydia Kane would help him deserve the girl he loved.

20

Outside the commissary, cold rain fell from a dreary sky. Eden sat at a round table with Barrett and Violet and absolutely zero appetite. Her fingers were icy. Her underarms, clammy. Her insides, jittery as she twirled noodles around her fork and Barrett talked around mouthfuls of garlic bread.

She tried to listen, but her mind was a whirl—spinning in a hundred different directions—and she couldn't stop checking the time. Cassian had left the safety of the Potomac Yard before Eden had a chance to say goodbye. He'd gone to the airport to meet the first group of travelers.

What if something went wrong? What if Cassian didn't return? What if she never saw him again? What if she did? What if he came back with another wall erected —a stronger one this time? What if he gave her the cold shoulder all over again? What if he pretended like nothing happened last night?

Last night.

Warmth pooled deep in her abdomen. The tiny hairs on her arms—on the nape of her neck—tingled at the memory. She shivered, but she wasn't the slightest bit cold. On the contrary, heat radiated all the way down to her toes.

Eden had no idea how Cassian felt on the other side of that encounter. She had no clue where they stood. Other than knowing why he was shutting her out, nothing else had been discussed. She recalled his outburst, his confession. He loved her. But he also felt rage. He was plagued with nightmares. He struggled with murderous thoughts. One hot and heavy, truncated make-out session didn't fix any of those things. They were serious matters that deserved serious consideration, for they didn't bode well for a relationship. They were headed for disaster. But then she would relive that kiss, and disaster didn't seem so terrible.

Eden checked the clock for what felt like the four hundredth time in the last hour. Beside her, Violet crushed saltine crackers in their packets and sprinkled the crumbs on her pasta. She took a crunchy bite just as Cleo swept into the commissary, her cheeks a rosy brown, her micro braids replaced by Bantu knots.

Eden's heart pounded in her ears as Cleo spotted

them at the far table and hurried over. "He did it!" she exclaimed, pulling out a chair. "He got all ten of them. They're on their way here now."

Eden set her fork on her tray and buried her face in her hands, relief hitting her with such force she felt woozy.

"He didn't run into a single problem. Everything went flawlessly. "

"That's awesome," Barrett said, tearing off another bite of garlic bread. "To have the first one go so well has to be an excellent indicator for the rest. Don't you think?"

"Definitely." Cleo flipped the chair around and sat on it backwards. She cast a look at Violet's concoction, then filled them in on all that had transpired. By the time she finished, Eden's dizziness had passed, the knot of dread in her chest had loosened into a tangle of anticipation, and her nerves were still buzzing.

Violet crumpled the saltine wrappers in her hand and stood, the legs of her chair scraping against the linoleum.

The three of them looked up at her.

Like usual, her dark hair obscured a good portion of her face. Unlike usual, she gave the smallest clearing of her throat. "I'm … going … to K-kaiser."

For a moment, Eden completely forgot about her nerves. Across from her, Cleo gaped. Violet had just talked. She spoke actual words in a voice that was soft and slow and scratchy with disuse.

Barrett nodded encouragingly and offered a comforting word as the girl collected her tray and scuttled away.

Cleo hitched her thumb over her shoulder. "Did she just ...?"

"She sure did," Barrett said, wiping the grease from his fingers with a napkin.

"She's talking."

"A little."

Cleo scratched her cheek. "What's in Kaiser?"

"Dr. Lydia Kane. Violet's been trying therapy. Asher told us about the possibility when we arrived."

"Asher?" Cleo repeated, like maybe Barrett had gotten him mixed up with someone else.

"He was with us when I first showed Eden the journals. He mentioned that there was a therapist here in Alexandria, and maybe she could help Violet." Barrett opened a small carton of chocolate milk. "Cass asked me about it last night. I think he might start going."

Eden did a giant double take.

Meanwhile, Cleo smacked both of her palms flat against the table. "To therapy?"

"I know," Barrett said. "I was shocked, too. I mean, the guy hardly talks. He usually just grunts at me. But last night, he finds me in the living room and starts asking me questions."

"What did he say?" Cleo asked.

"He wanted to know if it was working."

"Therapy?"

Barrett bobbed his head. "Crazy, right?"

Cleo turned, her body slowly revolving until she faced Eden, who had resumed twirling her noodles. "You're quiet."

Eden's face caught fire.

The visual cue only seemed to add fuel to Cleo's curiosity. She dipped her chin. "Did something happen?"

"No," Eden replied, one note too high.

Barrett coughed.

Eden gave him a sharp kick under the table.

He held up his hands. "I'm just saying—"

"Barrett," Eden warned.

"*Something* was happening."

"Oh my gosh," Cleo said, looking between the two of them. "Spill the freaking beans."

"It was nothing. Barrett just ..." Eden gave a shrug of her shoulder, a roll of her eyes. "He interrupted a kiss."

"You two kissed?" Cleo asked this question so loudly, several people at the nearest table stopped to stare.

The heat in Eden's cheeks intensified.

Barrett set his elbow next to his tray, cupped his

fingers over his lips, and said in a pointed tone, "That looked like more than a kiss."

Eden gave him another kick.

Cleo gawked—her mouth and eyes wide open. Then she got a faraway look in her eye and folded her arms on the back of her chair. "That's romantic as hell."

"What's romantic as hell?" Asher asked, taking Violet's seat in the same fashion Cleo had. Chair flip, straddle the back. But only after giving one of Cleo's Bantu knots a flirtatious tweak. "Nice hair."

She batted him away. "I cannot believe Cass is going to therapy."

"Is this the romantic thing?"

"Getting mentally and emotionally healthy in order to be with the person you love? Absolutely."

Asher frowned. "What ever happened to flowers?"

"A man in therapy beats flowers every day of the week."

"He's not *in* therapy," Eden said, finally finding her voice. "By the sound of it, he's *considering* therapy. And he's not doing it for me."

Cleo and Barrett exchanged a long look, then burst into laughter and said at the same time, "Yeah he is."

"Trust me, Six," Cleo added. "He would go to therapy for nobody else."

The pool of warmth that had collected in Eden's cheeks radiated through her body. She tried to squash it down, head it off at the pass. Getting her hopes up like this felt like a recipe for heartbreak. But then, so was reliving that kiss and she'd done it approximately twice every minute since wandering back to her apartment last night in a daze.

Asher helped himself to Eden's cold piece of garlic bread. "So, does this mean you two are a thing?"

Eden squirmed. She didn't know what they were. And everyone talking about it made her nerves a thousand times worse.

"Are you two going to be all PDA, making out in the hallways and stuff?" Asher took a wolfish bite of the bread and gave his eyebrows a waggle.

Cleo turned on him. "What are you doing here?"

"Besides complimenting your hair?"

She glared.

He swallowed his bite. "I thought you might like to know that Jericho radioed a few minutes ago. The new group has arrived."

Eden dropped her fork and lurched to her feet. The four of them hurried from the cafeteria and poured out into the wet, cold day.

Almost immediately, Eden saw them approaching through the mist—a group in v-formation with Cass at the lead. His shoulders were strong, his stride confident. Even more so when compared to the weary travelers behind him.

Ten lives, saved.

Because of his competence.

Her stomach swooped. Her heart ached. Oh, how she wished her parents were among those ten.

Cleo rushed forward to greet them.

Cass was smiling. A triumphant, genuine smile. One that made Eden weak in the knees. Then his eyes found hers and, wonder of all wonders, he didn't shut down. He didn't look away.

Best of all?

His smile—that rare, gorgeous smile—remained.

21

Eden wrung her hands while she paced in the empty corridor around the corner of Dr. Lydia Kane's office. In the flurry and fuss that followed the group's arrival, her eye contact with Cassian—their shared smile—had been cut short. Ten new residents were safe but not sound. Five needed a trip to Kaiser—four for significant dehydration, one for an alarming rash and a large, oozing blister.

The rest looked the way Eden must have when she'd climbed out of a steel shipping container after the botched prison break—hungry and tired and in sore need of showers.

Eden and Barrett helped them get settled. By the time they finished, she had no clue where Cass had gone. She checked his suite, the fitness room, and the commissary at The Landing before circling around to the west tower of the IDA.

Cass wasn't in the newsroom, either.

But Cleo had been.

"If I were you, I'd look on the fourth floor of Kaiser. In a certain … doctor's office." She'd given her eyebrows a knowing lift before rejoining Dayne at one of the round tables.

So, here Eden was. Pacing. Not directly outside the closed door, but around the corner, down the hall, humming the slow, dreamy melody of *La Vie en Rose* to drown out the conversation unfolding inside Dr. Kane's office. Cass was definitely in there, and as curious as Eden was, she would not infringe on his privacy by using her superhuman hearing to eavesdrop.

She was already infringing enough by simply being here. Cass had said nothing to her about therapy. He hadn't told her where she could find him when she was done. She twisted her fingers. She should probably go. Let *him* find *her*.

She reached the end of the corridor with her mind made up. She was going to leave. But then she pivoted on her heel and stopped dead. Her fidgeting fingers stopped. Her humming, too. Cass stood at the opposite end of the hallway.

A flashback burst like a firework in her brain. His lips on her neck. Her hands on the bare skin of his back. Her cheeks caught fire as he approached, his expression unreadable. It wasn't closed off, but it wasn't open either.

Her fingers resumed their wrestling match. "I promise I wasn't eavesdropping."

"I didn't think you were," he said, his voice measured. His breathing, too.

"Cleo said I could find you here." Eden bit her lip. She kept picturing him striding through the mist with his shoulders back, his legs long and powerful.

He stopped in front of her, his attention dipping to the waistband of her joggers. His heartbeat was steady. Meanwhile, hers galloped so maniacally she felt light-headed. She bent her ankles outward to stand on the sides of her shoes. Her hands kept fidgeting. She couldn't seem to help herself. Her anticipation was building, mounting in her chest. She needed him to say something. Do something. Kiss something. A thought that had the fire in her cheeks exploding anew.

He continued eying her waistband, as though trying to decide if he wanted to use it to pull her closer. Finally, he nodded toward an unoccupied room, where the muted light of a cloudy afternoon poured in through the windows. "Can we talk?"

A skitter of nerves raced up her spine. With a nod and a swallow, she followed him into the room and out onto the balcony, where the rain had stopped.

"Is this okay?" he asked.

Eden nodded. The temperature was mild for late November. It occurred to her, as she set her hand on the railing, that Thanksgiving was in two days. Her parents would spend it locked up in Fredericksburg. If the recon mission didn't go horribly south, she would spend it here. With Cassian.

He pushed his finger across his bottom lip. "We didn't resolve anything last night."

Her thoughts exactly.

There was an uptick in his heartbeat. He stared hard at her hand with a small twitch in his brow. "I meant everything I said, Eden."

Her stomach clenched.

"About the anger and the nightmares and … my feelings for you."

"I meant everything I said, too," she replied, her chin slightly lifted.

He *wasn't* his father.

He set his hand beside hers. "I don't want to be like him."

"You aren't."

"Sometimes I feel like him, though." His knuckles whitened, then relaxed with an exhale. He picked at the railing with his thumb. "When I saw him, when I had to sit there and listen to him talk, something went … crooked inside me."

She stared up at him fiercely. There was nothing crooked about him.

"He kept saying how much he loved my mom." He shook his head with a bitter twist of his lips. "He kept saying he loved her too much."

"That's not love, Cass. That's dysfunction."

"How do I know my feelings for you aren't just as dysfunctional?"

"Because. If I left you right now, you wouldn't hunt me down. You would let me go. You certainly wouldn't hurt me." She delivered the words vehemently, then added—with a tiny smile tucked in her cheek, "Not that you could."

Cass smiled back.

Her heart soared.

But then his smile melted away, replaced by an expression without a trace of amusement, and her soaring heart sank. "I have a lot of baggage I need to work through."

They'd come to it at last. The part where he was going to push her away. They were in the middle of a war. Her parents were in captivity. She didn't know if she'd ever see them again. Now wasn't the time for romance. But a knot of stubbornness tied tight inside her. There were only a few good things in her life right now. Cassian was chief among them. Eden needed good.

She braced herself for a rejection. For the argument

that would ensue. Instead, he took her hand—his touch so surprising, so electric, Eden lost her breath.

"So that's what I'm going to do," he said, lacing his fingers with hers, his attention traveling across her knuckles. "Then maybe one day I'll feel less like him, and more like the guy you think I am."

Her breath was still gone—her lungs on sabbatical as she waited for more. But more didn't come. She peeked up at him. "Is that it?"

He seemed thrown by the question.

"I keep waiting for you to get to the part where we can't be together."

"You said the only way I could ruin you was by shutting you out." His thumb traced a featherlight circle on the sensitive skin between her thumb and forefinger. "The last thing I want to do is ruin you."

Her stomach somersaulted.

He gave her hand a tug, pulling her close. Then he cupped the side of her face, the tips of his fingers on the nape of her neck, his thumb brushing her cheek, and with tantalizing slowness, drew her lips to his in a kiss that was achingly soft. It stirred in her a desire that didn't match the chasteness of the moment.

She could feel his desire, too, like a hot, thrumming heartbeat. She could also feel his restraint. He was holding back, then pulling away. She was left bereft, in want of more. But she wouldn't push. Not today, when he seemed so determined to maintain control.

With a shaky exhale, he set his elbows on the railing and looked down at the abandoned avenue and the train tracks beyond. "It felt good today. Helping those people."

Eden set her elbows on the railing, too, standing beside him with her arm pressed against his. "I hear you're pretty good at it."

He took her hand again and traced her fingers. Tomorrow loomed. Another big day. Another important mission. Neither broached the topic. Instead, they talked of other things, from the inconsequential to the profound and everything in between, until the sky grew dark and the air chilly.

It was the very best night in a very odd place with this boy she'd come to love with deep tenderness and fierce passion. When it came to an end, Cassian walked her to her apartment and kissed her sweetly goodnight.

22

The Verrazano Bridge was a skeletal monstrosity. A deteriorating behemoth held together by rusted bolts and brittle rivets and corroded joists that groaned and creaked and threatened to collapse with every gust of wind. Yet, they crept upon it, making their precarious way in the dark. 4,260 treacherous feet from one tower to the other, according to Barrett.

"The fort's named after James Wadsworth, a general who was mortally wounded in the first Civil War. People used to think the place was haunted. Visitors would see soldiers walking through walls, or out in one of the open fields. One lady claimed she traveled back in time inside the body of a nurse. She didn't come back until a healthy soldier grabbed her by the arm."

Eden suspected Barrett's monologue was for Violet.

Truth be told, it was helping her, too. Maybe it was helping all of them, for nobody told Barrett to shut up. He didn't need to. He kept his voice low, and the bridge was abandoned. Swarm members traveled to and from Staten Island via the motor boats docked at the marine terminal in south Brooklyn. Which made this their one and only clear path to Fort Wadsworth. Eden's muscles tensed with every fraught step.

They traveled four across—Cassian, Eden, Violet, and Barrett. An impenetrable wall with Lark behind them, locked in with laser-like focus. On Eden's left, Cassian's tension was palpable. On her right, Violet radiated vigilance while Barrett explained—with a false note of nonchalance—how the bridge was twelve feet lower in the summer because of the seasonal contractions and expansions of its steel cables.

Up ahead, a tower loomed like a spaceship in the sky. One made almost entirely of windows. Eden could tell by the moon's reflection off the glass. The tower's spotlight swept the water in front and the fortress behind. Thankfully, it didn't reach the bridge.

Still, the sight of it made her stomach hurt. She was much less worried about Barrett being heard, and much more worried about them being seen. Hence Jericho and Nairobi, waiting in what was once Lower Manhattan. Jericho, in an old Costco building. Nairobi, in an abandoned hospital. Both with five rounds of high-tech explosives.

Another gust of wind blew.

Steel groaned.

The bridge swayed.

They all stopped—frozen in fear, certain the edifice would collapse beneath them and they would plummet into the frigid, frothy water below.

Thankfully, the bridge held.

The wind passed.

The groaning stopped.

Barrett was the first to take a step. "Would you look at that," he said, pointing into the dark.

Eden followed the direction of his point and saw the unmistakable figure made small by the distance, her arm lifted high as she held her flame of liberty. Eden's skin prickled with wonder. She'd always wanted to see it, this gift from Paris. A symbol of freedom from a bygone era.

Lark placed her hand over her brow like a visor. "What are we looking at?"

Cassian was squinting, too.

"The Statue of Liberty," Eden said.

Lark and Cass couldn't find what Barrett and Eden could see. Perhaps it was only visible because of their superhuman vision.

They resumed their trek forward.

Barrett changed subjects. He was talking now about

the famous statue and how Paris possessed five of them, a fact Eden already knew. She stopped listening, opting instead to run through the plan in her mind once again.

Eleven minutes.

If all went according to plan, they would be back on this bridge in eleven minutes—the time Lark needed to get the drones through the entirety of Brahm's headquarters, from the catacombs underground to the control tower above the harbor. In order to get detailed and accurate footage without being detected, they would need a diversion. Hence, Nairobi and Jericho and their ten rounds of explosives.

When they reached the second tower, Barrett was no longer talking. They moved in silence, using hand signals to communicate as they rappelled from the bridge to solid ground and hunkered beneath a copse of trees to collect their breath, readying to climb up and over the wall that would bring them into the fort. Lark radioed Jericho and Nairobi.

Forty-two seconds later, a blast sounded across the harbor, so loud the deteriorating bridge rattled above them. The spotlight moved toward the detonation and the team leapt into action. They quickly and deftly scaled the wall as another explosion rocked the night.

As soon as they landed on the other side, Lark turned on the ring-like remote wrapped around the tip of her pointer finger and released the drones—tiny black sparrows in the dark, unnerving in their likeness to the Search and Kill drones Eden first encountered in the bowels of Washington, DC.

With that unpleasant memory front and center in her mind, Eden moved into position. The four of them fanned along the perimeter to cover Lark on all sides as she directed the technology with the flick of her finger.

Another bomb exploded across the harbor.

Eden wedged herself in the corner of a stone wall, her eyes tracking Lark, her body as still as Lady Liberty, impossibly transfixed as she took in her surroundings. This was where the soldiers had been raised. This was the place she herself might have called home.

Footsteps echoed up a nearby stairwell. She ducked into shadow and held her breath, her tranquilizer gun clutched to her chest as a pair of soldiers came into view, poised beneath the light of the moon. Both were female with long hair pulled back into a braid—one the color of burnished gold, the other a dark burgundy.

The dark-haired soldier pointed at the plumes of smoke billowing toward the stars as a fifth blast detonated.

Behind them, a tiny black drone zoomed down the stairwell.

The blonde spun around, her eyes wide, her breath escaping in a puff of white. "What was that?"

The other didn't look; she was too entranced by the fiery sky.

The blonde yanked on the brunette's arm. "Aurelia, did you hear that?"

Eden gasped, then immediately covered the sound with her hand.

But it was too late.

It had already escaped.

She pressed herself against the wall with her heart thumping in her throat.

Aurelia.

The dark-haired girl was *Aurelia.*

She turned, whether from the yank or the gasp, Eden didn't know. She peered toward the stairwell where the drone had disappeared, giving Eden a full view of her face. *Tycho's Aurelia.* With long bangs, a spray of dark freckles across the bridge of her perfectly straight nose, and blue eyes that were shocking against the dark shade of her hair.

Eden held her breath.

"I'm going to check it out," the blonde said.

Aurelia nodded. "I'll contact control and find out what's going on."

The blonde hurried down the stairs.

Aurelia climbed up them.

A sixth bomb exploded.

Eden hesitated, but only for a moment. As soon as

Aurelia was out of view, she signaled to Cassian across the distance. She was going up. She told herself it was for Lark, who was taking full advantage of the chaos, directing the drones across the grounds. What if Aurelia spotted her from the higher vantage point? They couldn't let that happen.

She followed Aurelia on silent feet, up the stone spiral staircase, into what had to be the soldiers' living quarters.

They were empty.

Dark.

Aurelia was nowhere.

Eden pivoted in a circle—her ears on high alert—when she heard the fast approach of someone behind her. She spun around, her tranquilizer gun aimed. But it was only Cassian. He'd left his post to come after her.

"What are you doing?" she hissed.

"What are *you* doing?" he whispered back.

Before she could answer, a gun cocked.

Aurelia stepped into view with her crystal blue eyes ablaze and a pistol aimed straight at Cassian's head. "Drop your weapons."

They quickly obeyed.

Aurelia took a step closer, her gun carefully aimed. "Who are you and what are you doing here?"

Eden grappled for an answer, for something to say. For a way to get them out of this. But her tongue was tied. She was frozen in terror at the sight of that gun pointed at Cassian's head.

Aurelia's finger curled around the trigger.

"We have Tycho!" Eden blurted.

Somewhere across the harbor, a seventh bomb exploded.

They were coming down to it now. The end of their mission. The eighth explosion was their cue to get to the bridge. But here they were, in the wrong place, being held at gunpoint by Tycho's Aurelia. The girl stood there breathing shallow breaths, staring like Eden's words were a physical thing that had slapped her across the face.

"*Where*?" she finally said in a low tone that quaked with emotion.

Eden glanced at Cass with his hands in the air.

With an aggressive step forward, Aurelia pressed the barrel of her gun against the back of his head. "Tell me right now or I will end him. And if you think for one second I won't be able to detect a lie, then you are a fool and he is dead."

Eden's throat went dry as bone.

Cass stared straight ahead, his mouth grim, his nostrils flared.

Aurelia shoved the barrel into his temple. "Three … two … "

"Alexandria!" Eden choked.

Cassian closed his eyes.

"He's in Alexandria."

Aurelia tilted her head, no doubt studying Eden's pupils, measuring her pulse. She would find no lie. Eden had told Aurelia the truth, and in so doing, she had handed their location to the enemy.

The eighth explosion fired.

"He loves you," Eden said, grasping for something —*anything*—that might get them out of this. Growing wilder with panic the longer that gun remained fixed against Cass's temple.

Aurelia's eyes glistened with unshed tears.

Cassian's were no longer closed. He was staring straight at Eden with muscles so coiled they were ready to spring.

"He says your name when he's sleeping," Eden said.

Aurelia's grip on the pistol loosened.

Cassian wasn't superhuman. There was no nanotech zooming through his veins. But he was highly trained, and he'd been sparring with Eden for months. As quick as a viper, he knocked the gun from Aurelia's hand. It clattered to the ground as Eden snatched up her weapon and took her shot.

The dart whizzed through the air and hit its mark, embedding itself into the soft flesh of Aurelia's neck. She wobbled for a moment, maybe two, then collapsed on the floor.

Eden froze—her eyes fixed on the unconscious girl.

"We can't leave her here," Cass said.

He was right, of course.

Aurelia knew their location.

She knew where Tycho was being held. As soon as she woke, she would alert *Pater* and he would comb every square inch of Alexandria until his five-star general was found.

Cass picked Aurelia up and positioned her over his shoulders in the same way he had carried Eden's father. Together, they hurried down the stairwell as the ninth explosion boomed.

23

"Aurelia!" Tycho rasped.

Cassian climbed down the ladder after Eden with the unconscious girl in a firefighter's carry.

Tycho attempted to get closer, but he could hardly lift his head, let alone fight his restraints. His dose must have been recent. "Aurelia," he said again, his eyes wild. Feral. Filled with terror. "What's happening? What did you do to her?"

Cassian set Aurelia on the other side of Tycho's bedroll. "We didn't do anything."

Unless, of course, you counted seven rounds of tranquilizer. Or the scrambling device they'd secured to the bottom of her boot.

Behind them, Dvorak descended the ladder with a needle in hand.

Tycho moaned—an indistinct sound in the back of his throat. "Please. Don't. Don't do this to her. I'm begging you, please."

It was the first time Eden had ever heard him beg. Not once over the past several weeks had he succumbed to it, despite being tortured on repeat. And yet, here he was, pleading. Not for his life, but hers.

Eden's heart squeezed.

Meanwhile, Dvorak looked indifferent. If not for the slightest twitch in her right eyelid, Eden would believe her to be. But there the twitch was, barely perceptible as she strode toward Aurelia donning a mask of utter impassivity.

Tycho's moan became a high-pitched keen. "Please. Please, no."

Eden stepped between them and held up her hand. "Don't do this."

The keening stopped.

So did Dvorak. She tilted her head, her gaze sharp and steady.

"It's the wrong move." Eden could feel it in her bones, in the very depths of her being. She knew it as certainly as she knew Erik loved pi. As assuredly as she knew the Notre Dame Cathedral was the most visited attraction in Paris. She knew it as confidently as she knew Cassian's eyes were golden brown, and burned brightest whenever he was about to kiss her. Every fiber of her being pulsed with the knowing. Poisoning Aurelia would be a grave mistake. "If you inject her with that, we will never get him on our side."

The tilt in Dvorak's head deepened. "I wasn't aware that was something we were trying to do."

"Maybe it should be," Eden said, heat rolling up her neck. "We keep trying to force our way into his network like a battering ram." So they could *use* him. Control him. And eventually, destroy him. "But that's not working. And it's not going to work, either. If Asher hasn't gotten in by now, he will not get in, period. So what's next? Where do we go from here?"

Dvorak's midnight eyes narrowed as she looked from Eden to the boy she'd given birth to, beside himself as he tried to get to the girl on the floor. Her lips thinned into a grim line. "If we keep using tranquilizer, we will run out before the night is through."

"What about the magnet?" Cassian asked.

The magnet!

Yes, of course. The magnet would buy them time. Give them space to figure out how to handle this new situation without resorting to callous torture.

Aurelia groaned.

Dvorak's attention snapped in her direction. She took a step toward the girl, but Eden placed a firm hand on Dvorak's shoulder.

Dvorak looked at it.

"Please," Eden said. "Go get the magnet. No harm will come from using it, I promise you. She's barely conscious. He can hardly move. Right now, Cass and I are stronger than both of them. And we have these." She lifted her tranquilizer gun. There were three more rounds inside. "If they devise some sort of mutiny, I'll shoot them both and we'll do it your way."

Dvorak studied her beneath heavily lidded eyes. Ever since joining the council, Eden had deferred to her leadership, respected her authority. For the past two weeks, the two of them had worked side-by-side, united in purpose and determination. Eden accepted the council's vote about her parents, even though it killed her to do so, and she never once complained about her nighttime security detail. Slowly but surely, she was earning Dvorak's trust, and here now was the moment she needed that trust to work in her favor. She waited with bated breath until finally, Dvorak called up to Asher, inquiring about the magnet.

"It's in the lab at Kaiser," he called back.

Dvorak told him to fetch it. "I'll be up in the booth, watching," she said to Eden. "If anything goes wrong, it's on your head." With one last uneasy look around the bunker, she climbed up the ladder and exited the room.

Eden exhaled as Tycho tried and failed, tried and failed to get to Aurelia, his eyes glued to the girl who was slowly coming to.

Eden and Cass backed away with their tranquilizer guns at the ready, watching carefully as Aurelia gained consciousness and bolted upright. As soon as she registered Tycho, she released a strangled cry and threw herself upon him. She wrapped her arms tight around his neck. When he didn't hug her back, she noticed his restraints. She grabbed them—ready to tear—but Tycho stopped her. "There's no point."

"No point? Of course there is, Tycho. We can get out of here right now." She surveyed her surroundings—the doorless room, the hatch in the ceiling. The ladder. "My powers have come. We can defeat whoever stands in our way. Nobody can stop us."

"She can," Tycho said, his breathing labored.

Aurelia looked at Eden. Her piercing blue eyes shuffled from surprised recognition to aggravated confusion to utter contempt.

Cass squared his shoulders, like he was ready to fight should her contempt turn violent.

"She's one of us, Rails."

Rails.

Tycho had given her a nickname. Such a human one, too. Like Cass or Pru or Fran.

"What do you mean?" Aurelia asked.

"She's one of the six."

Aurelia shook her head. "That's impossible."

"I thought so, too. But four of them are alive. Pater

has one of them now."

"He does?"

"He must."

Aurelia sank beside him. She reached into Tycho's lap and took his hands, her expression filled with tenderness and concern. "What have they done to you?"

He licked his parched lips. "They have … a poison. It's terrible. I won't let them touch you with it. I'll find a way to get you out of here."

"I'm not leaving you."

"Aurelia." He lifted his arms—a herculean effort, Eden knew—and with his wrists bound, brushed his thumb down the girl's cheek. "Please."

She sucked in a sharp, loud breath—the kind a person took when they were side-swiped by pain. The kind Eden took whenever she glitched. Aurelia's face contorted. She collapsed onto her side and writhed, like the poison had found another way in.

Eden took a lurching step toward them, but Cassian grabbed her arm as Aurelia arched off the ground and screamed.

"What are you doing to her?" Tycho demanded, coming to his knees.

"We're not doing anything," Eden replied.

Aurelia grasped her head with knuckles that had gone bone white.

"What's wrong, Rails?" Tycho asked. "What's happening?"

But Aurelia couldn't answer. She was bearing down like a woman in labor, the tendons in her neck protruding. She clawed at Tycho's hands, her face red, her veins bulging. "I can't be here," she wheezed. "He's going—to kill me!"

"Who, Aurelia?" Tycho shouted. "Who's going to kill you?"

"Pater," she screamed.

"Pater?" Tycho shook his head, trying to calm her. But the girl thrashed and flailed. "He can't, Aurelia! He wouldn't. He—he's not here."

"He's inside!" She clutched her skull. She pulled her hair. She dragged at her cheeks. She begged like Tycho had begged. "Please, I don't want to die. Don't let him kill me, Tycho. Please don't let him!"

Tycho shouted. He screamed. He yelled for help. But what help was there to give? How could they stop a man who wasn't there? Eden watched, her horror expanding like a cosmic yawn. A black hole that sucked her into the past. She landed hard in a familiar forest with smoke and fire all around and a guard with no legs, clutching her hand with a claw-like grip. He'd begged for his mother. He'd begged for his life. He didn't want to die like Aurelia didn't want to die. Both of them enemies. At least, they were supposed to be.

Cassian's voice broke through her mental time warp, loud but muffled, like he was yelling from under water. Shouting at the ceiling. Shouting for Asher. Because Asher was retrieving the magnet, and the magnet would save Aurelia. It would shut her down. It would boot Oswin Brahm out of her head. Eden started shouting, too. Moving and yelling as she jumped on the ladder, but a horrible sound stopped her.

Aurelia was convulsing, frothing at the mouth. Choking on her own spit.

Tycho tried to still her, to help her. But Aurelia kept spasming. And Tycho started screaming. Even when Aurelia stopped, his screaming continued. He screamed and he screamed and he screamed as she lay there with open, unseeing eyes and a blood-red tear trickling down her temple.

24

Several things happened at once.

Asher arrived with the magnet. He and Dvorak stormed down the ladder, demanding answers. Tycho made unhinged accusations with eyes deranged and spittle flying. Cassian took Eden by the arm and pulled her behind him like he could protect her from all three.

Dvorak averted her gaze from the spectacle that was Tycho. She stood with her nostrils slightly flared, her face pinched. "What did she mean when she said Pater was *inside*?"

Tycho clutched Aurelia to his chest and rocked. "He didn't do it. It wasn't him. It couldn't have been him."

Eden spoke his name gently.

He only rocked faster. "They did this. They had to have done this. All of them are in on it."

"In on what?" Asher jabbed his hand into the air with his palm upturned. "Nobody even touched her."

Tycho kept muttering. "He loves us. He loves her. He didn't use it. It doesn't exist. He wouldn't have created one."

"Shut up!" Asher shouted.

Eden jumped.

Tycho buried his face in Aurelia's neck.

Cass kept hold of Eden's arm. He stood beside her, his grip tight, his tension palpable.

Dvorak looked from his hand to Eden's face, the wheels in her mind almost visibly turning. "What is he muttering about?" she asked. "What wouldn't he have created?"

Eden stared at the drop of blood that had trickled from Aurelia's eye. She had just witnessed the self-destruct command in real time. Oswin Brahm had carried it out. He killed Aurelia in front of Tycho. He murdered one of his own.

Eden shuddered and said slowly, "We have something built into our systems."

Dvorak cocked her head.

Cassian's grip tightened. He spoke her name—a taut plea to be silent. To say no more.

But Eden said the words anyway. "It's a self-destruct command."

Dvorak blinked.

Cassian swore.

Asher ran his hand over the top of his head, flattening his hair before it sprang back up again. "Why didn't you say anything about this?"

"Why would she say anything about it?" Cass retorted.

"We've been studying networks together for the past two weeks."

"It's a command you can use to destroy her."

"Nobody's going to destroy her."

Eden ignored their back and forth. Her eyes were on Tycho, who kept rocking. He'd lost the girl he loved. The man he worshipped so unwaveringly had killed her.

"Tycho," she said, trying to break through. Wishing she could soothe his pain.

He pressed his chin against the crown of Aurelia's head.

"We didn't do this. We couldn't have. We weren't inside her network. After all these months, we still can't get into yours."

He closed his eyes like doing so might block out her words. Might erase his new reality.

"I'm sorry, Tycho." Eden's voice broke.

His deranged expression crumpled into pure grief. It opened wide and swallowed him up as he cradled Aurelia and wept—a lament laced with pain infinitely worse than any poison could cause. His agony filled the entire room.

Asher couldn't talk over it.

Dvorak couldn't endure it.

The two of them left.

Eden stayed.

And because she stayed, Cassian did, too.

By the time Tycho finished, his eyes were swollen shut. His shoulders bent like each one weighed a thousand pounds. "I must lay her to rest," he whispered in a voice so ravaged it was barely there. He lowered her from his chin and straightened her hair. "I must bury her in the catacombs."

Eden and Cassian exchanged a look, then she took a step closer. "We can't go to the catacombs, Tycho."

"Please." He sniffed, then wiped his nose with one of his bound wrists. "She deserves to be honored."

"She does," Eden replied, grappling for a solution. She recalled something Tycho had shared when he talked about his upbringing, belligerently romanticizing it like doing so might prove she was wrong and he was right. Pater was good and everyone else was bad. Tycho and Aurelia used to swim together in the New York Harbor. She loved the water.

With utmost care, Eden placed her hand gently on his shoulder and crouched in front of him. "What if we lay her to rest by the river?"

Eden scooped another shovelful of earth from the grave she and Cass were digging. They worked side by side, a labor of compassion and sympathy for a young man who lost the love of his life. The girl he'd grown up with. The girl he called for when he slept. Eden tried not to imagine what it would feel like if she were Tycho right now. The pain of it took her breath away.

Cass scooped one last shovelful, and together they climbed out of the grave and onto the bluff overlooking the Potomac. Beyond, a petal pink sky on the cusp of sunrise outlined the decimated silhouette of Washington, DC.

Eden was running on instinct. She had been ever since she stopped Dvorak from poisoning the girl. She'd let her gut take the lead. Not impulsively, as she'd done in the past. But intentionally. Mindfully. Convinced this was the right way to go, even if the other council members weren't too pleased with the direction.

In the distance, Lark watched. Her tranquilizer gun at the ready. It was an unnecessary precaution. Tycho was still weak from the poison and crushed by grief—barely able to hold himself upright as he sat near a thicket of wild violet, holding Aurelia in his arms.

Eden pushed the blade of her shovel into the dirt.

The grave was dug. It was time to place Aurelia inside. But Tycho didn't look ready to let her go. Cassian pulled Eden close. He brushed his lips across her temple and whispered that he wouldn't be far. Even though his own tension was palpable, he seemed to understand that Tycho needed privacy. While Eden's presence might not infringe upon the moment, his certainly would.

A biting wind blew across the bluff. It caught a lock of Eden's hair. A lock of Aurelia's, too. Tycho took it between his fingers. He was no longer rocking or muttering or weeping. His deranged accusations had ceased. His face was dry and pale and drawn. His eyes, lifeless.

Quietly, Eden sat beside him and fixed her gaze upon the sun rising over the horizon, bathing the land in golden shafts of light as it slowly ascended in the sky. Beauty over destruction. Time marching onward amid profound sadness.

Tycho's shoulders rose and fell with a trembling breath. "Maybe this is my punishment."

"For what?"

"Loving her more than him."

The statement broke Eden's heart. It also ignited her ire. She wanted to scream at the sky. She wanted to grab Tycho by his shoulders and tell him how totally messed up that punishment would be, especially from a *good* father who was supposed to love Aurelia, too. But instinct held her tongue.

His entire world had been ripped from him. Not just the girl he loved, but the father he trusted. One was dead. The other, a lie. This was plenty to process without Eden adding fuel to the flame.

Another breeze blew. A patch of pink clouds rolled across the sky.

Together, they wrapped Aurelia in a linen sheet and laid her gently in the grave. Tycho placed a bouquet of pansies—plucked by Eden from the IDA's courtyard—over Aurelia's heart. Then he took the shovel in a movement so replete with exhaustion, Eden objected. She could do this part. But Tycho insisted—shovel after painstaking shovel—until Eden's walkie-talkie beeped and Asher's voice cut through the slow and rhythmic scoop-dump, scoop-dump that was Tycho's final goodbye.

"Headquarters are ready to explore, over."

Francesca's voice followed. "The asset is overdue for his dose, over."

Eden stepped away, lifted the walkie-talkie to her lips with a jerk, and spoke in a firm, hushed tone. "Giving him a dose would be the cruelest, most foolish thing we could do. Now is not the time to treat him like an enemy, over."

"He is the enemy," Francesca replied.

Eden jabbed the button. "Not anymore."

A moment of radio silence ensued.

Dvorak broke it with a question. "What do you suggest we do?"

Eden glanced at Tycho sorrowfully filling Aurelia's grave—either oblivious to or disinterested in the unfolding conversation. "I propose we let him grieve." She proposed they treat him like a human for once. Deserving of dignity, just like Aurelia was deserving.

More radio silence.

"I can watch him," Cass said from his own walkie-talkie. He was standing several paces away with his tranquilizer gun strapped around his shoulder.

Eden's chest flooded with appreciation as she brought the walkie-talkie to her lips. "I'm on my way to the boardroom, over."

25

After all this time, Tycho was finally free. In the open air with no restraints on his wrists, no poison in his veins.

He could feel his strength returning, growing with each scoop of earth. Not fully, but enough to make a move. There was only one watching him now. The others had left. He had a shovel in his hands and years of training at his disposal. He could run. He could fight. He could kill. At the very least, he could contact his brothers and sisters.

Instead, he scooped and he dumped and he tried to remember to breathe, his heart a ravaged wasteland. All his life, he'd been trained—in combat and arms, in direct action and reconnaissance, in sabotage and intelligence gathering. But never had he trained for this.

She wasn't supposed to die. None of them were

supposed to die. And yet, Aurelia was dead. He was pouring dirt over her body right now. But even as he did it, he didn't believe it. This wasn't real. It couldn't be.

But then her voice would scream through his mind. *"I don't want to die. Don't let him kill me, Tycho. Please don't let him!"*

He couldn't stop seeing her. He couldn't stop hearing her. Writhing. Frothing. Clutching her head. Begging for her life. His jaw clenched as a wave of white fiery anger swept through him. But it had nowhere to go.

There was a bottomless chasm in his brain between Aurelia's death and the rest of his existence. Pater as murderer kept falling inside it. They were his prized possession. His beloved. His chosen. Why would he ever kill them?

"Three buttons and your life is done. That's how easily he could end it."

Eden had said those words.

A soldier who wasn't supposed to exist. But then she'd sliced open her hand and proved she was one of them. He'd been so sure she was wrong. She was lying. She'd been led astray. In her wrongness, she had spun a story to mess with his head, to plant seeds of doubt.

Pater would never create such a command. And yet, here was more proof. Eden wasn't lying. She hadn't been led astray. At least not about this. Not only did Pater create the command, he'd used it.

On Aurelia.

The thought sprinted headlong into the chasm. Tycho continued to scoop, wondering if everything Eden said was true, and everything he believed was false. If Pater killed Aurelia, then didn't it stand to reason he might have killed the Great Mothers, too?

It was a treasonous question.

The Great Mothers died giving birth. Each one had willingly sacrificed her life for the cause. For *Caelum In Terra*. All of them except for his—the treasonous backstabber named Prudence Dvorak. Somehow, she was strong enough to survive his birth, only to run away and build an army of her own. But why? Why would she run from honor? Why would she build an army to fight utopia? The story he believed was growing convoluted. Eden's story was making more sense.

His mind waged war.

He should run.

He should fight.

He should murder his snake-of-a-mother.

Return to Pater and be cleansed.

Tycho leaned against the shovel and looked across the river, toward the city Pater had destroyed. A visual reminder of all the people he'd killed. Tycho had never thought twice about it before. He'd grown up knowing it, accepting it, embracing it. The act was easily justified. Excused. Necessary. Those people weren't really people.

They were history and numbers. Contaminated and unworthy.

But Aurelia?

She was loyal.

She was good.

She was … everything.

The chasm in his mind shrank. From it came the echo of her laughter, its cadence contagious. Her smile, too. Especially when she won a competition. She made a point of doing so as often as she could, for she had a competitive spirit. She craved adventure. She couldn't wait for her power to come. She had marveled at Tycho's.

While in captivity, he had done his best to repeat passages from Sanctus Liber. To fortify and re-fortify his allegiance to Pater. But it was Aurelia who had gotten him through. Aurelia who had kept the madness at bay. The memories they shared. The hope of seeing her again.

Now Aurelia was dead.

The chasm had closed.

The truth had nowhere to fall.

Tycho would never see her again. Never swim with her again. Never explore with her again. Never train with her again. Memories were all he had left.

His chin trembled.

His throat tightened.

He gnashed his teeth, refusing to cry as another wave

of rage swept over him. The truth, too. Stark. Obvious. He clenched the handle of the shovel so tightly it crumbled in his grip.

Pater killed Aurelia.

Tycho would make him pay.

26

"Our goal is to gather as much intel as possible," Asher said.

"What are we looking for?" Cleo asked.

"Data. About his operations. His resources. Infrastructure. Vulnerabilities. Anything that might give us an advantage."

Sanctus Liber, Eden thought.

That would definitely give them an advantage. She'd first learned about the book right here, in this boardroom. It had been teeming with tension then. It was teeming with tension now. Everyone listened to Asher's spiel, either tight-lipped and stone-faced or wide-eyed and fidgeting. All had been debriefed on the latest. The unconscious soldier they'd taken from Fort Wadsworth was dead. Oswin Brahm killed her remotely using a self-destruct command the council wasn't aware existed.

Tycho was roaming free. And Dvorak was trusting Eden to call the shots.

A surprise to Eden. A betrayal to Francesca, whose bandages had finally been removed. Her head and hands were no longer wrapped in gauze. Scabs and shiny pink patches marred one side of her face as she sat beside Dvorak, glowering with her hair shorn and her arms crossed.

Eden might reassure Francesca if she thought it would help. Nobody was in danger; Cassian had Tycho under control. But the words would be a waste of breath. Confidence couldn't be forced. If Eden was right about this plan—and she knew she was right—time would tell the story.

"Once you're inside, you'll be able to access your own blueprint via a virtual wristwatch." Asher swiveled his laptop to face them. On it, a two-dimensional avatar stood in the courtyard of Fort Wadsworth. The avatar lifted his arm as though to check the time. With the push of a button, a holographic blueprint appeared in front of him.

"You can jump from space to space with the tap of your finger." He enlarged the blueprint, tapped on a location marked *living quarters,* and the background changed. Just like that, the avatar was standing somewhere else.

"Cool," Barrett said under his breath, elongating the

word. He was sitting on Francesca's other side, bouncing his knee and twisting the tab on his soda can. "It's like apparating."

"Like what?" Asher asked, distracted by the comment and visibly annoyed by the distraction.

"You know, apparition."

Asher very obviously *didn't* know.

"From Harry Potter? Wizards learn how to apparate from one place to another when they turn seventeen. It's like magical teleportation."

Asher blinked at him dryly, then turned to address the group. "Whether you magically teleport is up to you. You can walk from place to place if you want. Point being, you'll want to use the blueprint. The location is expansive. There are living quarters, training quarters, labs, the catacombs, the control tower, and the biggest data center I've ever seen."

He tapped from one place to the next. "If you find anything noteworthy, touch the location and mark it on your blueprint. When we're done, we can collect our information and decide what to do next."

Eden couldn't help but marvel. Judging by the look of grudging admiration on Cleo's face, nor could she. Creating this at all required a fair amount of brilliance. Creating it in such a short time required a lot.

"We should split into groups," Asher said. "We can cover more ground that way."

"We'll take the control tower." Dvorak motioned to Jericho on her left, Francesca on her right, whose scowl lost some of its edge. She was pleased to be included in Dvorak's *we*. Or at least, mollified.

"I'd like to check out the labs first," Lark said. "I didn't get a good look yesterday, but I believe he's keeping people in them."

"Keeping people?" Eden inquired.

"To experiment on."

She didn't know why she was so aghast. It was hardly the worst of Brahm's sins. Even so, warmth drained from her face as she pictured lab rats in cages. Only instead of rats, humans.

"This isn't anything new," Dvorak said. "Brahm's been experimenting on people for as long as I can remember. It's how Amir's father died. Moshe volunteered, but still ..." She swallowed hard, her eyes going cold and flat.

Asher plugged coordinates into each of their headsets. When he reached Nairobi's, she volunteered to go with Lark. When he reached Cleo's, he asked if she wanted to join him in the data center, which he was eager to explore. He knew how some of his father's operations worked; he was ready to learn more.

"I wouldn't mind seeing it myself," Dayne said.

Meanwhile, Eden couldn't stop thinking about Aurelia, dead. Tycho, wanting to give her an honorable burial.

And the book called Sanctus Liber with prophecies about the future. She looked at Barrett and Violet. "Do you want to head to the catacombs?"

"Sure," Barrett said with a shrug.

Asher programmed their headsets. Then he moved to his computer to make some final adjustments before pulling his own headset over his ears. "Recon mission number ten, underway."

Eden could feel the temperature drop before she opened her eyes. She could smell dust and old stone. She could hear a steady drip-drip from somewhere in the distance. And beneath it—all around—the ambient sound one might hear when holding a conch shell to one's ear. Somehow, Lark's drones had captured not just visuals, but a complete sensory experience.

"Whoa," Barrett exclaimed.

Eden opened her eyes.

Whoa, indeed.

They were standing in a subterranean passageway lit by torches. The light of flickering flame danced up the stone walls and cast eerie shadows on the ground. Eden walked a few paces forward to read the words etched into a decorative plate made of marble.

"Here lies Rosalyn Berkovich," Barrett read aloud. "The fallen mother of 022."

They looked at one another.

Double whoa.

Not only were the tombs marked with names, those names came with numbers. Each superhuman soldier would know which great mother carried them in utero.

It was so very bizarre.

Eden kept going. A quick-paced jaunt along the narrow passageway, stopping briefly at each marble plate until she'd followed the curved path in a giant circle.

Unsurprisingly, numbers 001 through 006 were missing. So was 007, which had to be Tycho, Brahm's five-star general. Dvorak wasn't down here, enshrined in a tomb. Dvorak was exploring the control tower.

Barrett nodded toward a narrower passage—as black as pitch. "Where do we think this leads?"

"There's only one way to find out," Eden said, before ducking inside and following it with her hands. Violet followed behind her and Barrett played the caboose, offering words of comfort as Violet's heartbeat tripled in speed.

Thankfully, the darkness was short-lived, for not more than a minute later, they came into a circular sanctuary. On either side of the entrance stood two votive stands filled with candles, all ninety-three of them lit. In the sanctuary's center was a raised circle of stone. And in the center of that, a golden lectern upon which sat a book.

With goosebumps crawling across her skin, Eden

scurried toward it. She hopped on top of the altar in a manner that was undoubtedly sacrilegious. Behind her, Violet crouched into a squat and ran her palm over a monarch butterfly that had been etched into the stone.

Eden imagined lighting a votive candle in offering to her great mother. She imagined worshipping alongside her brothers and sisters in some sort of cultish ritual while Tycho read passages aloud from this book. With an aggressive shudder, she opened it and flipped through its pages.

"They're blank," Barrett said, looking over her shoulder.

Herein lay the first flaw of Lark's drones. As thorough as they might be, they didn't have x-ray vision. They couldn't peer through the cover of Sanctus Liber and record Brahm's prophecies. This replicated virtual space gave them nothing but the book's location. Perhaps this was why Lark and Dvorak hadn't cared to come to the catacombs. Still, Eden took a note on her holographic blueprint.

They carefully searched the sanctuary for anything noteworthy, then took another lap around the tombs to do the same. Eden filled Barrett and Violet in on the details of Aurelia's death while they went. When they finished, they made the joint decision to leave the creepiness behind. They exited the hallowed space and stepped into one much more clinical.

The Mecca of all data centers, enormous in scope just as Asher had said, filled with rows upon rows of encased, blinking servers.

Violet pointed to Cleo and Dayne across the way. As they approached, Cleo pressed her palm against the plated glass. "Can you imagine how much intel we could get for *America Underground* from this place? We could expose his entire operation in a single issue."

Asher joined them, too, nodding over his shoulder. "There's a whole case full of microchips over there."

All of it was highly intriguing and just as torturous. A tease, like the book. They could study the layout of Brahm's gigantic data center to their heart's content, note numbers, rows, and labels, but they couldn't extract any information from within.

Their watches beeped with an incoming message from Lark. She wanted everyone to join her in the labs.

With a tap and a blink, Eden was there, standing in a long, sterile hallway lit with fluorescent lights that reflected off the glossy, white flooring. One of them flickered. Dvorak and Francesca arrived, too. Sans Jericho, who was walking from the control tower to get the lay of the land.

Rooms with large observation windows lined the corridor on either side. Rooms with people inside. One per room, frozen in whatever position the drones had captured them in. Eden shuddered once again. The place reminded her of an insane asylum.

A door swung open at the end of the hallway. Jericho appeared. He'd exited the tower via a spiral staircase that led here. According to the blueprints, the laboratory hallway acted as a walkway between the tower and the rest of headquarters.

Lark stood by the door next to one of the windows and tapped on the doorplate. *Subject 005.* Ellery. Here, in Fort Wadsworth. Alive, just as Tycho had insisted.

"Didn't you say she was captured by the RRA?" Lark asked Barrett.

"Yeah," Barrett said, blanching as he beheld the girl in a gown, asleep on an examination table.

"Then why is she here?"

"He must have gotten her from the RRA."

Bile rose up Eden's throat. She swallowed it down as the group chattered, discussing things they already knew. Like the government being in Brahm's pocket.

Somewhere in the middle of it, Violet let loose a garbled shriek—half choke, half scream—that silenced everyone. She pressed her back against the window behind her and stared in frozen horror at the window directly in front.

Barrett rushed to her side. Eden saw the reason for Violet's distress. A man stood with his face pressed against the glass, as familiar as Ellery Forrester. Eden recognized him from a photograph in Violet's file.

Oswin Brahm had her father.

Asher's watch beeped.

He looked down at the incoming message. "We have visitors in the boardroom. Time to disengage."

Eden was one of the last to leave. By the time she pulled off her headset, Francesca was on her feet looking murderous.

Cassian was the visitor.

He'd brought Tycho.

"What is he doing in here?" Dvorak demanded.

"He wanted to speak with you," Cass answered, his tranquilizer gun pressed firmly against Tycho's spine.

Dvorak glared at the young man.

He glared back. "From the very beginning, I was taught to despise you. If given the chance, I was encouraged to kill you."

Dvorak's mouth tightened. Francesca stepped in front of her like a small bodyguard, her good eye twitching.

"All my life, I was told the Great Mothers died in childbirth. It was a sacrifice they willingly made. You were the only survivor. Physically strong, but mentally despicable." He shot a brief glance in Eden's direction. "She tells me a different story."

"What story is that?" Dvorak asked.

"The Great Mothers survived childbirth. They were

tricked into drinking poison. You were the only one smart enough not to drink it."

Dvorak gave him a slow, singular nod.

"Why would he do this?" Tycho asked.

"So he could be the sole, authoritative influence over your lives."

Tycho didn't move. He stood still and resolute, with a fire burning in his eyes. And in that moment, Eden knew. She knew it all the way down to her toes. This was what her instincts had been waiting for.

"You want to get your hands on Sanctus Liber," Tycho said.

It wasn't a question, but Dvorak answered anyway. "Yes, we do."

"You don't need it."

Her eyes narrowed. "No?"

Tycho shook his head. "I have every word memorized."

27

"On the 88th day of the last year of Chrysalis, as the world celebrates a new beginning and the gathering is complete, the Great Winnowing will usher forth like the rising sun. There will be weeping and gnashing of teeth until the circle is perfect and desecration is no more. The faithful will emerge. The sleeping martyrs will be reborn. Together, we will step forth into a new era. *Caelum In Terra*. The Monarch reigns."

As Tycho finished the recitation, shivers rippled through Eden's body. Perhaps the whole room.

"That was never part of my bedtime reading," Asher said, leaning back in his chair.

Tycho cocked his head curiously, like he didn't know what Asher meant by such a statement. "It's from the Passage of Epiphany."

"The passage of what?" Cleo asked.

"A concealed chapter from Sanctus Liber. Only those worthy to enter the sanctuary may lift the veil and read from it."

Cleo clucked her tongue. "I take it Amir was never considered worthy?"

"Obviously," Francesca said, shooting a protective glance at Dvorak, whose mood darkened whenever Amir was mentioned. "If he was, we would have known the location of headquarters a long time ago."

"You know," Cleo said, "you should really take that stick out of your butt."

Asher snorted.

Francesca glared.

"Who is Amir?" Tycho inquired.

"He was a spy," Eden replied. "His last name was Kashif."

"Mother Lillian's son."

Mother Lillian.

The term was almost as creepy as the prophecy. Eden ran her teeth over her bottom lip. "She gave birth to soldier 012."

"How do you know that?" Tycho asked, his face paling.

"I saw it on the plaque outside Lillian's tomb."

"You were in the catacombs?"

"We took a virtual tour."

His pallor intensified. Even knowing the truth, he clearly still believed the catacombs to be sacred. He buried his fingers in his hair. Eden could only imagine the minefield his thoughts had become. Sorting fact from fiction, truth from lies—a task that would take years of unlearning. He hadn't even had a day.

"These 'sleeping martyrs' who will be 'reborn' …" Dayne used air quotes around the words. "Is that referring to the mothers—Lillian Kashif and the rest?"

"It pertains to anyone who has given their life for *Caelum In Terra*."

Cleo gaped. "So, Brahm has y'all believing what, exactly—these people are gonna get up out of their tombs and join you in his utopia?"

"That is the commonly held belief, yes."

Cleo released a low whistle.

Jericho scratched his goatee. "What is Chrysalis?"

"The era of transition," Dvorak said, her tone as dry as sand. "Between the old world and the new. I assume we're in its final year."

"How do we pinpoint the 88th day?" Jericho asked.

"Count from the first," Dvorak answered.

"And that would be …?"

"Sanctus Diem," Tycho and Dvorak said together.

October fourth.

The day of The Attack, and four years after that, the birth of the Electus. Eden pulled up a calendar in her mind and made a quick computation, counting eighty-eight days forward. Barrett must have, too, in a more efficient manner, for he beat her to the punch.

"That's New Year's Eve," he said, then brightened. "'As the world celebrates a new beginning.'"

Beside him, Lark looked appalled. "If that timeline is correct, then the Great Winnowing hasn't even started yet."

"Ozzy's still 'gathering'." Asher nodded toward the large screen behind him, where satellite footage captured a bird's-eye view of the detainment facility in Fredericksburg.

Eden's parents were in there. New Year's Eve was only a month and a few days away. According to Tycho's prophecy, the Great Winnowing would come like the rising sun. "The sun rises in the east," she said, dread sinking into her stomach. "Fredericksburg is in the east."

"That'll be where he starts then," Asher said. "After that, he'll move west to Shenandoah. Then Wendover."

"Until what?" Dayne asked. "Every illegal resident is eradicated?"

Cleo scoffed. "Ten to one, he's not stopping with illegals."

Everyone around the table looked at Tycho, who obviously knew the answer.

"He plans to get rid of all contamination. Until the circle is complete and the world is ready."

"How is he going to decide who's contaminated?" Nairobi asked.

"By reading minds," Barrett said.

Jericho pulled a face like it was a ridiculous suggestion. But it wasn't ridiculous. It was already happening.

"CogniFuse," Cleo whispered.

The room went silent. The tiniest of pins could drop and everyone would hear it. At this very moment, as they were sitting together in this room, people were willingly inserting chips into their brains. Chips created by Oswin Brahm. A man who had the CEO of CogniFuse killed so he could swoop in to acquire the company. Now he was orchestrating attacks that had the country on lockdown. Americans were stuck inside their homes, cut off from the world. Unless, of course, they ordered a CogniFuse drone to swing by and make an insertion.

More shivers rippled up Eden's spine.

He truly was the grandmaster, moving the pieces and making a fortune while doing so. Eden could see it all so clearly—every facet of his plan. First, he would eradicate illegals. Then he would move on to citizens—through CogniFuse, a technological advancement that would enable the government to police not only actions, but thoughts. And that government was in Oswin Brahm's pocket. At his command, they would keep going—rounding up and killing off the unworthy until all that remained was a giant, brainless *swarm*.

This was what he called unity. This was how he imagined utopia.

"We have to expose him," Eden said, breaking the silence.

"We've been trying," Dayne replied.

"I'm talking wide-scale, impossible-to-ignore exposure. The whole world needs to know what he's done and what he's planning to do before everyone is as brainwashed as his inner circle."

"How do we do that?" Nairobi asked.

Eden turned to Tycho. "What kind of information is stored in his data center?"

"Everything. Recordings. Plans. Highlights. Accomplishments. Celebrations. From the very beginning of Chrysalis."

"Is there something in there that would link him to The Attack?"

"Of course."

"Then we need to go back. We need to break into his data center, find something undeniably incriminating, and share it with the world."

Jericho began shaking his head. "If getting into Fort Wadsworth was tricky before recon, it will be impossible now."

Eden's frustration flared. She was tired of the naysaying. According to the council, they couldn't get into Fredericksburg, either. So what, they were just supposed to hide here in safety and let everyone be winnowed?

"I can get in," Tycho said.

The silence returned, heavier than before.

"Send me back and I will be your spy."

Francesca scoffed. "Not a chance."

"Why not?" Tycho asked.

She gaped at him like he was dumb. "You're his five-star general."

Cleo pulled on her earlobe. "Which means he has access to things nobody else does."

"It also means Brahm can control him. Probably more efficiently than he can control any of the others."

"He won't control me. Not if I play the part well." Tycho's lip curled. "Loyal soldier. Loyal *son*."

Francesca continued staring, her expression appalled. Unamused. Disbelieving.

Meanwhile, Dvorak looked intrigued. She studied Tycho like she was seeing him clearly for the first time. "You'd really be willing to do this?"

"For them, I would do anything."

Them.

The Electus.

"My brothers and sisters deserve to know the truth."

Francesca touched her temples. "I can't believe we're considering this."

"I have to side with Fran here, Pru," Lark said. "The

second he tells his brothers and sisters the truth, they will run and tell Oswin."

"I know who I can trust," Tycho said.

"You didn't before Aurelia died," Francesca retorted.

Eden grimaced. While true, it was a heartless thing to say.

To Tycho's credit, he didn't break down. He didn't back down either. He looked at Francesca, his gaze unwavering. "They won't turn on me. They might be worried, but they won't tell Pater. They know what will happen to me if they do."

Eden stared—in wonder, in awe—at this boy who had just revealed Brahm's fatal flaw. With this army he created, he failed to consider a very real factor. They were super, yes. But they were also human. Which meant they weren't just capable of love, they were bent toward it. They were bound to form attachments, bonds. Maybe not with their dead mothers, but certainly with one another. Killing Aurelia had been his biggest mistake. For in so doing, Oswin Brahm had made an enemy of his greatest asset.

"Here's an idea," Cleo offered. "Why not let him go back? Only instead of feeding us information, he can kill the psychopath the first chance he gets."

"The pleasure of that belongs to me," Lark objected.

"You might have to take one for the team here. If the kid has a clear shot—"

"If I kill him," Tycho interrupted, "I'll mark myself as an enemy. My brothers and sisters will be lost."

"Members of Swarm will step in and take the mantle," Asher said. "My father will be immortalized."

"Your father?" Tycho choked.

Asher's eyes gleamed. "Did he tell you I died of a drug overdose? Or did he fail to mention he had biological spawn at all?"

Judging by Tycho's expression, the second option was the correct one.

"Oswin Brahm, the martyr, will be even more dangerous than he is now," Eden said. "And Swarm will be all the more united."

It was a truth the Monarch understood. A truth he capitalized upon. *Tragedy unites.* The assassination of Oswin Brahm would turn Swarm into an unstoppable, unified force. They wouldn't quit until their leader's vision had come to fruition. Even in death, the Monarch would win.

"Killing him won't cut it," Jericho agreed.

"We need to crush his ideology," Eden said.

"Tear Swarm apart," Cleo added. "Exposure's the only way this will end in our favor."

Most everyone in the room seemed in agreement. Even Francesca looked like she might be coming around.

"If we go forward with this," Dvorak finally said,

addressing her son. "If we let you go, how do we communicate?"

"We could use the ring," Asher suggested. "The one that belonged to the guard."

Dvorak shook her head. "If we can use that ring to spy, then I'm sure they can use it to spy in return."

"We don't need rings," Tycho said. He looked from Eden to Barrett to Violet. "We simply need a connection."

Asher gave his eyebrows a lift. "Care to elaborate there, Tych?"

"It's part of our design. We're built to communicate with one another. Now that I'm no longer incapacitated with poison, I could communicate with my brothers and sisters right now."

Eden's breath caught.

Fear swept through the room.

It was a jarring statement.

"Have you?" Cleo finally asked.

"No."

There was a collective exhale, followed by a shaky inhale.

Asher crossed one leg over the other. "How do we establish a connection?"

"If I let you inside my head, I'm sure you could figure it out."

Asher's eyes went bright at the suggestion. The poor

guy had been trying and failing to get inside Tycho's head for months now.

"I would think twice if I were you." The words belonged to Cassian, who had yet to speak since Tycho repeated the prophecy. He did so now in a deep vibrato that shook with warning.

Everyone looked at him.

"He told us Brahm's end game. I think it only fair we tell him ours."

Eden shifted uncomfortably. "Cass."

But he didn't stop. His expression was hard as granite. "They want to take out Oswin Brahm by destroying the Electus."

"Plans change," Dvorak cut in, her voice sharp with warning.

Cassian was undeterred. He stood with his legs splayed, his gun still pressed against Tycho's spine. "You let them inside your head, you give them access to the same command Brahm used to kill Aurelia."

And here it was. The source of Cassian's tension, the reason for his suppressed anger. The self-destruct function. The cat was out of the bag. The Resistance knew about it. They also knew how to get inside Eden's network, which meant they could use it on her if they wanted.

Dvorak came forward in her seat. "That *was* our plan,

when we thought it was a necessity. This doesn't seem to be the case any longer."

Tycho studied them, his attention swiveling from Dvorak to Cassian, from Cassian to Dvorak. All of this would take an astronomical amount of trust.

On his part.

On theirs.

But honestly, with their purposes now aligned, what other choice did they have?

The last time Cass celebrated Thanksgiving, he was twelve. His mother had just died. He was recovering from Dad's baseball bat, but strong enough to sit at Beverly's dining table and eat with several members of her extended family. Along with her nosy eleven-year-old daughter, Cleo.

It was a holiday designed for families. Cass didn't have one, so Cass didn't celebrate. Last year, he'd been tracking down overdue payments for Yukio. The years before that, he trained. This year, he sat at a table in the commissary with turkey, mashed potatoes, corn, and stuffing on his plate.

He should be ravenous. Instead, he had to force down the food. Back in the boardroom, Prudence Dvorak had patched in Harlan Wallace and Emmett the Irishman in order to call for an emergency vote among the council members. They'd all agreed, even Francesca. So long as Prudence reached a place of confidence regarding Tycho's newfound allegiance, so long as Asher could establish a connection that would allow them to communicate securely, they would set the asset free. He would return to headquarters and become their new mole. After the decision, Dvorak excused everyone but her son from the boardroom.

"Go to the commissary," she'd suggested. "They're serving a Thanksgiving feast."

Her words elicited a momentary bout of bewilderment. The holiday caught everyone off guard. On the way, Eden filled Cass in about Ellery and Violet's father. Now, Violet was mixing cranberry sauce and corn on her plate while Asher and Cleo flirted and Barrett told a long-winded story with animated hand gestures.

Beside Cass, Eden quietly picked at her food. Meanwhile, he couldn't stop seeing Aurelia die. It played on repeat in his mind—making his throat hot. The muscles across his chest, sore. He gripped his fork in a clenched fist, wishing he could rip the self-destruct command from Eden's system. Maybe even more than the Queen Bee. The traitorous thought left him thankful Eden's superpowers didn't include mind reading.

When everyone finished, they threw away their

scraps and returned their trays. Francesca found Asher and told him he was needed in the boardroom.

"Do you want to watch Concordia Nightly with me and Cleo?" Eden asked, taking Cassian's hand.

"I'll catch up with you soon," he replied, eying Asher's back as he walked away. Before Eden's curiosity could turn into a question, Cass pulled her against his chest, pressed his lips against the top of her head, and went after him.

Night had fallen. The air was cold. His breath frozen as he jogged forward.

Asher glanced over his shoulder. When he saw it was Cass trailing him, he looked more amused than surprised. "What's up, Gray?"

"I need to speak with you about something."

"Cleo said you would."

Cass came beside him, frowning at the statement. He didn't like the idea of Cleo talking to Asher about him.

"Let me guess. It's about this self-destruct command."

"I need your word that you will not use it."

Asher rolled his eyes. "She's part of the council. We're on the same side. What reason would I have to use it?"

"She'll probably ask you."

Asher pulled back, like Cass was speaking nonsense. "Why would she do that?"

"Because," Cass replied. "She's done it before, with me."

Asher's confusion only grew.

Cass rubbed his brow and shook his head. "If she's given a choice between death and hurting someone against her will, she'll choose death every day."

28

Violet left her fourth therapy session feeling like a pile of clothes after a spin cycle. She found Barrett on the tail end of his surveillance watch, debriefing the girl who'd come to relieve him of his duties.

"It's some sort of transmission tower," he was saying, pointing to satellite footage of Fredericksburg. He zoomed in and peered at the screen, as if taking a photograph with his mind.

A new tower was there. One that hadn't been yesterday.

"Now look at this." He shifted to the satellite footage on Staten Island and zoomed in to Fort Wadsworth's control tower. "This is new, too," he said, pointing at the transmission-like apparatus on top.

Violet cleared her throat.

The moment he spotted her in the doorway, he smiled with his whole face. She smiled back with only a fourth of hers. The last two days had been different in Alexandria, without Tycho screaming every four hours. The reprieve might have loosened the knots in her chest, if not for Father. The shock of seeing him behind the plate glass of that observation window stuck to her like glue, even two days later.

Some might call it karma. Payback. What goes around comes around. He experimented on her for the first seventeen years of her life. Now he was being experimented upon. Maybe she should feel a sense of vengeance or justice. But Violet only felt unsettled. What kind of experimenting was Oswin Brahm doing?

Barrett joined her in the hallway. "I want to take a closer look at the control tower. Care to join me?"

Violet nodded hesitantly.

Asher had set up a quasi-permanent HQ exploration room across from his lab in Kaiser. Anyone who'd been part of the recon mission could visit at their discretion, so long as they shared their findings. Since being part of that first exploration, Violet had yet to return.

Dr. Kane encouraged her to go. Face her fear. Father couldn't hurt her anymore. She knew this in theory. But in practice, her heart fluttered and her palms grew clammier the closer they got to that room. Halfway there, they ran into Eden, who'd been heading to the same place.

Barrett updated her on the new transmission towers. Eden updated him on the magnet. They'd sent a tiny piece of it to Harlan to see if he could decipher its composition. If they could replicate the magnet, they'd have the ability to disable Brahm's entire army without causing any harm. "The material is extraterrestrial," Eden explained. "He must have acquired it from his galactic mining project."

"Funded by SubTech," Barrett said.

Eden nodded. Then sighed. "Unless we have a spaceship that can get us to Mars, there's no way to make more of them."

They reached the room, which blinked with technology. A variety of blueprints lined the walls with notes scribbled on nearly all of them. There were five chairs, each with its own headset.

A few moments later, after several reassurances from Barrett, Violet was standing in a circular glass tower filled with control panels and surveillance monitors, where guards could oversee every area of headquarters, from the underground catacombs to those awful labs to the docks across the harbor where motorboats came and went.

In the center of the tower was a pneumatic tube. This was what Barrett called it, anyway. He told her that banks used to use them, once upon a time, at drive-up windows. Except this one was big enough to hold an entire person. Maybe even two. Barrett had already seen it. So had Eden. This was Violet's first time, however.

She circled the tube, grazing the glass with her finger as Barrett followed its trajectory upward, toward the new transmission tower overhead. Violet stopped in front of the retinal scanner and dragged her thumb along the keypad. This tube had been the source of many a conversation. Nobody knew what it was, where it went to, or why it existed. Still, Eden and Barrett continued to theorize like the speaking of words might lead to answers.

As they referenced their blueprints, Violet fixed her gaze eastward, toward the endless sea of blue. She'd first learned about this ocean on the map she used to carry around in her pillow sack. For a long time, she fantasized about swimming across it, right off the edge, where Father could never reach her.

"It's the Atlantic," Barrett said.

Violet startled. She hadn't noticed him standing beside her.

He slid his hands into his pockets. "Did I ever tell you about the time my brothers pretended to be sharks?"

Sharks.

The word caught in Violet's brain like a bit of snagged fabric.

"We were in Maine for a summer holiday. I was eight —maybe nine. My brothers were out there in the Atlantic. Mom thought I was too young to go out with them, so I was stuck on the beach, watching them when they pulled a little prank involving a fake shark fin and an Oscar award-winning performance that was so realistic, I might have peed my pants. To my parents' chagrin, I didn't step foot in that ocean for the rest of the summer."

Barrett laughed a little under his breath, then looked down at his palms. "It's baffling to think that now, if I wanted, I could fight a shark with my bare hands. Barrett Barr verses a Great White." He began to bob and weave, punching the air with his fists.

The snagged bit of figurative fabric caught harder as Violet stared at the horizon.

Sharks.

Sharks.

Sharks!

With a gasp, she tugged on Barrett's sleeve. He stopped his shadow boxing as she looked pointedly from him to the tube, then back again. She swallowed and whispered, "W-weapon."

Barrett's brow furrowed.

Violet kept looking. Meaningful, pointed stare downs —from the tube to Eden, from the tube to Barrett. From the tube to Eden, from the tube to Barrett. Until finally, Eden gasped, too.

"Sharks are messing with the weapon again," she said in a tumble of words, repeating the soundbite they'd intercepted several days ago.

Understanding dawned across Barrett's face.

"What if it isn't code?" Eden pressed her hands against the glass. Her nose, too, as she peered down the length of the tube. "What if literal sharks are messing with a literal weapon?"

"What kind of weapon?" Barrett asked.

Eden didn't have an answer. Nor did Violet. Oswin Brahm already had weapons. Ninety-three, to be exact. What could he possibly do with another, and why in the world would he store it in the New York Harbor?

29

"There it is." Asher highlighted a command on the command log. Over the past several days, he'd created a copy of Tycho's system, turning it into a three-dimensional interface. He was currently standing inside that system like a young Tony Stark—zooming and highlighting and exploring with the tap and drag of his finger.

Eden set her hands on her hips. "He has one."

"That, he does," Asher said.

Up until this point, she'd been hopeful Tycho wouldn't have a self-destruct command. Perhaps this was what set him apart.

Tycho believed Brahm made him his five-star general because they both had unworthy mothers. Asher was confident his father picked Tycho because he was the firstborn, the strongest, and the most obedient. Eden wasn't convinced either told the full story. Her gut said there had to be more. Maybe this was it. Brahm made Tycho his five-star general because he didn't have this particular feature. Eden narrowed her eyes at the highlighted command. Apparently, she was wrong. Tycho had a self-destruct command.

He had a Queen Bee, too. Asher found it yesterday, then used his Queen Bee to establish a connection with Eden's. Now they shared an unnerving, telepathic portal that could be opened and closed at will, like pushing the talk button on a two-way radio. She imagined having the same connection with ninety-three others. Or rather, ninety-two.

It seemed horribly intrusive.

"So," Asher said, dragging the command to one side. "Is Mr. Therapy still freaking out?"

"Who?"

"Your boyfriend."

Eden pursed her lips. She didn't think Cass would appreciate the nickname. "Freaking out about what?"

"This command."

"What makes you think he's freaking out about it?"

"Because he all but told me so." At Eden's furrowed brow, Asher continued. "He hunted me down a few days ago, after our Thanksgiving meal. Made me swear not to use it on you."

Clarity fell into place. She'd wondered what Cass had been up to.

Asher kept exploring, his attention not on her, but on the many parts that made up Tycho's system. "Look, I get it. If the girl I loved could be destroyed with a few taps of a button, I'd probably go crazy, too."

Eden's cheeks warmed at the phrase. *If the girl I loved*. It made her long for more time with him. The rare moments they did find were almost always interrupted. Their days were jam-packed. She was busy planning for Tycho's departure. He was busy preparing to intercept a second group of refugees at the airport. They both had important jobs to do, and those jobs pulled them in opposite directions.

The laboratory door swooshed open. Barrett marched inside holding a stack of printouts. "Look what I found," he said, setting them on the standing desk next to Asher's laptop.

Eden leaned forward to read them.

The first one was an article featuring Oswin Brahm, taken from a scientific journal written a decade and a half ago, five years before he founded SubTech. The article discussed the cutting-edge research he was investing in through the acquisition of a company called Seven Seas. Eden picked up the papers. According to the author, the company had just discovered a new type of electromagnetic wave more powerful than any of the rest. Generated *by the ocean*. In theory, these waves could be transmitted anywhere through mineral-dense water supplies found deep in the Earth's crust.

"The deeper the depth of the ocean, the stronger the wave," Barrett said.

"How deep is the harbor?" Eden asked, picking up the papers.

Barrett had her shuffle to a color-coded map. "Most of it's shallow, five feet or less. That's this whole yellow section there. But here—" He pointed at a spot where the harbor narrowed, between Brooklyn and Staten Island. This was colored a deep blue. "It's ninety-six feet to the bottom."

Eden moved the map to the back of the stack. "That's still not super deep though, right?" At least, not compared to the depths of the ocean.

Asher turned away from the interface. "What are you two muttering about?"

"The weapon," Eden said.

Asher wrinkled his nose. It drove him nuts that he didn't know what it might be. That in all fourteen years of living under his father's roof, of spying on his father's operations, he never once heard any mention of a weapon. He scratched his cheek. "I have a hard time believing Tycho doesn't know what it is."

"The control tower has always been off limits."

Asher snorted derisively. "Exactly my point. You

make a thing off limits, and every kid on the planet is gonna check that thing out. It's Forbidden Fruit 101. We're supposed to believe Tycho and his freaky siblings never even tried?"

"We're not dealing with typical rebellious teenagers here, Asher," Eden said, rereading the article. The possibility of a weapon had turned into an obsession. She'd already been visiting virtual headquarters every chance she got—early in the morning, between meetings and assemblies, before bed. Now, she kept returning to the control tower, circling that pneumatic tube.

Barrett took the stack from her and turned to the final sheet. "Check this out."

He handed Eden a different article, one that hadn't been copied from a scientific journal, but an entertainment magazine. A chilling first-hand account from a diver who had lost two of his friends while exploring a lake underneath Lake Superior. A story so over-the-top, Eden felt like it had to be satire.

She looked up. "You think there could be something like this in the New York Harbor?"

"It's possible."

Asher was peeking over Eden's shoulder now, reading bits of the story aloud. "'We descended toward the abyss like reverse astronauts, reaching a depth of six hundred feet with no sign of the bottom … the current began pulling at our legs with such force, we could no longer control our buoyancy … Their screams filled the com as their helmet lights slowly spun into blackness. Where was the bottom?'" Asher released a long, low whistle. "Think Tycho's up for some scuba diving?"

He was joking.

But Eden chewed on the possibility. Could Tycho swim to the bottom to see what was there?

"Can you find him for me?" Asher asked. "I need to do some final checks before he leaves, make sure I have everything replicated correctly."

He directed his question at Eden.

With a deep breath, she tapped into their connection, trying not to feel like a total intruder. She focused her attention until a strong wave of grief rolled over her. A breathtaking sadness, along with familiar imagery. She knew exactly where to find him.

Sure enough, there he was, sitting in the grass on the bluff in front of Aurelia's grave as a biting wind blew in from the east. The season was changing—fall slipping into winter. New Year's Eve would be here in thirty days and her parents were still stuck in Fredericksburg.

Eden shifted her weight and gave her mental voice a clear. *Hello,* she thought, as unobtrusively as possible.

Tycho turned.

She smiled sheepishly and lifted one shoulder in a shrug. *Do you want some company?*

He didn't object.

She crept closer, then joined him in the grass. After a long, quiet moment, he finally spoke. "I'm afraid," he said.

Eden understood his fear. She was afraid, too. Their plans came with a terrifying amount of what-ifs, a margin of error so thin it felt paralyzing. And she wasn't the one headed back into the dragon's lair, trying to save ninety-two brothers and sisters she knew and loved.

Tycho drew up his knees and rested his elbows on them. "That girl with the weird eye?"

"Francesca?"

He plucked a blade of grass and twirled it between his fingers. "She wasn't wrong. He *can* control me."

She understood this, too. Viscerally, with memories that made the horrendous possibility all the more possible.

Tycho dropped the blade. "What if I go back and I tell them the truth and he finds out? What if he gets really angry and forces me to do things I don't want to do?"

Eden looked out at the river and the decimated Washington, DC, beyond. Brahm's penchant for violence and destruction literally surrounded them. "If that happens, if that's what it comes down to, you can fight it."

Tycho's chin jerked. "How?"

Eden shared her story. She told Tycho about being on the rooftop of The Sapphire during the Prosperity Ball. She told him about Mordecai, about the device, about how he'd used it to get inside her head. How he ordered her to shoot her own mother. She told Tycho about fighting it. Not forever. Not even for very long. But enough for help to arrive.

"You can do the same thing," she said. "You can fight it, Tycho. And if you need help, you can send me a message." She gave her temple a tap. "I promise I won't leave you high and dry."

30

Tycho sat in quarantine, knees bouncing as he cracked his knuckles. Two guards had brought him here, then left to alert Pater of his arrival. Now he waited. Anxious. Angry. Bereft. Stuck in a holding cell.

Seeing such a familiar sight—the harbor, the bridge, the glass tower, the fortified stone walls of his home—had filled him with a longing that twisted into a deep and piercing ache. Here was the home he'd longed for. Only Aurelia wasn't there. She never would be again.

Betrayal coursed like hot lava through his veins. He fisted his hand, wrapped the other around his fist, and held tight to his anger. He needed to channel it. To pull himself together. To play the part and play it well. For Aurelia. For the others.

He had less than a month to convince them of the

truth, to locate incriminating evidence that would bury Pater, and to figure out what sort of weapon might hide in the harbor. He would have to work quickly and strategically while giving nothing away. If Pater found out—if he even so much as suspected—Tycho would end up as dead as Aurelia. Of that, he was certain.

The light inside the cell flickered. The projector set in the cement wall behind him hummed to life, then flickered, too. A few times before holding steady. Pater in hologram form appeared several feet in front of him, looking as put together as always in a three-piece suit that fit his lean build to perfection. He wasn't too short and he wasn't too tall. His salt and pepper hair was neatly styled and his carefully groomed beard had gone mostly silver.

Tycho stopped bouncing his legs. With bile in his throat and vitriol on his tongue, he slid off the bench and onto one knee with his head bowed.

"My son," Pater said in a voice thick with fabricated emotion. "I never thought I would see you again."

Tycho kept his head bowed, afraid his face might betray him. "Nor did I," he replied.

"Look at me."

After carefully schooling his expression, he looked up at this man he once trusted.

His blue eyes pooled with tears that only stoked the fire of Tycho's fury. They were as fabricated as his emotion. Pater was a master of deceit. Because of him, Tycho hardly knew what was true and what was a lie. The only way to keep the two sorted was by constant, willful reminders.

Lie. Pater loved him.

Truth. Pater only loved himself.

"I must know everything," Pater said. "How did you get away?"

Steeling himself for the performance of a lifetime, Tycho launched into the story he had devised with the council in advance, one that was similar enough to the truth. He'd been kept in a nondescript, underground room. They injected him with a debilitating poison that stole his strength. They experimented on him. They tried to get information from him. He'd given them nothing, of course.

Then one day, when he was due for another injection, nobody came. Tycho took advantage of their error. He escaped by the skin of his teeth with hardly any strength at all. He snuck onto a barge and collapsed amongst shipping containers, where he remained until the barge reached port in Philadelphia. He walked the rest of the way. He didn't know the exact location from where he'd come, but he did know it was somewhere in Delaware.

"You weren't followed?" Pater asked.

Tycho shook his head and with his shoulders quivering, allowed anxiety and fury to get the best of him. He let the tears come. Hot, angry tears he hoped would pass for remorse. "I am so sorry," he choked. "For allowing myself to be captured. For putting you through this. For failing to kill her when she was so close."

His mother.

Prudence Dvorak.

Lie. She was a conniving traitor.

Truth. She was a hero.

Pater shushed him. "You mustn't blame yourself for the evil they have committed. As for the snake, you will have another opportunity. As I did with my own mother."

Tycho wiped his eyes. "The only thing that kept me going was the hope of seeing you again. Of seeing my brothers and sisters. Please, I must be cleansed as quickly as possible so I can join them."

"Most of them are not here," Pater said.

Tycho feigned surprise.

"So much has transpired while you were away. Your siblings have been awakened. Their powers have come, and they are now working to fulfill their duties. Those who remain here do so to keep our home secure." Pater frowned. "It saddens me greatly to have to tell you this, my son, but we have lost one of our own."

Tycho's heart pounded in his ears.

"Dearest Aurelia was taken from us."

"Taken?"

"They captured her. And they ..." Pater's voice cracked. He brought his fist to his mouth, then combed his fingers through his beard with the slow, mournful shake of his head. "They destroyed her."

Tycho ground his teeth.

Lie. The Resistance killed her.

Truth. Pater did.

Because he wanted no more of his weapons in enemy hands. That's all they were to him—weapons. His grief was a show, a charade. No different from the one Tycho was putting on now. He only hoped he was the better actor. "But that isn't possible. We cannot be destroyed."

"There are ways, my son. Cruel ways that even I could not anticipate when I created you. The enemy did not hesitate to use these methods."

"But then ... why didn't they destroy me?"

"Evil knows no rhyme or reason."

Tycho breathed through his nose, chewing on his rage. He ground it between his teeth. Masticated it with his molars. His jaw tightened with such aggression, he thought his muscles might snap.

Pater noted his fury. He nodded as though to encourage it. "So long as the enemy exists, your siblings are in danger."

Here was the first true thing Pater had said. Tycho's siblings *were* in danger. He was determined to share that truth with as many of them who would listen.

31

Sunlight glittered off a thin layer of snow coating the frozen grass. At least thirty people stood on the lawn, broken into pairs, their breath visible in the cold as they worked through the move Cass had just demonstrated. Eden watched him as he traveled from one to the next, offering constructive feedback.

At the request of the council, the two of them led twice-a-week, voluntary training for anyone in Alexandria who wished to take part. Neither Cass nor Eden objected, as it seemed to be the only time they had together.

He guided a young woman's wrist in a specific way, eliciting a spark of jealousy in Eden. She longed for that wrist to be hers, certain his touch would make her feel better than she was currently feeling. She was restless and rattled. Tycho had discovered a weapon, only this one wasn't in the New York Harbor. This one was in the detainment facility in Fredericksburg, connected to the air ducts.

Her stomach twisted. The 88th day of Chrysalis drew nearer. Time was slipping through her fingers and progress was so painstakingly slow, she felt the near constant urge to crawl out of her skin. The winnowing would start in Fredericksburg. It seemed that winnowing would involve the dispersal of a deadly toxin that had already killed tens of thousands. And Tycho had yet to find the ironclad, nail-in-the-coffin evidence they were looking for. But even if he did, the council still couldn't figure out how to share it. At least, not in the broad scale way that would be required for such evidence to have its desired impact.

The only council member with anything positive to report was Dayne. *America Underground* was doing its job, priming a growing percentage of the public. If they could find that irrefutable evidence and figure out a way to share it with the world, it would at least land on fertile ground.

The newsroom didn't sleep. They worked around the clock to increase their counter-propaganda efforts, using the drastic proliferation of the metaverse to their advantage. Oswin Brahm wanted to push CogniFuse? Fine. They took to strategically hijacking its airwaves—interrupting virtual concerts and sporting events, infiltrating virtual chat rooms to challenge the narrative and plant seeds of truth.

Twice a day, Tycho sent messages to Eden, passing along the intel he had gathered. So far, he'd visited the patients in the labs and confirmed that Brahm was experimenting on both Ellery and Violet's father, often together. He discovered a treasure trove of information regarding the makeup and design of the Electus, along with a list of updates they'd received through the years. He'd also narrowed his search to one specific bay in Brahm's data center, which housed every video taken before, during, and after The Attack twenty-one years ago. This one might feel like real progress if not for a simultaneous discovery—the data in this bay had been coded for corruption upon transferring. Even if he found the right footage, he couldn't send it to them.

Then there was the matter of Tycho's latest message, which arrived earlier this morning like a swift kick to the gut. While he had no clue what weapon might be submerged in the harbor, he had discovered the existence of another. It seemed the Great Winnowing would bear an eerie resemblance to Hitler's gas chambers.

Eden was beyond disturbed.

Meanwhile, Cassian was on a roll. The Secret Passage was working. Two more groups had joined them in Alexandria. By the time the toxin hit Fresno, its entire off-the-grid community had been safely evacuated to Mexico.

Eden watched him as he continued helping the young woman in training. She wasn't getting the move. Or maybe she was only pretending not to get it to keep Cassian nearby. Eden could hardly blame her if that was the case, but such understanding did nothing for this sudden, intense bout of jealousy.

He stopped and called the group's attention forward, then invited Eden to help him with a demonstration. It was a defensive maneuver they'd practiced a hundred times before. Her insides coiled in anticipation. The second his hand curled around her hip, the coil sprung. She burst into action, but he was ready, too. She spun. He parried. She struck. He hooked her arm. She pivoted and threw him over her hip. He landed flat on his back with Eden over top of him, her knees straddling his waist.

Their eyes locked.

Desire electrified the space between them—a palpable, magnetic charge that made her toes curl. For one heart-thumping, blood-pounding moment, she forgot about the weapon. She forgot they had an audience. She wanted to kiss Cassian Gray. He obviously wanted to be kissed.

But then a sharp pain stabbed her temple. Wincing, she covered the spot with the heel of her palm. Cass's strong hands moved to her waist. He shifted her as he sat upright, his face a mask of concern. Only it needn't be. The pain had already receded.

Someone coughed—an acute reminder that they were far from alone. With her cheeks flooding with heat, Eden clambered to her feet and helped Cass to his. He cleared his throat and told everyone to partner up and practice. Then he scratched the back of his neck and asked, "Is it happening more often?"

He was referring to the burst of pain in her temple.

"It's holding steady at twice a day," she said. She shuffled to a nearby building and leaned against its outer wall. She always felt shaky after these bursts. Thankfully, that weakness was almost as brief as the pain.

"I noticed Barrett has another name on his hand," Cass said.

That he did, which made six altogether. Violet was the only one of them improving. Eden suspected that improvement could be attributed to the absence of Tycho's screams.

"There's nothing Asher can do?" Cass asked. "No way to update your systems so the glitching stops?"

"Not that he knows of."

His eyes filled with concern. With care. Just like they had before the training session started, when Eden told him about the latest news from Tycho regarding the toxin disperser.

"We'll get your parents out before it's activated," he'd said, conviction swimming in his golden irises.

Tomorrow morning, he was leaving to bring a fourth group to Alexandria. Herein lay the second reason for her restlessness. Every time he left, she turned into a useless tangle of nerves. She was good for nothing but pacing and worrying.

He leaned against the wall with his shoulder pressed against hers. He propped the sole of his shoe against the brick and set his gaze beyond the sparring trainees, his attention lost somewhere in the far distance.

She curled her pinky around his. "Penny for your thoughts?"

He spread his hand wide—palm to palm with hers—and threaded their fingers. The touch made Eden feel as though her entire body was sinking into a pool of sunshine. One corner of his mouth turned upward in a sad, barely there smile. "I was thinking about my mom."

She blinked at the confession. Of all the things he could have said, his mother wasn't on her radar.

"She doesn't have a grave site."

Eden glanced toward the spot he was looking and realized his gaze wasn't lost, but set toward the bluff where they'd laid Aurelia to rest.

"I think it's good that you gave her a proper burial," he said.

"So did you," she said back.

"It was your idea." He traced his thumb over the tip of hers.

A delectable shiver raced up her arms.

"I never asked anyone about my mother, what happened to her ... *after*." His expression turned somber. "It was the first thing Tycho thought about with Aurelia."

Eden turned to face him. "You were twelve." Still a kid. One who had just endured unimaginable trauma.

She wished she could reach that twelve-year-old boy now. She wished she could wrap him in a hug and give him a different story. He deserved a better one. But that was as impossible as Cass predicting the future. He didn't know if they could get her parents out in time, no matter how strong his conviction. And the past was the past. It couldn't be undone. But it could be worked through. She suspected this was exactly what he was doing in his therapy sessions with Dr. Lydia Kane.

"Hey!" The breathless greeting grabbed their attention. Cleo clomped toward them, her breath escaping in frozen puffs.

Cass didn't let go of Eden's hand.

Cleo didn't tease him about it, either. She looked too distracted for teasing. Troubled, too, as she pressed her tongue against the inside of her lip, making her snakebite lip piercings bulge.

"What's the matter?" Eden asked, trying not to feel so alarmed.

Cleo twisted her crossbones ring around her thumb. "Asher found something. He wants you to come to the lab."

Eden and Cass ended the training session early and made a beeline for Kaiser. Upstairs, Asher had all four networks on display—Tycho's, Eden's, Barret's, Violet's. He stood in the center of them, zooming in on a node Eden recognized. The Queen Bee. He'd pulled up Barrett's, too, then swiped to Tycho's. Only it looked different from the one he'd already pinpointed.

"What is that?" Eden asked.

"I think you might have been right," Asher said.

"About what?"

"The reason Tycho's the five-star general."

Cass took an aggressive step forward. "You said he was the five-star general because he was first born."

"I guess I was wrong. It doesn't happen very often, but when it does … " Asher let the statement go unfinished as he scratched his chin and scrolled from the odd-looking Queen Bee to one that was much more familiar.

Eden's eyes went round. "He has two master nodes."

"Apparently," Asher said.

"Why does he need two?" Cleo asked.

Asher shook his head, cross-referencing this new discovery with the slew of information Tycho had provided regarding the Electus—their design, the updates they'd received through the years. He scribbled notes Eden didn't understand. Until finally, he stepped back and said, "It's like a hive mind."

Eden glanced at Cleo, discomforted by the lack of coloring in her face. "What is?"

"His army." Asher made a few more cross-references. He zoomed in on one of the master nodes. Then zoomed in to Barrett's. "My scumbag of a dad pre-programmed his soldiers to work like a hive."

"What does that mean?" Cass asked, a bite in each word. He didn't like when people dillydallied around a point.

"He doesn't need their locations. He doesn't even need to breach networks. If he controls Tycho using this master node," Asher gave the strange Queen Bee a tap, "then he controls his whole army."

"Who's included in that army?" Cass all but growled.

"Any soldier connected to the general."

Every ounce of warmth drained from Eden's face.

After a silent, tense beat, Cass pulled at his jaw. "What do you mean—connected?"

Nobody replied. Nobody had to. The question wasn't necessary. They all knew the answer. Tycho was connected to his brothers and sisters. And now, thanks to Asher, Tycho was also connected to Eden. It had been a necessity—the only foolproof way they could remain in communication.

Cass muttered a curse. "You need to disconnect them."

"That's impossible."

"Surely you can find a way."

Asher scrubbed his palm down the length of his face. "The only *way* is by eliminating her Queen Bee."

And that, they had decided, was unattainable. Eden had pored over the journals. So had Asher. Together, they had brainstormed until they were blue in the face only to reach a profoundly frustrating conclusion. Eliminating the Queen Bee was nothing more than a giant distraction. A massive time suck. If Eden didn't want to be controlled, her only option was taking out the people seeking to control her.

Cass and Asher started to argue—heated words that had Cleo stepping between them. Meanwhile, the full weight of the situation was slowly sinking in. Before Tycho left, he told Eden he was scared. He was afraid of being controlled. She promised that if that were to happen, she would come to his aid. But her words were a lie. For now it seemed that if Tycho was controlled, she would be, too.

32

A snowflake landed on Eden's eyelash. She blinked it away. She lay on the train tracks with her hands crossed behind her head as flurries fell from a dark sky.

The snow reminded her of Christmas, which was only two weeks away. If she was in Eagle Bend with her parents, they'd be celebrating in a new home. The tree would have been up for a while now, since the Friday after Thanksgiving. Four stockings would be hung; there was always one for Christopher. Presents would be wrapped and under the tree. Outside, icicle lights would twinkle from the gutters. From ages eight to ten, a giant blow-up Santa had joined those icicle lights. But somewhere during the move from Seattle to San Diego, Santa got lost. At this point in the season, all the classic movies would have been watched. Loads of hot cocoa and candy canes would have been consumed, Christmas music playing on repeat. Eden loved this time of year. Even with Christopher's sad stocking hanging above the fireplace, her parents loved it, too.

This Christmas, there would be no tree or lights or stockings or wreaths or candy canes or carols or wrapped presents. The country was in a panic, her parents were trapped in that detainment facility, the people of Alexandria were too busy to celebrate, and apparently, Eden might not be herself for very much longer.

She'd come here to the train tracks looking for quiet and solitude so she could work up the courage to contact Tycho and tell him about Asher's discovery. But Tycho had beat her to the punch, and for the first time, she hadn't felt a wave of anger or fear or grief in the connection. Instead, there'd been relief and a newfound sense of determination. Tycho had swayed two of his brothers to the truth, who then helped him sway eight more, most of whom were stationed in Fredericksburg. He had *ten* on his side. Eden didn't have the heart—at least not in that moment—to tell Tycho it might not matter in the end.

Someone approached. The crunch of boots on gravel drew nearer and nearer until that someone stood above her with his hands in his pockets and snowflakes in his hair. "Care for some company?"

Eden shrugged.

Barrett lay beside her on his back, his eyes on the sky, and for once, he didn't fill the space with words. He was uncommonly quiet as the snow fell and the soft silence embraced them. Eden was pretty sure he'd heard the news from Cleo or Cassian. Probably Cleo.

She took a deep, slow breath in through her nose. "Are you a fan of the zombie genre?"

"Zombies," he said with a chuckle. He checked his hand to read one of six names written there. "Graham loves Zombie movies. Can't say I've ever been much of a fan." He turned his head. "Are you?"

"Not particularly." She'd watched them with Erik from time to time, but they weren't her favorite. She'd never watched a trailer and thought, *Ooo, I can't wait until that one releases.*

"Why are you out here thinking about zombies, Eden?"

"I don't know." She shifted ever-so-slightly. "They look like themselves, in a gross sort of way. But they aren't. The person they once were before they were infected is just … gone. All that's left is their bodies, moving around, doing these really awful things."

Barrett made a noise—a short hum of understanding. He knew why she was thinking about zombies. And Eden knew she'd rather be dead.

The choice between zombie and corpse wasn't even a contest. And yet, it wasn't as simple as she originally thought when she first learned about the self-destruct command. Death sucked, too. She only had to remember Aurelia's final moments, or the guard who'd lost his legs. Both of them had begged for life in the end. Neither had wanted to die.

Nor did Eden.

She wanted to live. She wanted to see her parents. She wanted to see Erik. She wanted to introduce him to Cassian. She wanted to spend year after year kissing the boy she loved under the mistletoe.

"Do you think this will come to an end?" she asked, giving her hand a wave as though to indicate their general predicament.

Barrett seemed to consider. "Did I ever tell you about my great-grandpa?"

"I don't think so."

"He used to be a soldier in the United States Army. He was sent to Afghanistan two months after he married my great-grandma. He said it was awful. He was far from home, stuck in the middle of a desert, surrounded by sand and heat and blood and death with twelve more months ahead of him. He thought he would die there in that desert, missing his pretty, young wife. But he didn't die in Afghanistan. He died sixty-five years later, in a hospital in Maine. Surrounded by his pretty, young wife who wasn't so young anymore and his three gray-haired sons. He would always have sand in his teeth, as he liked to say, but he wasn't in the desert anymore.

"My family paid him a visit in his final days. I have this super vivid memory of him lifting his finger and looking me straight in the eye and saying, 'Barrett, my boy, everything must come to an end. The good stuff, and the bad.'"

Eden blinked another snowflake from her eyelash.

Barrett wiped one from his cheek. "I think it's normal for our imaginations to fail us when we're in situations like these. I think it's hard to see beyond the desert, to whatever happy ending waits on the horizon."

"You think it'll be happy?"

"I hope so." He smiled at the sky. "I really want Violet to see Maine. I want to take her to The Captain's Hat so she can taste the most delicious lobster rolls on the face of the planet. And I really think she'd get a kick out of hunting for ghost crabs on the beach. She'd have a lot of fun doing something like that. She deserves to have some fun, you know?"

Yes, she did.

Violet's quality of life had been crap. So much so that it had actually improved since waking up in Dr. Norton's basement. Compared to Dante's inferno, the desert of Afghanistan would probably feel pretty nice. Especially with a guy like Barrett to keep her company.

"What about you?" he asked. "What are you gonna do when this is over?"

"Go to Paris."

"Ooo. 'Respirer Paris, cela conserve l'ame.'"

Eden laughed. "That is the worst accent I've ever heard."

"Hey, I'm just proud of myself for knowing some French, even if the quote comes from a book that is totally depressing. I will not be subjecting Violet to Les Miserables."

Eden laughed some more. "It's Lay Miser-ah!"

Barrett laughed, too.

The quote was written by Victor Hugo.

Breathe Paris in, it feeds the soul.

She hoped to one day.

She really, really hoped.

"Hey, Barrett?"

"Yeah?"

"Has anyone ever told you what a great guy you are?"

"Most people are too busy telling me to shut up." He folded his hands over his abdomen and shot her a wink.

But Eden wasn't joking. She looked at him with all the sincerity she could muster. "You are a great guy, Barrett Barr."

Maybe Violet Winter wasn't lucky in general, but she sure was lucky to have him in her corner.

Cass pinned the photograph of the young boy on the bulletin board on his cubicle wall. He would meet this young boy, along with twelve others, at the airport tomorrow morning. He didn't typically sleep much on the eve of an airport run. He was too antsy. Too eager. Too hopped up on adrenaline.

Tonight, his adrenaline was for a different reason, and he wasn't antsy so much as slowly losing his mind. It was the kind of issue one might work through with one's therapist. But the hour was late. And therapy was hard. The whole thing put him on edge. Had him second-guessing why he was doing it. Therapy in the middle of mass destruction? It felt like something a person should do later, when the world wasn't on fire. He had expressed as much to Dr. Lydia Kane at his last appointment. She told him there would always be a reason to put it off.

"Everyone deserves to heal," she'd said. "Even amid mass destruction. Or maybe *especially* amid mass destruction. Tomorrow isn't guaranteed."

He knew this.

His past told the story.

One minute, he was a twelve-year-old kid with a mother. The next, she was dead and he was one nose bleed away from joining her. He sat on the edge of his chair, shoved his fingers into his hair, and began bouncing his knee.

"Knock, knock."

He looked up to find Cleo stepping into the cubicle. "I thought I might find you here." She took a seat on their desk and held out a box of chewy lemon heads.

He declined the offer with the shake of his head.

She rattled a candy onto her palm. "Wanna talk about it?"

"About what?"

"The reason your knee's bouncing like that."

Cass made his leg stop.

"The reason you tore out of the lab like a man on fire."

He leaned back in the chair. He set his forearms flat against the armrests with his fingers curled over the edge and bit back a choice word. "You know what she's gonna do."

Cleo popped the lemon head into her mouth.

"She'll go to your boyfriend—"

"He's not my boyfriend."

"And she'll ask him to do the same thing she asked me to do after Forrester discovered that command."

Take her out of the ring.

This time, he didn't bother to bite anything back. He let the curse fly. "I made her promise to never ask that of me again. Now I wish she would."

"Would you do it if she did?"

His hands clenched into fists. No, he wouldn't do it. He'd find some other way to pry her from Brahm's control. He'd kill whomever, destroy whatever was needed to keep her breathing. His knee started bouncing again. He bent forward and buried his fingers in his hair. He kept seeing Aurelia, writhing on the floor, frothing at the mouth.

"Look," Cleo said. "I think you're jumping to the worst-case scenario here. We don't even know if this hive mind thing will work on her."

"She's connected to Tycho."

"With an outdated system. We keep trying to fix those glitches, figure out how to run whatever updates are needed to make them stop. But maybe those glitches are a blessing in disguise."

The suggestion took the edge off his mounting insanity.

Cleo made a valid point. Eden's system didn't work like Tycho's and Aurelia's. She was an old model, evidenced by the pain she experienced approximately twice a day. What if old models couldn't take part in the hive? He dragged his hands down his face and looked up.

Cleo was studying the board, rattling another candy from the box. There were thirteen photographs, but her attention held steady on the boy. "He can't be much older than six."

He was five and a half.

Their youngest traveler to date.

A little boy and his mother, on the run. Searching for safety.

33

He moved like a ghost through the concourse, armed with a Heckler & Koch semi-automatic pistol courtesy of Harlan. The cold metal was reassuring in his grip; it wasn't loaded with tranquilizer. Cleo and Jericho were on standby. Four more were hiding along the route, watching to ensure the coast was clear.

Cass crept closer and ducked into position, his sights set on the carousel farthest away. If they were there as they should be, they were ghosts, too. He couldn't hear them. He couldn't see them. Cass brought his fingers to his lips and whistled twice—two sharp tweets.

There was a beat, maybe two.

Then, a group of thirteen slowly came out of hiding. They rose from their crouched positions with squinty eyes and shell-shocked expressions, all of them travel worn. The Secret Passage was working, but it wasn't kind to its passengers. Between train hopping and perilous hikes without food or water, it was a wonder anyone made it at all. And yet, made it they had, their faces covered in grime, their clothes torn and dirty. With a five-year-old among them. A little boy with an unruly cowlick.

He wasn't standing on his own feet. He was being carried in his mother's arms, despite her thin, frail frame. She straightened with her hand cupped around the back of his head, her expression one of fiercest protection. Mother and son. Isla and Huck. These were the names that came with the photographs.

Cass showed himself.

The group clambered forward—beaming with relief.

With his finger to his lips, he pulled a map and a small flashlight from his back pocket. He switched on the light and unfolded the map and showed them the route he'd shown the previous two groups. It wasn't to Alexandria. Nobody was privy to that information until they arrived at the Potomac Yard. This was a route to a meeting spot should an emergency arise. "If anything goes sideways, you go here and you hide until someone arrives to get you."

Fear flashed across faces.

"We haven't run into any trouble so far." They'd done the hard work. Compared to what they'd been through, the rest was easy. But they still had to move carefully. Diligently. Cass wouldn't let his guard down until all thirteen of them were safely inside Alexandria. He pointed along the map. "We'll move in groups of two. Each group needs to get to this covered walkway here. Follow the signs to the DC Metro. Once you reach the station, hide and wait for the rest to arrive and we'll go from there."

Huck lifted his head from his mother's shoulder. "Are we safe now?" he asked with a slight lisp. He was missing his two front teeth.

"Almost, baby," his mother said, her eyes brimming with tears. "Almost."

She looked dead on her feet. Cass thought the kid could walk on his own, but then he noticed why he was being carried. His left shoe was missing and his foot was wrapped in a soiled, bloodied t-shirt. Isla shifted the boy in her arms, struggling with his weight. "He was injured after the last stop," she said, noticing Cass's attention. "He needs a doctor."

So did she, by the looks of it. She sported more than a few cuts and scrapes, with one nasty gash on her forearm that looked in need of stitches. How many miles had she carried him? And why hadn't any of the men offered to lighten her load? With a frown, he refolded the map and slid it into his pocket. He sent groups of two onward, holding Isla and Huck back. They would go last, and they would go with him.

"I can carry him for you," Cass said when it was just the three of them.

At his words, Huck pressed his face into the crook of her neck and clung to her more tightly.

"We'll get there faster this way, honey. And I'll be right here. Right beside you." Isla didn't pry him away. She didn't force him to go. She held him close, making a gentle shushing sound in his ear, until the boy gave Cass a wary look over his shoulder. After a moment, he reached out and Cass took him.

He had no idea how much a five-year-old should weigh, but surely it should be more than this. Huck was featherlight, his arms skinny but strong as they wrapped themselves around Cass's neck.

"Thank you," Isla whispered.

Something in his heart shifted. Steeling himself against the sensation, he nodded gruffly and looked at his watch. "It's our turn. We have to be really quiet."

As if on cue, the boy's stomach growled.

"I'm sorry," he said with that adorable lisp again.

Cass's heart shifted some more. He swallowed. "Do you like mac and cheese, Huck?" he asked quietly.

"With hot dogs," Huck replied.

"Well, of course, it's the only time hot dogs are acceptable."

Isla wiped a tear.

"You stay really quiet, try your hardest not to make a sound, and you can have a whole bowl of mac and cheese and hotdogs as soon as we get there."

The boy nodded.

Isla smiled tremulously.

Together, they crept into the open. Isla walked with a noticeable limp. Cass moved at a speed she could tolerate, his eyes and ears on high alert. As they reached the rental car kiosk, his walkie-talkie squawked, a jarring sound followed by indecipherable shouts and a spray of bullets.

Cass hit the ground, pulling Isla with him.

The kid screamed.

They crawled for cover, hiding behind the kiosk.

Isla was right there, shushing Huck. "It's okay, baby. We're okay."

But the words were a lie.

They weren't okay.

RRA officers poured inside. Cass had no idea where they'd come from. He only knew they were blocking their escape, guns ablaze, mowing down the twosomes ahead. He switched off his walkie-talkie. Isla cupped her hand over Huck's mouth, her eyes locked onto his until he was no longer trying to scream. Then she pulled her hand away and turned to Cassian.

"I'll distract them," she whispered. "You take my boy and you run."

Cass stared at her, appalled. If anyone was going to provide a distraction, it would be him. He moved to place Huck in her arms. "You need to get to the security checkpoint on the south side. Stay hidden until someone comes for you."

"I'm not strong enough. If I try, neither of us will make it."

The boy whimpered.

She pressed her hand against his cheek. But her eyes remained on Cass. "Please. Please save him." She slid a backpack from her shoulders. She pulled a well-loved teddy bear from the pouch and pressed it into Huck's arms. "This man is going to keep you safe, sweetheart. You hug Eddy tight, okay? Super, super tight. I need you to be brave and close your eyes for Mommy."

Cass was still shaking his head.

But the woman wasn't listening.

She kissed her son's cheek. She closed his eyes for him and crossed herself, like Cassian's grandfather used to do once upon a time, in a different life. "Get him to safety," she said, fiercely, vehemently. Then she stepped out from hiding with her hands held in the air.

Guns turned in her direction.

RRA officers barked commands.

"Please don't shoot," she begged, hobbling forward. "Please, please don't shoot."

They commanded her to stop. To get down on her knees with her hands on her head. As soon as she obeyed, they circled her and cuffed her and Cass took the boy and did what Isla said—he ran.

He turned into a ghost once again, Huck miraculously silent in his arms, holding on to Cass like a spider monkey. They made their way to the south security checkpoint and hid with three others.

Only three.

The rest were dead or captured.

He found the five of them a secure hiding spot and settled in to wait. The officers swept the entire airport, missing them by inches. Huck buried his face into his teddy bear and wet himself. When the officers finally cleared out, night had fallen. Cass waited some more, unwilling to move until he was positive nobody was there to follow them.

At two in the morning, he extricated himself from his spot. With Huck still in his arms, he waved at the others to follow.

An hour later, they were in the Potomac Yard. Huck was sound asleep. The other travelers were shivering and traumatized as Jericho radioed for help and Cleo and Eden rushed out of the IDA into the night.

Eden ran to him with wild eyes, her hand going to the boy's back as a team of nurses joined them outside.

One of them took the boy.

"His foot is badly injured," Cass said.

Then Eden was there, in his arms, hugging him tight. He tried to hug her back, but the image of that mother on her knees with her hands on her head, begging the officers not to shoot felt like a hot branding iron to his brain. And before that, familiar, haunting words.

A mother, telling her son to be brave.

The nurses escorted the travelers to Kaiser, leaving Cass outside in the dead of night, his muscles quivering, his teeth grinding as Dvorak and Jericho and Cleo stared at him like he was an apparition—like they weren't sure they believed he was actually there.

"What happened?" His words exploded in a bellow, a roar—so loud Eden startled away from him and a sleeping crow took flight from a tree, releasing several alarmed caws.

Dvorak shushed him, like RRA officers might hear them all the way from Arlington. Cass fumed while she ushered them inside the foyer of the IDA with her eyes on the sky, in search of any government drones that might be circling overhead.

Cass pushed through the door with fire in his lungs. "Why wasn't there a warning? Where was backup?"

"Backup was dead," Dvorak said.

He blinked, momentarily stunned from his rage.

"Officers shot them down. We're lucky they didn't find us here."

Cass shoved his fingers into his hair, then dragged them down his face. He couldn't stop seeing it—Isla handing herself over like a sacrificial lamb. Her words to her son before doing so. Her voice blending with his mother's. *Be brave. Stay in the closet. Close your eyes. This will be over soon.*

He spun around and slammed his fist into the wall.

Cleo jumped.

Eden stared.

With his chest heaving, Cass strode toward the boardroom.

Footsteps followed him. He didn't look to see who. He didn't stop until he was inside, snatching up a device the council used to contact people outside Alexandria.

"What are you doing?" Dvorak asked.

Eden and Cleo followed her into the room.

"I need to contact Amanda Hawkins."

"It's the middle of the night."

"I don't care." With his grip like a vise, he plugged in the correct sequence of numbers, then hit the button to send the alert. The device emitted a holographic scrolling ellipsis, chirping intermittently.

There was a *bloop*.

The ellipse disappeared.

Cass tried again.

And again.

Until Amanda Hawkins appeared, her miniature hologram floating two feet in front of him—at first rumpled and bleary-eyed, then almost instantaneously alert as she recognized who was contacting her.

He didn't waste time on pleasantries. "Location Zero was ambushed by RRA officers." He glanced at his watch. "At 0900 hours yesterday morning. One traveler was a woman named Isla Coffelt. White female. Twenty-eight years of age. Petite frame. Brown, curly hair. Birthmark behind her left ear. I need to know if she survived and if so, where she was taken."

Amanda jotted the information on a notepad with her bottom lip captured between her teeth, nodding along. When she finished, she looked up from the paper. "I'll see what I can find out."

With a nod, Cass ended the call.

Close your eyes for Mommy.

The words whispered through his mind.

This man is going to keep you safe, sweetheart.

Positive he was going to punch another wall or claw out of his skin, he pocketed the device and stalked from the room.

Eden exchanged a worried look with Cleo, then went after him.

"Cass," she called, her body humming, her knees shaking. She'd been worried to death. All day. All night. Her mind abuzz with scenarios that grew increasingly worse the longer Cassian remained out of pocket. Then suddenly, he was back. Not with thirteen, but three. Along with that little boy in his arms. When she'd hugged him, his body had been as tense as a bowstring ready to snap.

He didn't wait for her.

He kept going, his stride long, his pace fast as he exited the IDA and headed to The Landing. He didn't stop until he reached the walk-in refrigerator in the cafeteria kitchen. He swooped inside, grabbed a package of hotdogs from the shelf, set them on the prep table, and began searching through the industrial-sized pantry, sifting through crates of canned foods and dry goods.

"Cass," Eden said. "What are you doing?"

"Does this place have macaroni and cheese?"

Macaroni and cheese?

Eden had no idea what was going through his head, but she recognized single-minded determination when she saw it. For whatever reason, Cass wanted mac and cheese, and he would not stop until he found it.

She joined his search and found several boxes in a

crate in the back. "What is this for?" she asked, setting a box by the package of hotdogs.

"I promised the kid mac and cheese."

Something cracked, like a fault line across her chest. He wanted to make that little boy macaroni and cheese. But the boy was sound asleep. He hadn't even stirred when Cass handed him off to the nurse. She took a tentative step closer, trying to get him to meet her eye. "He's sleeping, Cass. He'll be sleeping for a while."

At her words, he set his hands on the prep table and leaned forward with his head bent like he didn't have the energy to hold it up. "I should have stopped her," he whispered.

"Stopped who?"

"The kid's mom. She gave him to me and she just … she turned herself in."

The fault line cracked wider. It felt like someone was pouring wet cement inside.

"I should have saved her."

Eden took another step. "You saved her son."

"I let her go. I just … let her go." His knuckles whitened. "I didn't argue. I didn't fight it. I just got in the closet."

Eden stopped.

Got in the closet.

They weren't talking about the boy's mother anymore.

He looked up, his golden eyes lost in a storm-tossed sea. "Maybe if I wouldn't have gotten in. Maybe if I would have just—"

"No," she said—decisively, definitively—taking one last swift step forward. She held his face between her hands, inclining her head, forcing him to meet her eye. "There was nothing you could have done. No way you could have stopped it. Your mother is dead because of your father, full stop. And you went into that closet because you were a kid doing what your parent told you to do."

His eyes shone with unshed tears.

She stared into them, wishing she had the power to convince him, to make him see the situation from her perspective.

The device in his pocket chirped.

He pulled it out and answered.

Amanda Hawkins floated in front of them.

"A woman matching the description you gave me was brought into Fredericksburg yesterday at 4 pm. I wasn't able to get all the way into the system, but the initials on the intake file were IC."

Isla Coffelt.

"She's alive?"

"Yes," Amanda said. "She's alive."

He set the device down with a clatter.

Eden picked it up. She thanked Amanda and she

ended the call, then she stared at Cassian's back—the broadness of it, the defined outline of muscle, even through his black shirt—as it rose and fell with deep breaths. Tentatively, she reached out and set her hand on his shoulder.

He pulled her into his arms and didn't let go.

34

Be brave. Stay in the closet. Close your eyes. This will be over soon.

His mother stared down at him with eyes as resolute as Isla's. She shut the closet door and turned the bolt.

Cass lurched awake.

Sunlight flooded through a window and pooled across the floor. He stretched his neck, which had a horrible crick thanks to the uncomfortable way he was positioned in the chair. Silverware clinked, followed by a small, shy giggle.

He straightened.

He had fallen asleep in the corner of Huck's hospital room. Last night, the boy had been sound asleep while a monitor beeped beside him. This morning, he was sitting upright with shadows beneath his eyes, but a shy, gap-toothed smile on his face. He held a fork in one hand and watched as Eddy the Teddy performed a silly dance, courtesy of Eden.

She spotted Cassian—awake—and the bear stopped. She followed the direction of his gaze, toward the bowl on Huck's tray. "We got him some mac and cheese," she said. Then she held Eddy up straight and threw her voice toward the stuffed animal with a funny intonation. "With extra hotdogs."

This elicited a giggle from Huck.

A swell of warmth in Cassian.

Man, he loved her.

He scrubbed his hand down his face.

"She said my mommy is with her mommy," Huck chirped.

Cass came forward in his chair with a nod, watching as the boy scooped up a big bite of mac and cheese. A slice of hotdog fell from his fork. He swallowed the bite, took a long drink of milk from the glass by his elbow, wiped his milk mustache with the back of his hand, and smacked his lips. "When will I get to see her again?"

Cass set his elbows on his knees. He failed to save his own mother. He would not fail to save Huck's. "As soon as we can get to her."

"Are you going to get her mommy, too?" Huck asked.

"Hers, too." His gaze connected with Eden's. They shared a look filled with every word they couldn't say as

Huck ate more mac and cheese, and Cleo knocked on the door.

She stepped inside with a bright-eyed expression that looked like worry in disguise. She greeted the kid, then she asked Eden and Cass if they could join her out in the hall. Eden flipped on the television. She changed the channel quickly from Concordia News to cartoons. Then she gave Huck's unruly hair an affectionate ruffle and they stepped into the hallway.

"Brahm just made an announcement," Cleo said, waving at them to follow. She stepped inside the first empty room she came upon. She, too, turned on the television, but she didn't change the channel.

Cass watched the news unfold.

Oswin Brahm's team of scientists had successfully created an antidote to the toxin. At this very moment, they were hard at work creating more of this antidote. Enough to stock hospitals and workplaces. Enough for every American citizen to have one on hand with more in their medicine cabinets at home. The whole country was rejoicing. Brahm promised the people their lockdown was coming to a close. This nightmare would soon be behind them. Better times awaited.

So did the 88th Day of Chrysalis, when the Great Winnowing would begin.

"To celebrate this monumental turn of the tide, I plan to host a New Year's Eve Party right here in Chicago—

the very city our enemy tried to destroy. If joining us physically isn't possible, you can be with us virtually. Together as a nation, we will raise our glass to new beginnings. We will raise our glass to victory. For now, more than ever, our enemy is on the run!"

Finally, the council had their *how* and their *when*. They would expose Oswin Brahm during his New Year's Eve party—a broadcast so expansive in scale, the entire country and a good portion of the wider world would tune in.

This called for an emergency meeting in the war room. The full council attended, along with Cassian, Cleo, Barrett, Violet, Amanda Hawkins, and Dr. Beverly Randall-Ransom, who'd been helping with the Secret Passage. Together, they formed a circle around a virtual table. Eden sat between Cassian and Emmett with her hands on her thighs, her leg bouncing, her pointer finger tapping.

"We're missing a vital piece of the equation," Asher said, ten minutes in.

Dvorak tented her fingers. "The incriminating footage."

"Tycho has it narrowed down to Bay 13 though, right?" Nairobi asked.

"Bay 13 is large," Dvorak replied.

"He needs to work faster," Francesca said—her face unmarred by burn scars here in this virtual reality.

Dayne rubbed the stubble on his cheek. "He works any faster, he'll start blurring the line between aggressive and stupid."

Cleo leaned back in her seat with a skeptical brow. "Isn't this all a moot point? Even if he finds exactly what we're looking for, he can't send it without corrupting the file."

"We don't need him to send it," Asher said. "We'll broadcast the footage from his very own control tower."

Francesca laughed humorlessly. "How do you plan on doing that, Ash? Soldiers are stationed there. Not to mention a slew of regular guards."

He shrugged. "Regular guards are easy enough to evade. Plus, we have Tycho."

"And ten more of his counterparts, according to her." Jericho nodded at Eden.

"Only two of them are at headquarters," Cleo said. "The others aren't on our side."

"*Yet,*" Asher replied. "Maybe in two weeks they will be."

Dvorak cut in. "We will not carry out plans based on maybes."

"Okay, then. We tranquilize the ones who haven't come around."

Francesca folded her arms. "What about the tower's security system? A tiny drone might be able to slip in unnoticed, but surely not a full-grown adult. An extra large one, if we're talking about you."

Asher rolled his eyes. "C'mon, Fran. I spent the first fourteen years of my life getting around the old man's security systems. His control tower won't be any different."

Eden's leg bouncing had morphed into leg jack hammering. The pressure inside had reached capacity. She felt like a tea kettle ready to scream. "What are we doing about Fredericksburg?"

Everyone looked at her.

Sure, the New Year's Eve party gave them a way to broadcast incriminating footage to the watching world, but such exposure would come at the eleventh hour. Even if Asher could break into headquarters and pull this off, Brahm would carry out genocide in secret. Her parents would be two of his victims.

She tapped a button in the center of the table. A projection appeared—live satellite footage of RRA-East. Four guards patrolled the grounds, circling the facility and the transmission tower that had been erected a couple weeks ago. Since then, identical towers had been erected in Shenandoah and Wendover. Nobody knew what they were for. Not even Tycho, their new mole.

"We have to stop the toxin from dispersing," Eden

said. "Otherwise, a thousand people will die while we're exposing the enemy."

"One thousand twelve," Amanda Hawkins corrected. "That's the latest head count."

Francesca massaged her temples. "If breaking into headquarters is going to be difficult, breaking into Fredericksburg will be suicide."

"I don't care!" Eden shot back. She clutched the armrests of her chair, her attention zipping to Dvorak. "We can't just leave them. Surely that's not our plan."

"Of course not. Doing so would make us no different than Brahm." Dvorak tapped the table, her lips twisted to the side. "How many soldiers are stationed at RRA-East?"

"Thirty-one," Hawkins replied.

"Eight of those thirty-one will help us," Lark said.

"Supposedly," Francesca emphasized.

"Plus three of our own."

"Hold on a second there, Lark." Asher held up his finger. "I may be confident, but I'm not foolish. I will need *some* superhuman protection."

"I'm going to Fredericksburg." Eden spoke in a voice that left absolutely no room for debate. She would not be playing bodyguard while her parents were in mortal peril elsewhere.

"I can go with Asher," Barrett offered.

Which meant Violet would go, too. The assumption

went without saying—they were a package deal. As of this moment, it would be Eden and eight super soldiers squaring off with the other twenty-three. The numbers were far from ideal, but they weren't hopeless either. Especially when adding the element of surprise to their side.

Eden tapped the button again. The projection shuffled from live footage to a static three-dimensional blueprint of RRA-East. According to Tycho, the machine was in the boiler room. Loaded with toxin, ready to disperse. An observation deck circled the facility. A team of soldiers took turns patrolling from above. A couple more patrolled the grounds outside. The rest patrolled inside, on the floor, moving between cages stuffed with people.

If they could get the eight soldiers on their side plus Eden up on that balcony armed with tranquilizer guns, they might be able to render the others unconscious.

The plan came with several glaring problems. RRA-East had surveillance monitors everywhere. Swarm members were undoubtedly keeping tabs on such surveillance. Even if they weren't, as soon as that first dart flew, surely at least one soldier would be able to radio Brahm and alert him of an ambush. There was also the matter of the tranquilizer itself, which only worked on the soldiers for a short period. Perhaps long enough to disable the machine, but certainly not long enough to free over a thousand captives and get them to safety. Not to mention, the dose of tranquilizer required to take a soldier out for even fifteen minutes would kill a regular person. How could they ensure the people in those cages didn't get hit in the crossfire?

Eden wasn't willing to take such a risk. Not with her parents. Judging by the tension radiating off Cassian, he wasn't willing to take that risk with Isla Coffelt. Not when he'd promised Huck to save her.

They talked over one another, brainstorming solutions. Asher could take over surveillance. He would have no problem looping in false footage. Anybody watching would have no idea RRA-East was under attack. Jericho could use the Atax to create another dead zone, just like they'd done during the prison break. It was possible, with enough of them, to make the whole facility a dead zone. Of course, this would shut down their communication, too, but they could sacrifice a short window of time to ensure nobody sent an SOS to Brahm.

"Will that stop them from communicating with one another?" Barrett asked. "You know, with their special … communication connection?"

All eyes turned to Eden.

She shared that connection with Tycho.

Jericho rubbed his chin. "I'm not sure, but we could try it out."

"We can also tranquilize the soldiers at HQ beforehand," Asher said. "If anyone tries communicating with them, they'll be out of commission."

That was great, except for the twenty-six soldiers stationed in RRA-West, and the twenty-five in RRA-Central, none of which they could tranquilize. Not to mention the problem Eden and Cass were most concerned about. Killing the innocent.

"I'm afraid it's a risk we're going to have to take," Dvorak said.

Shaking her head, Eden turned to Dr. Beverly Randall-Ransom, who up until this point, hadn't said a word. "What about an antidote? Some counteracting agent we could inject in a person if they get hit."

"It wouldn't be quick enough," she said in that calm, cool voice of hers. "As for the brevity of the tranquilizer's effectiveness, I believe I could help." She folded her hands on the table. "I don't think it would be terribly difficult to create a slow-release function that could expand the window of unconsciousness."

"That would be incredible," Dvorak said, before turning to address Eden's growing concern. "I don't see how we can mitigate the risk of hitting a bystander. In my eyes, the only solution is impeccable aim. We'll have to gather a team of our best marksmen."

Except for Lark, their very best.

She was as adamant as Eden about her location. Lark Shangguan would not be joining them in Fredericksburg.

Nor would she be helping in headquarters. She would be in Chicago at the New Year's Eve party, in position to use the bullet she'd been carrying in her pocket for the last thirty years. The same bullet composed of nanotech that allowed the Resistance to meet in this very war room, plotting the Monarch's demise. As soon as she received the go ahead, she would send that bullet straight into Oswin Brahm's head.

"Poetic justice," she said.

If it worked.

From where Eden sat, the plan didn't seem likely to succeed. There were too many moving pieces. Too many substantial unknowns. Strategizing felt like a giant game of whack-a-mole. Smack one potential problem, only for another to rise in its place. They plotted and devised, creating contingencies for their contingencies, until patience wore thin and stomachs growled.

The meeting was adjourned.

Eden pulled off her headset and waited while the boardroom cleared. She told Cass and Cleo to go ahead; she would catch up with them in the commissary. She had one last contingency to make. When only she and Asher remained, she shut the door with a soft click.

He typed on his laptop, his attention fixed on the screen. He always had technological housekeeping to attend to after meetings in the war room. "What's up, Pruitt?" he asked.

Figuratively? A thundercloud. The very one that had been hanging over her head ever since Asher discovered Oswin Brahm's hive mind two days ago. It had been the proverbial elephant in the room today. Of all the potential problems, nobody brought this one up. To Eden, it was the most glaring. If activated—however such a thing *was* activated—it would not only work on the soldiers they'd won to their side. It would work on Eden, too.

He stopped typing and leaned back in his chair. "Cleo warned me you'd hunt me down."

Eden took the seat across from him. "I can't be his pawn, Asher."

He set his elbow on the armrest of his chair and tapped his chin. "There's no reason to think you will be."

"I've been controlled before. I can't let it happen again. This tranquilizer pump on my arm will not protect me from that in Fredericksburg."

"You shouldn't need protection. So long as my father remains in the dark, he'll have no reason to activate anything."

"But if he does—"

"Then we'll tranq you."

"There are circumstances in which I can't be tranquilized." The most obvious, if nobody was present to tranquilize her. Because they were all dead. A shudder rippled down her spine. "If a circumstance like that arises, if he activates the hive mind and I'm in a position to hurt someone, I need you to—" She choked on the words.

Thankfully, she didn't need to finish them.

Asher's expression sobered into utmost sincerity. It was a look she'd never seen on him before, without a trace of condescension, of arrogance, of flippancy. His hazel eyes held hers with kindness, with understanding as he gave her a singular nod. "I've got you, Pruitt."

Eden exhaled, feeling grateful in the weirdest way. That Asher understood. That he was willing. That he would not make this harder than it needed to be. That he didn't even make her say the words. He would not let her be a zombie. She curled her hands on top of the table. "You promise?"

He nodded again. "You have my word."

35

Tycho blinked—heart thumping, mind spinning, unable to believe what he'd just watched. This was it. After weeks of searching, after weeks of failing, he'd finally found the footage that would drive the nail in Pater's coffin.

He replayed it—a recorded meeting between Pater and his most revered disciple. Karik Volkova, a man who had sacrificed his life in service to Pater. He'd played a part, and he'd played it well. The world's most hated terrorist had taken responsibility for The Attack and was publicly executed several years later. The footage was time stamped—twenty-one years ago on October fifth. In it, the pair lifted flutes of champagne and toasted to victory. Afterward, Karik Volkova bent in a subservient bow to hail his master, Oswin Brahm.

The world would flip.

So would Eden. Only her reaction wouldn't be shock or outrage, but relief. The New Year's Eve party was only a few days away. There was too much of Bay 13 left to search. Tycho couldn't get through it all. They both thought they'd run out of time. But here it was. He finally found something not just useful, but perfect. He knew its exact location.

With a thrill in his bones, he strode from the data center. The hour was late, long past curfew. He should already be in bed, asleep. Chances were, Eden was asleep, too. Even so, he would certainly attempt to contact her once he reached his quarters.

Halfway through the snow-covered courtyard, footfalls stopped him. Ten sets. Soon after, he spotted a guard leading his nine siblings down the stone staircase. Tycho froze, looking first at Nikos, then at Knox—the two brothers who believed him about Aurelia. With their hair unkempt and their shoelaces untied, they looked as startled as he.

"What is going on?" Tycho asked.

The guard stopped and saluted. "I have an order from the Monarch, sir. He wants all of you transported to Fredericksburg."

"Now?"

"Yes, sir."

Tycho looked about as if the guard had just told him a riddle, and the answer was hiding somewhere in the darkened courtyard. "If we leave, our home will be wide open for attack."

The guard bowed. "We will be here, sir. We will protect this home with our lives."

Their lives were weak. They were regular humans. Tycho's gaze flicked to Nikos, then Knox. They were as baffled as he. "Did Pater say why he wanted us to make such a transfer at this time?"

"No, sir. But he promised to explain upon your arrival. Please, follow me."

With a nod, Tycho stepped into the front of the pack per usual. In the past, Aurelia would flank him to his left. Nikos on his right. Now Nikos had taken Aurelia's post. Knox marched to his right. They were headed to Fredericksburg, where they would join eight more who also believed him about Aurelia. Tycho would have access to the machine in the boiler room. He could greet Eden and the others when they arrived on New Year's Eve. Meanwhile, headquarters would be left wide open. Asher could break in, retrieve the data he'd just located from Bay 13, and expose Pater for the lying roach he was.

Excitement zipped through his veins. He could hardly wait to send the news to Eden.

36

Snowflakes danced in the courtyard. They spun and twirled against a curtain of black before coming to rest on a blanket of white. The snow on the ground was three inches deep and climbing.

Inside the boardroom, Eden sat beside Cassian. Cassian sat beside Barrett. Barrett sat beside Violet. Violet sat beside Cleo. And Cleo sat beside Asher. They had formed an assembly line down one side of the conference table—first, loading and programming two boxes full of high-tech explosives, then filling guns with Dr. Beverly Randall-Ransom's innovative tranquilizer, which Harlan had transported from Beverly's home in Chicago to Emmett's speakeasy in Bethesda. Lark had stepped in from there, bringing it the rest of the way to Alexandria.

Now, it was the eve of New Year's Eve. Tomorrow morning, their group of six would split in three and go their separate ways. Barrett, Violet, and Asher would travel northeast to Staten Island. Eden and Cassian would go southwest to Fredericksburg. Per Dr. Beverly Randall-Ransom's request, Cleo would remain here with Dayne.

But that didn't mean she was sitting out. As soon as Asher infiltrated the metaverse, mentor and protégé would broadcast live in front of a green screen. According to Dayne, every groundbreaking story needed a reporter. This one was set to be so groundbreaking, it could use two. Tycho hadn't just come through on the footage, he had knocked it out of the park.

The once iconic anchorman who had been made into a scapegoat—a truth-teller accused of being an agenda-driven crook—was raring to go. He couldn't wait to return to the airwaves. His protégé had never been very interested in broadcast journalism, but for this, she would make an exception.

Upon Tycho's arrival in Fredericksburg, he recruited two more of his siblings. They had thirteen soldiers on their side. He sent mental snapshots of each one, along with their names and numbers. Eden sat down with Alexandria's very own sketch artist, and a day later, they had digitized photographs. Asher added them to an intel board in the war room.

Brahm's party would go live at 8 pm central time, which gave them three hours to infiltrate RRA-East, tranquilize the soldiers who hadn't joined them, disable the machine, and get over a thousand captives to an abandoned community center two miles north. Meanwhile, with the help of Cleo and Dayne, Asher would have sweet revenge on his abusive father, exposing Oswin Brahm from his very own control tower. And Lark would be in position, ready to take her long-anticipated shot. She'd left for Chicago yesterday.

Jericho had called for one final assembly. Francesca and Nairobi were playing gopher for Dvorak as she made last-minute preparations. Which was how the six of them came to be in the boardroom, forming an assembly line, readying the weapons.

When they finished, the snow was still falling. They were sitting in a snow globe. Standing on a precipice. Looking down the edge of a steep and perilous cliff. Tomorrow night, they would jump. The plans they made would fly or fail.

Eden felt nauseous.

Asher spun his queen like a top on the table. "What now?"

Cleo stretched her arms toward the ceiling.

"We should go sledding," Barrett said.

Cleo laughed.

It was an absurd suggestion. A ludicrous thing to do the night before the end. But Barrett shrugged, like he wasn't being absurd at all.

Eden agreed.

Why not?

Maybe tonight of all nights was the perfect time to do something as frivolous as sledding. Maybe tonight, more than ever, they were due for a little fun.

"We don't have sleds," Asher said.

"Actually ... " Cleo tilted her head, then gave her eyebrows a jaunty lift. "We have a whole stack in the cafeteria."

Which was how they ended up on top of a snow-covered hill, not far from Aurelia's grave. The six of them were dressed in an eclectic assortment of winter clothing and held cafeteria trays as snowflakes fell in their hair.

Barrett grinned at Violet, obviously eager to show her how this was done. He backed up several steps, then took a running start. As soon as he reached the downward slope, he leapt. His knees hit the tray and he zoomed down the hill with a yip and a holler.

Violet stared, her face curtained by her hair, her mouth spreading in a slow, wondrous smile. She peeked to her left, then her right. Then she took a few steps back and did the same thing Barrett did, only her yip was a scream. A jubilant, high-pitched shout that continued all the way down the hill.

Behind Eden, Asher chucked a handful of snow at Cleo. She shrieked and ran after him. He juked and rolled and sidestepped and backpedaled as she chased and laughed and attempted to tackle him.

Cass scratched the back of his head and peered down the hill skeptically. Perhaps he'd never gone sledding before. Perhaps he thought this was as silly as Cleo had before she thought of nabbing the trays. Whatever the case—on this night of all nights—Eden felt brave. She felt bold. She felt … a little frisky.

She took Cassian's tray and set it on the ground. "Sit," she said with a point.

He arched his eyebrows.

She inclined her head.

Cassian obeyed. He sat cross-legged on the tray, then looked up at her like, *now what?* With a shaky breath and a lot of resolve, she climbed on his lap with her face to his and wrapped her legs around his waist.

The skeptical look on his face vanished.

Asher wolf-whistled.

Cleo exclaimed, "Go get 'em, tiger!"

Eden wrapped her arms around Cass's neck, and with their eyes locked, he pushed them forward, paddling his hands along the ground until they were zipping down the hill, spinning in circles, Barrett and Violet a blur as they ran up and Eden and Cass flew down. Faster and faster and faster until they reached the bottom and tumbled off the tray and lay together in the snow, laughing. Then kissing. Then laughing some more.

Until he pulled her to her feet and they were running back up the hill.

This time, they went in a group of six. All together. They set their trays in a line. They backed away holding hands. On the count of three, they ran forward and jumped aboard. Eden missed her tray, but it didn't matter. Cassian held onto her left hand. Cleo held onto her right. They pulled her along as they flew down the hill in a fit of shrieks and giggles.

Cassian landed on top of her, smiling the best smile. The kind that made his golden eyes crinkle in the corners. And she was overrun. Head over heels. She loved him. She loved him, she loved him, she loved him. With an overwhelming, all-consuming, buoyant love that made her believe in impossibilities. On this night of all nights, she needed to believe.

Eden traced the scar on his chin, wanting to remember this moment forever. Capture it for as long or as short as she lived. This bright, shining, pure moment in the snow, unmarred by the fact that somewhere out there, great evil was underway.

Tears pricked her eyes.

Not because of the evil, but because of *this*. Life. Beautiful, messy life. Fun and frightening. Good and bad. Euphoric and painful. A person couldn't have one without the other. Life didn't work that way.

The world was too filled with juxtaposing forces.

Light and dark. Laughter and tears. Love and hate. Angels and demons. Existing together. Fighting each other. From time immemorial. In the world all around, and in every human heart, reminding her of the sentiment Cassian had alluded to on the back deck of Dr. Norton's cabin after she'd nearly killed her mother on the rooftop of The Sapphire.

"You don't think we all have the same struggle—a battle inside that has us doing things we don't want to do? If you're good, you fight it. You starve it. I'm telling you right now, I'm looking at one of the best."

So was she.

Cassian Gray was one of the best.

And these people playing in the snow were the best, too. She loved them all. Barrett and Violet and Cleo and maybe even Asher.

Tomorrow, they would fight this evil.

Tonight, they were clinging to the good. Holding on for all they were worth.

Barrett clambered to his feet. "Let's do that again."

37

"It's gone." Barrett blinked at the dark expanse where the Verrazano Bridge used to be. Thirty-five days ago, Violet had walked upon it. All 4,260 terrifying feet. She didn't want to walk upon it again. She was sure she would plummet into the choppy waters and sink to the bottom of the harbor, where she would remain—in the cold, dark depths. All alone. Waiting for someone to find her. Because she couldn't swim. But she couldn't drown either.

Asher shoved his large hand into his hair. "He knows we've been watching."

"What do you mean?" Barrett asked.

"We have surveillance teams monitoring headquarters. Someone would have noticed a bridge being demolished. But nobody noticed, which means he must have covered it up. The bastard looped in faulty footage."

The fear in Violet's belly quadrupled.

She had a bad feeling. A terrible feeling.

"Why wouldn't Brahm tell Tycho about the demolition?" Barrett asked.

The unspoken answer dangled ominously in the cold night.

A biting wind whipped Violet's hair.

They quickly retooled their plan. If they couldn't take the bridge, they would have to take a motorboat, which would put them significantly behind schedule. By the time they arrived at the South Brooklyn Marine Terminal, they should have already been in the control tower. They scouted the area for signs of life while a rusted crane groaned overhead and the motorboats rocked.

Nobody was there.

This didn't bode well either. For some reason, the terminal had been completely abandoned. Almost like Oswin Brahm was baiting them. Violet shook the thought away and climbed aboard a boat while Barrett removed the anchoring ropes from the pier and Asher searched for keys. When he found a ring of them, he took the captain's seat and began trying one at a time.

"Have you ever driven a boat?" Barrett asked.

"Can't be too different from a car," Asher said.

"Do you want me to—"

With a choke and a spit, the motor growled to life. Propellers chopped through the water. Asher hit the gas and Barrett fell into a seat. Violet clutched the side of the boat with one hand and Barrett's arm with the other. They sped over the choppy, black waves, the small boat rising and crashing, rising and crashing until they reached the other side.

Violet shrieked, positive Asher was going to crash their boat into the docks. Asher must have thought the same thing. He relinquished the wheel to Barrett, who brought them safely ashore. Violet's legs wobbled as she stepped onto solid ground. They hurried into the facility, toward the control tower—stopping once along the way so Asher could create a temporary glitch in the security cameras.

Violet tried to take steadying breaths. But this wasn't virtual. This was real. She couldn't tap a spot on a holographic blueprint and magically appear in a specific place. To get to the control tower, she had to move through a tunnel. She had to go past the labs. The fear in her gut tightened into a fist. Violet didn't want to go past the labs.

Perhaps they would be as abandoned as the rest of Fort Wadsworth. Perhaps the patients inside the lab rooms had evacuated the premises with everyone else. Violet clung to this hope as tightly as she could for as long as she could. Which wasn't nearly long enough. All too soon, she could hear heartbeats. And breathing. And then, there they were, inside their rooms, visible through the glass paneling.

Violet sucked in a sharp breath and held it. She dug her face into Barrett's back, pushing him from behind, when a jarring knock made her jump. It was followed by the loud squeak of a hand sliding down glass.

"I knew you'd come!"

"Don't look," Barrett said, his pace quickening.

But Violet couldn't help herself. She looked. And Father was right there, his face—that deranged, horribly familiar face—shoved so close to the window, she reared back. He cackled like her fear was funny. Then he rapped on the glass, his eyes bright and wild as he followed her down the length of his room. "He told me you would be here!"

Violet hunched up her shoulders and covered her ears and scuttled down the tunnel, into the stairwell. Father's muffled, manic shouts chased her the entire way as Barrett spewed questions in front of her.

What does he mean?

What is he talking about?

Asher didn't respond. He climbed the stairs wearing a look of grim resignation. Meanwhile, Violet's heart was beating frantically. So much so, Barrett answered his own questions, as though doing so might calm her wild heart.

It's probably nothing.

The ramblings of a madman.

He's deranged.

Out of his mind.

More so now than ever before.

When they reached the top, Asher stepped toward the keypad on the door. He punched in numbers and code with his bottom lip captured between his teeth, stopping now and then to glance at a camera. After several prolonged beeps, he lifted his watch to the scanner, which he'd programmed with the stolen retinal profile of a control tower guard.

The doors slid open.

Automatic lights turned on, one after the other, until the cylindrical command center was aglow, a bright orb floating in the night. Asher slid his backpack from his shoulder and took a seat at the panel, powering up computers and an entire hub of surveillance monitors. He slipped on his earpiece and began patching in to the various groups he would be coordinating. The team in Chicago. The team in Alexandria. The team in Fredericksburg. All while footage loaded on the monitors.

United Center on the west side of Chicago, home to the Chicago Bulls, filled three of them—a jam-packed arena with a giant stage and a raucous, celebratory crowd. Somewhere among that crowd was the bad man who had done this to her and Barrett and Eden. The bad man who wanted to take over the world. He was there with his wife and every other member of America's Board.

The detainment facility in Fredericksburg filled five more—a large and lonely warehouse-of-a-building in the middle of nowhere, surrounded by fog and fence. Somewhere in those woods were the good guys who were going to stop the bad man.

Asher pulled Eden's device from his bag. He commanded Barrett to power it up, to get Eden's network projected. It was the only way they could tell if the bad man activated the hive mind.

Down below, Father continued pounding on the glass. In the room beside his, a familiar red-headed girl sat catatonically on an exam table with her eyes open, her bare feet dangling above the ground.

Violet stared at the tube in the center of the room.

Sharks are messing with the weapon again.

The fear in her stomach churned. What, exactly, did this weapon do?

38

Eden hunkered beneath a row of trees lining the hillside, her focus fixed on the detainment facility below. An extensive but rudimentary storehouse wrapped in mist. Lights made hazy with fog illuminated the snow-covered grounds. It created a haunting picture—that fog. A swirl of ectoplasm. A multitude of corporeal ghosts reaching up from the frozen ground, eager to collect more souls.

How many would it grab before tonight was through?

She pushed the creepy thought aside as her teammates shifted restlessly beside her. Cassian, Dvorak, Francesca, Jericho, Nairobi, and five of their best marksmen from Alexandria. They were fully loaded with tranqs and semi-automatics, their belts clipped with explosives. They had comms in their ears and specialized watches around their wrists. Each one contained soldier bios, blueprints, timelines, and alarms that would go off accordingly. Two already had—a quiet buzz against Eden's wrist, first at 7:45 pm and again two minutes ago.

Asher was late.

And now, so was Tycho.

Such a foreboding start to an evening so dependent on timing set her nerves on edge. She squinted into the foggy night, searching in vain for the flashing morse code that was supposed to be Tycho's invitation.

The night remained dark and quiet.

Her heart drummed faster.

She tried tapping into the telepathic connection she and Tycho shared.

Where are you?

The question went unanswered.

Dvorak repositioned herself. "We're due at the meeting spot in five minutes."

Cassian peered through a pair of night-vision binoculars. "The soldiers at the gate aren't on our side."

"So we tranq them," Francesca said.

"They'll hear the darts coming," Eden replied.

Francesca released a tense breath. "Then what do you propose we do?"

Eden looked down the embankment, toward a thicket of shrubs to the left, another further away to the right. "Attack twice. From two different directions." She addressed Cassian. After herself, he had the best shot. It was almost as deadly as Lark's, and she'd been practicing for thirty years. "See that thicket of shrubs there?"

He nodded.

"Wait for my signal. When I give you the go ahead, shoot. They'll hear the darts coming. I'll piggy-back fire from over there." She nodded at the other thicket of shrubs.

"Won't they hear those darts, too?" Francesca asked.

"I'm hoping they'll be too distracted with the first set."

Cass slid down the embankment and got into position.

So did Eden.

Halfway, Asher's voice sounded in her ear.

"Where have you been?" Dvorak demanded, her relief clear. Her aggravation, too.

"The bridge was gone. We had to improvise."

The bridge was gone? What did he mean? Bridges didn't disappear. They had to be demolished, which wasn't a commonplace endeavor. If Brahm demolished the Verrazano Bridge, Tycho would have told her. Or they would have seen it on surveillance. And yet, they had no idea.

"The broadcast is going live in T-Minus two," Asher said. "I'm looping in false security footage now. Are you inside?"

"We're working on it." Eden ducked from view and peered through the scope of her gun, using it to locate Cass.

He was in position.

"Ready when you are," he said.

"Two quick shots when I say fire."

"Copy that."

Eden turned her gun from Cassian to the soldiers. "Ready …" She curled her finger over the trigger. "Set …" She took a deep breath in through her nostrils. "Fire."

Cassian's darts sliced through the air.

Zip-zip.

Anticipating the soldiers' reactions—the precise trajectory of their movements as they avoided attack—Eden shot.

They dropped like rocks.

She waved at the others and jogged to the gate. "Asher, I need a ping on Tycho's location. He's currently MIA."

She heard the typing of keys. The crunch of gravel as the others joined her by the gate. She reached through the bars and lifted a soldier.

"He's in the northwest quadrant," Asher said.

"The boiler room?"

"Looks like it."

Eden tried to imagine why he would be there. That

was step three of the plan. They were still on step one. Had something bad happened? Was Tycho there now trying to stop an early dispersal? If so, why would he keep her out of the loop? She tried tapping into their connection again, but it was like shouting into a void.

Eden grabbed the soldier's hand, peeled off his glove, and set his thumb against the fingerprint access pad. The gate unlocked. She pushed it open as Jericho stuck an Atax into the frozen ground. He had five more to plant around the fence's perimeter, which he would activate as soon as they sent him word. The dead zone would last a quarter of an hour.

This was the maximum time they were willing to fly deaf and blind. Anything longer felt too risky. They'd rehearsed and practiced and felt confident that with the number of soldiers they had on their side, they could tranq the rest within fifteen minutes.

Jericho left to plant the rest.

Eden and her teammates hurried inside, around the building to the back doors of the facility. She knocked four times. A line of waiting soldiers filed outside. There were supposed to be thirteen, but Tycho wasn't there, and another was missing, too. His final recruit, a burly young man named Morpheus.

Dvorak ran quick checks on those who were there, making sure they matched the bios Tycho had sent.

"Why is Tycho in the boiler room?" Eden asked the young man named Nikos. "And where is Morpheus?"

Nikos didn't know.

Neither did any of the others.

Nairobi passed out tranquilizer guns.

When everyone was armed, Eden led the way inside, running straight into a wall of stench. The place smelled like an outhouse. She buried her nose into the crook of her elbow and made a spontaneous decision. The group was headed to the observation deck. They would quietly tranq any soldiers they met along the way. Then they would take their positions. As soon as Jericho activated the dead-zone, they would let the darts fly.

Eden separated herself from the group. She needed to find Tycho. So instead of going with the others, she pulled up a blueprint from her wrist device and put a ping on the boiler room. She made her way on silent feet through the halls, blocking her eyes anytime she passed an opened doorway. She didn't want to see them. All those people stuffed inside cages—their clothes filthy, their faces gaunt, their eyes haunted and much too big.

Concordia News called them vermin.

Oswin Brahm treated them accordingly.

Babies cried. Children whimpered. The elderly coughed. Some looked dead. She resisted the urge to search for her parents. Finding them now would only distract her from her mission. She focused on the blinking dot that was Tycho and lengthened her stride. She didn't stop until she reached the steel door to the boiler room. With her gun at the ready—because who knew what she might walk into—she tried turning the handle. The door was locked. The handle didn't budge. She glanced over her shoulder, aware that if she tried forcing it open, she would create a significant amount of noise.

She looked up at the exposed ceiling, where a criss-cross of pipes and wires and air ducts ran like a roadmap. Off to the left, a stack of crates. She climbed to the top—as nimble as an acrobat—silently pried off a vent and shimmied inside the air duct. She crawled forward until the boiler room was beneath her, then dropped through another vent.

Tycho was there, just like Asher said he would be. Standing with his back to her, as still as a statue.

"Tycho?" Her voice echoed in the cavernous room.

He didn't turn around. He didn't react at all.

She tiptoed forward—uneasy, uncertain—until she stood right beside him.

His eyes were open but unseeing.

"Tycho?" she said again.

Nothing.

"We're ready and in position," Dvorak said through the comm.

"Activating dead zone," Jericho replied. "In five … four …"

Eden snapped in Tycho's ear.

Nothing.

"Three … two …"

"Tycho," she said again, as loud as she was willing to say it, giving his arm a tug when her wrist-device buzzed.

"One."

Her earpiece crackled with static, then went completely silent. Outside, Cassian shouted, "Everybody down!"

Screams filled the air as darts began to fly.

39

Violet stayed up in the tower with Asher.

Barrett went down. Past manic Father. Past catatonic Ellery.

Violet walked in a circle around the tube, wringing her hands, waiting and watching as Barrett stepped inside the data center.

"Row seven, third unit on the left," Asher said, instructing Barrett as he went. All the while, his fingers flew across the control panel keyboard, his attention jumping from monitor to monitor. Several captured footage from the party in Chicago. Several more had gone black and would remain so for thirteen and a half more minutes. The others covered the grounds of Fort Wadsworth.

Violet tried not to look at those. But her eyes had a mind of their own. They kept returning to one screen in particular, where Father wrung his hands just like Violet wrung hers.

Barrett began unplugging the processing unit, carefully following Asher's instructions. It took eight painstaking minutes. Sixty-five nervous laps around the tube.

"Got it," Barrett finally said, carefully lifting the unit from its shelf.

With a flood of relief, Violet stopped her circular pacing. Barrett had done it. He was on his way back. Only instead of finding Barrett on the monitors, she found Father. No longer pacing, but standing on a chair, his entire face filling the screen as he stared directly into the camera. Directly at *her*.

Violet choked and ducked behind the tube. But it was too late. That giant, horrible face was dragging her into the past, when she was the lab rat and he was the mad scientist.

The door swung open.

Barrett hurried inside.

He set the unit on the ground next to Asher, who used a special attachment that allowed him to transfer the footage to the mainframe. When the transfer was complete, he ran a search for Karik Volkova.

The search came back with one video. But when Asher clicked on it, the footage wasn't viable. Every file had been corrupted.

Outside the boiler room, chaos reigned.

Darts whizzed.

Captives screamed.

Soldiers fell.

Bullets flew.

They were three soldiers short. Morpheus was missing. Eden wasn't there. Neither was Tycho. He was here, standing perfectly still, like he heard none of it. Whatever trance had ahold of him, Eden couldn't snap him out of it.

She pivoted slowly and beheld the machine *he* was supposed to disable—the same shape and size as the steel shipping container she'd hidden inside when she rode to and from Chesapeake for their botched prison break. Only this one wasn't in the back of a semi. It was here, in this detainment facility with tubing connected to the air duct she'd just crawled out of. Along with valves and a pressure gauge and a keypad and a digital clock with red numbers that told the time.

If only she could contact Asher. Given his skill set, he might have some way to disable the machine remotely. But she couldn't reach Asher. Not for another—she checked her watch—eleven and a half minutes. That's how much longer the dead zone would last, and when it was over, how was she supposed to know if they'd immobilized all twenty-one soldiers? What if one of them escaped only to contact Oswin Brahm the second the dead zone lifted? Who was to say he didn't have some remote with him in Chicago, one that could immediately activate this machine?

With shaking hands, she searched for a power source. There wasn't one. She stared hard at the keypad, her mind racing, her breath shallow. What was she supposed to do—attempt to deactivate it herself? What if, in trying, she accidentally set it off? She moved back to Tycho and tried rousing him. She clapped in his face. She shouted in his face.

He didn't even blink.

She looked again at the keypad. Dare she push a button? Guess at the code? What if she pressed the wrong button? She checked her watch. *Seven minutes.* Her attention jumped around the room, frantic. Desperate. There had to be something she could do. Some way to shut this thing down. She slid her hands down her face, pulling at her cheeks.

Then she stopped.

Her hands.

She stared down at them like they were something she'd never seen before. Her hands. Strong enough to topple trees. Strong enough to *bend steel.* She studied the machine's steel tubes. If she tried snapping them, would the toxin escape? She looked at the vent she'd dropped through. She searched for more vents, but there was only the one. She raced through the room, looking for windows. Looking for cracks. Looking for any way a toxin might leak through. There were none that she could find. She ran to the door and began feeling around the frame. It seemed air tight.

Her heart pounded. Her breath came quick as she searched for something to seal the vent. She peeled off her jacket with absolutely no clue if it would work. She wasn't Dr. Beverly Randall-Ransom. She didn't know if the toxin particles were tiny enough to get through the fibers. Nor did she work maintenance. She wasn't familiar with boiler rooms. She had no idea if there were other leaks she should be aware of. She only knew that she had to do something.

Operating on panic and instinct, she turned her jacket into a barrier. When she finished, only three minutes remained. The machine was connected to the air duct—a guaranteed death sentence for everyone in this building should Brahm decide to activate it.

She set her palm against her stomach and took a breath—a determined intake of resolve. Then she burst into action. She climbed atop the steel. She took one of the metal tubes between her hands. She squeezed and twisted and just like that, the tube snapped. An error code on the keypad beeped. Quickly, Eden clamped the ends of the severed tube. Then she moved to the second tube and did the same thing. Another error code flashed.

She bent the valves. She tore off the keypad. She yanked at the exposed wires beneath it—electricity searing through her fingertips and pulsing up her arms. Ignoring the pain, she kept tearing until the beeping stopped and the red digital clock went black and the noises outside went silent.

Her chest heaved.

Her charred fingertips revived.

Her watch buzzed.

The dead zone had ended. Jericho's voice sounded in her ear—a staticky patch of noise she couldn't decipher. Followed by more from Dvorak. Eden could make out only two words. *Soldiers down.*

She closed her eyes and slid off the machine. They did it. The soldiers were down. The machine was disabled. They had over two hours to evacuate the captives and get them to safety. Her parents included.

Eden buried her face in her hands—filled with praise and gratitude and the sweetest relief—when the door opened and closed behind her, and a slow *clap-clap* filled the room.

"Bravo, bravo. You have saved the day."

Eden's relief curdled into dread, for she recognized that voice. There was nothing staticky about it.

Oswin Brahm stood in the boiler room, or at least, his

hologram did. Dressed in his best, smiling pleasantly beside the burly soldier named Morpheus as he pushed a button to seal the door shut. Morpheus wasn't a hologram. He was real. In the flesh. And decidedly *not* on their side as he held a familiar device in his hand, identical to the one that had controlled Eden at The Sapphire, only it wasn't projecting an image of her system. It was projecting an image of Tycho's.

Brahm folded his hands behind his back and walked a predatory circle around her, his smile unwavering. "You looked so hopeful, my dear. So proud. But, oh." He chuckled softly with a paternal shake of his head. "You didn't actually think it would be this easy?"

40

The captives lay prone on the floor, covering their heads. More than a thousand—whimpering, crying, slowly peeking out from beneath their arms at the fallen soldiers all around.

They were down.

Every last one.

Cass gripped the banister and peered into the facility, searching the cell blocks from his bird's-eye view while Eden's voice cut in and out in his ear—more out than in, making her words indecipherable.

Dvorak's voice blared through the sound system. "Attention captives, we need your full cooperation as we evacuate everyone quickly and safely. The soldiers still standing are on our side."

Slowly, people rose from their prone positions as cries

turned into shouts of relief and joy. If any of the innocent had been hit, nobody was vocalizing it.

In cell block four, Cass spotted someone familiar. Thinning hair atop a tall, thin frame. Jack Forrester, holding tight to a frail woman Cass recognized as Annette. Beside them—Dr. Norton. And beside him, Ruth and Alexander Pruitt. They were all there. Together and alive.

He scanned the rest of the facility. His attention sliding from cell block four to cell block five to six to seven, when he finally found her. Huck's mother. Isla Coffelt. She was alive, too.

"Evacuate blocks four and seven first," Cass said into his comm—authoritatively, uncompromisingly—as he raced down the stairs. By the time he reached the ground floor, the soldier named Nikos already used his thumb print to release the captives in four.

Ruth Pruitt collapsed into his arms. She hugged him like her life depended on it, asking over and over about Eden. *Was she okay? Was Eden okay?* When he assured her she was, Ruth went incoherent with relief. Alexander took her by the arms, his eyes locked on Cassian's.

"I need you to follow Francesca to the exit," Cass said. "We have to get everybody evacuated as quickly as possible."

Alexander nodded.

Ruth cried for her daughter.

Alexander promised they would be reunited soon while ushering her away. When block four was evacuated, Cass moved immediately to seven, skipping five and six to protests and shouts. Dvorak assured them nobody would be left behind. They would be released in an orderly fashion for the sake of expediency and injury mitigation. The last thing they needed was a stampede for the nearest exit.

The prisoners in seven poured out a little more aggressively—with pushes and shoves and cries to hurry. Isla was the last to exit, hobbling forward with a limp that had only grown more pronounced since the last time they met. Her mouth was tight, her face ashen, her focus so intent on the ground before her, she wouldn't have seen Cass at all if he didn't reach out to offer his support.

Her eyes lifted to his and went round with recognition. Her chin trembled as she grasped his hands in a claw-like grip. "My boy," she croaked. "Where's my boy?"

"He's safe and sound," Cass said. "And very eager to see you."

Tears spilled from her eyes, creating streaks down her dirt-caked face.

Cass refused to pass her to a soldier. He would escort this group to the exit. He wouldn't let this woman out of his sight until she had Huck back in her arms. He left the rest of the evacuation efforts to Dvorak and escorted the prisoners from block seven to the exit.

When he arrived, there was a logjam.

Francesca was still there with the captives from cell block four. They were packed into the corridor like sardines.

"What's going on?" Cass called, his muscles tense, his tone aggravated.

"The code isn't working," Francesca called back.

He wound his arm around Isla's waist and pushed his way through the crowd, parting the captives until he was at the front with Eden's parents, Dr. Norton, and the Forresters. Francesca stood by the keypad, pushing a sequence of buttons that was supposed to release the door's locking mechanism.

Jericho spoke through the comm. "I'm at the north quadrant. Code's not working. I need someone to let me in."

"It's not working in the south quadrant, either," Cass replied, trying the code himself.

Behind him, the captives grew restless.

"We need a soldier at the south exit," he commanded. "Delay release until we have this figured out."

A moment later, Nikos arrived.

He pushed his way forward. He tried the code. He tried his thumbprint. When neither worked, he kicked the door with his superhuman strength. Unnervingly, it didn't budge. Nikos backed up and tried again. His boot landed against the steel with a loud, echoing *boom*.

The door remained stalwartly in place.

Cass turned away with his hand over his earpiece. "Asher?"

"I'm here," came his reply.

"We need you to unlock the exits."

"Sure thing." There was a brief pause. A few clacking keys. And then, a muttered curse.

"What?" Cass barked.

"Someone changed the override sequence."

"What do you mean *someone changed it*?"

"From inside your facility. While the dead zone was active."

Cass looked around, his attention on high alert. Who would have changed it? *How* would they have changed it? "Can you override the override?"

"I'm working on it," Asher said, his frustration apparent. "I still have access to the cell blocks. Do you want me to unlock them?"

Cass shook his head. The corridor was already congested. They didn't need more people pushing toward the exit. "That won't help us."

A patch of static shot through his earpiece. Eden's voice—her words chopped to pieces.

"What's happening with Eden?" he asked.

"I'm trying to get eyes on her now," Asher replied.

Nairobi ran into the corridor, breathless on the other side of the crowd. "East and west exits are locked."

Restlessness morphed into fear.

In the captives.

In Francesca.

In Cass, too.

"Move back," he shouted, pulling his gun from his belt.

The crowd shifted.

He aimed at the lock and fired.

A loud *pop-pop-pop* echoed through the boiler room—the unmistakable sound of gunfire. Someone outside was shooting, and they weren't tranquilizer darts. With her heart in her throat, Eden tried sending another SOS through her comm—a warning.

Get out.

Get out, get out, get out!

But all she could hear was static and indecipherable noise. Something was bungling the reception. Her warning wasn't getting through.

She tracked Oswin's movements as he continued his predatory circle.

Around her.

Around Tycho.

Around Morpheus standing at attention with that ominous device in his hand.

"I think they just realized they're trapped," Oswin said with a note of enjoyment in his voice. "The code isn't working. The override sequence has changed. And not even my soldiers can breach those doors. Isn't that right, Morpheus?"

"Sir, yes sir," the burly soldier replied.

Oswin smiled. "We practiced. No matter how hard he tried, they would not give way."

More gunfire erupted.

Followed by frightened cries.

Oswin chuckled and shook his head, like they were silly little children and he was an amused but patronizing father. "I think it's time to rouse Tycho from his nap."

Morpheus brushed his hand across the projection of Tycho's network, creating a path of red light in its wake.

Tycho inhaled long and loud, like a person surfacing from the bottom of a lake. With his shoulders rising and falling, his attention darted from Morpheus, standing at attention to the device projecting his network to the busted machine with the severed tubes to the hologram of Oswin Brahm to Eden, all the while his expression shifting from confusion to horror.

"Tycho, how good of you to join us." Brahm spread

his hands in a welcoming gesture. "We didn't want you to miss the show. I know *I* certainly didn't want to miss it. But I couldn't leave my own party." He looked down at his holographic body, taking particular delight in his designer shoes. "Look at me, in two places at once. It's amazing, the physical bounds science and technology can bend. Omnipresence is a uniquely godlike quality. And here I stand, well on my way."

He tightened his circle, strolling closer to Eden, taking her in with an enigmatic gleam in his eye. "You are a beautiful specimen, my dear. One of my very first." He lifted his hand like he might caress her cheek, then thought better. "Tragic, when I think what could have been. What *we* could have been together. Instead, you turn Tycho against me."

Tycho paled. "How long have you known?"

"I suspected as soon as you returned. My suspicions were confirmed when you attempted to poison Morpheus, just like I warned him you might."

Tycho's attention shot to his brother. Morpheus stared straight ahead with his massive shoulders squared.

"You have no idea how grieved I am to have lost my dearest son."

Tycho seethed. "I am not your son."

Brahm lifted his eyebrows.

"And she didn't turn me against you."

"No?"

"You did that yourself when you killed Aurelia!"

"Ah, sweet Aurelia. Is that what did it?"

Tycho's chest heaved. His nostrils flared. "You destroyed her like she meant nothing."

"Destroyed her?"

Tycho's face twisted, so ravaged by pain it broke Eden's heart. Meanwhile, Oswin stood there looking completely and utterly unaffected.

"She died in my arms," Tycho whispered.

Oswin resumed his prowl. "You loved her. Which is fine. I want my children to love one another. The problem arose when you decided to love her more than me."

Tycho lifted his chin in defiance, but shame clouded his eyes like an old, persistent friend.

"Thou shall not put any other before Pater. These rules exist for your own good, to spare you from pain." Oswin clucked his tongue. "You know this. Or have you fallen into doubt so quickly? One small hardship and you completely dismiss my wisdom, my authority? I did not destroy Aurelia, my son. She will join us in *Caelum In Terra*."

Tycho's face crumpled.

"How convenient," Eden said.

Brahm pivoted on his heel. "Convenient?"

"This Utopia you've promised. It sure does cover a multitude of sins."

Brahm stared at her as impassively as he had stared at Tycho. "I am a forgiving father. It is never too late to return. Even now."

Eden's attention jerked to Tycho. Brahm may have been facing her when he spoke, but the words were obviously meant for his *dearest son.* To her relief, Tycho only lifted his chin higher, mutiny glinting in his ocean blue eyes.

Oswin frowned. "So much anger. Does it leave no room for remorse?"

Tycho held his tongue.

Oswin turned to Morpheus, who continued to stand at attention with that device in his hand. "Perhaps if he refuses to feel it on his own, we can help him along."

"Sir, yes sir!" Morpheus shouted, swiping his hand through the projection, creating waves of bright orange that had Tycho falling to his knees.

With a wince, Eden moved her hand to her temple, where a noticeable twinge grew in strength as Tycho clutched his head and released a loud, low, agonizing bellow.

She stepped toward him. "Stop it!"

Brahm lifted his palm.

Morpheus removed his hand from the projection.

The radiating waves disappeared.

Tycho knelt on his hands and knees, panting.

With a tut, Brahm skimmed his fingers down the

length of the machine Eden had destroyed. "Did you really think you could outsmart me? You are clever, of course. Resourceful, no doubt. I would expect nothing less from one of my daughters. But did you honestly believe I wouldn't know every part of your plan? That I didn't know you would come here? That I'm unaware of another group in my tower right now, trying to expose me to the world? That I don't have a plan for them, too?"

Eden's stomach went sour.

"Did you think I wouldn't know about this connection the two of you established? Did you never stop to consider how it might play to my advantage? That perhaps I might tap into that connection? There were some holes, of course, but Morpheus was kind enough to fill them in." He smiled indulgently at his obedient soldier.

"You're a betrayer," Tycho wheezed, still on his hands and knees.

"No, Tycho," Morpheus replied. "You are."

Brahm's indulgent smile melted away. "He is right, my son. You have gone astray. I feared this outcome after you were taken. I knew you would endure corruption, contamination. But I held on to hope that you, of all my children, would remain faithful."

More gunshots sounded outside.

Followed by the loud bang of steel.

Eden needed to keep Brahm talking. She needed to

stall for time so Cassian and Dvorak could evacuate the captives. The longer Brahm talked, the more time they would have. She searched about as though frantically grasping at invisible straws. "You keep calling him your son," she said in a voice that rang with anger. "But he isn't really your son. Not in the way Felix was."

This caught the monster off guard. *Felix.* Asher's given name—the one on his birth certificate. The one on his death certificate, too. Oswin seemed to know every part of their plan, but did he know this? She ran through all the information she and Tycho had passed back and forth through their connection. Did they ever discuss Asher? And if so, would Brahm have put the pieces together?

Eden clenched her fists. Her fingers were like ice. "I read your biography. I memorized every line. Read between them, too. Felix never struggled with addiction. He didn't die of a drug overdose. You fabricated that story, and then you had him killed. Your own flesh and blood."

Brahm listened with his head slightly cocked.

Eden's attention darted to the door, then back again. "You're a liar. A murderer. A psychopath. And we are going to expose you."

"Ah, yes. The big reveal. You don't really think I would allow such footage to be shared?" He smiled an amused smile. "Those files have been corrupted beyond repair."

"I wouldn't be so sure."

He exhaled through his nose—a soft, derisive puff of air.

Eden watched him, studied him. Tried to decipher what he knew. She licked her bottom lip. "I don't think any files are too corrupt when you have a cyber genius on your side."

"Pray, tell. Who is this cyber genius?"

"Your dead son."

His face went pale. She could see the shock ripple across his features, quickly followed by a white, hot flash of rage. There and gone, as quick as a lightning strike. And in its wake, a mask of forced indifference. He polished his nails on the lapel of his suit coat, then looked down to examine them. "Felix is alive, is he?" He pursed his lips. He was trying so hard to keep up the charade, to act unaffected. Like he hadn't been duped. "How … lovely. It's a shame that life of his won't last through the night."

He slid his fingers over the machine. "I could have used this toxin to carry out my plans." He caressed one of the severed tubes. "But I must admit, I was hoping for something a little more … theatrical. This is shaping up to be an excellent show. And now, it seems, my dear Felix will get a front-row seat."

His words sent a chill down Eden's spine.

"Let's get to the first order of business, shall we?" He sauntered to Morpheus. With his hands folded behind his back, he whispered in his ear, "Let's see how indestructible my wayward children really are. Order him to kill her."

Eden's attention shot to Tycho on the ground—his expression confused, frightened. She took a step back, then made a break for the door. Nobody stopped her. They didn't need to. She couldn't open it.

Morpheus manipulated the projection and with a bright wave of red, Tycho gripped his head like his skull was being cleaved in two.

Eden could feel it.

The pain.

Excruciating, debilitating pain.

And beneath, an insistent, demanding urge to attack. To kill.

"Tycho," she said. His name. Only his name. But in it, a plea to fight. To resist. To not give in to Brahm's command.

Tycho roared, his agony reaching such a fever pitch, she herself was grimacing. She could feel it in the connection they shared. She didn't understand how Morpheus didn't feel it, too. Her entire body cried out for relief. For release. With her heart pounding, she locked eyes on the device, knowing that relief would only come in one of two ways. Tycho's obedience, or the destruction of that device.

As quick as a viper, she spun in a roundhouse kick, her boot flying straight at Morpheus's hand.

But he wasn't Mordecai. Morpheus had instincts as strong and fast as her own. He dodged the kick like one swatting a fly and made the waves of red go brighter. Until the entire projection was a ball of radiating crimson.

Tycho pushed himself to his feet.

He lifted his head and set his murderous gaze upon Eden.

She backed away, begging him not to do it. Fight. Resist. But he couldn't any longer. The pain had won.

Tycho charged.

41

Cass kicked the door, a useless waste of energy. If Brahm's soldiers couldn't open it, if bullets couldn't bust it, then his foot didn't stand a chance. Chatter sounded over the comm, fast-paced back-and-forth, mostly between Dvorak and Asher. He couldn't override the locks. Every time he tried, something glitched. And the footage they needed to expose Brahm wasn't currently viable. Brahm used a virus to corrupt the files. But this, Asher could handle. He recognized the virus, for it was one he, himself, had created. One his father had stolen. Asher knew how to fix it, but the fix required time.

Cass cupped his hand over his ear. "What's the status on Eden?"

"I don't know," Asher replied.

Cassian turned away from the soldiers and the

captives. From the escalating fear and panic. "What do you mean, you don't know?"

"Someone tampered with the surveillance camera in the boiler room. The screen is a blackout."

"Can't you get through it?"

"Not when it's a physical obstruction."

His steadily rising alarm skyrocketed. Why had that surveillance camera been tampered with? Why were the exits locked? Why couldn't the soldiers break them? With his muscles clenched, he tapped a button on his watch, projecting a three-dimensional blueprint of the facility. There had to be a way out of here.

"Is Tycho in there with her?" Cass asked.

"Yeah," Asher said.

So was the machine. Hopefully, they were working on disabling it. But then, why Eden's indecipherable shouts? What was she trying to communicate? Was the toxin about to be released through the air ducts?

The air ducts.

He looked up at the ventilation system overhead. Alexander Pruitt was standing beside him now, looking up, too.

"You think we can get out that way?" Cass asked him.

"Maybe," he said. "But only a few."

He was right, of course. There was no way over a thousand people could crawl to freedom one by one in the time they had left. And yet, it was the only option Cass could think to investigate. Investigating was better than standing next to an impenetrable door as Eden shouted things none of them could understand.

He asked Isla to stay with Alexander and Ruth. He asked Alexander and Ruth to stay with Isla. Then, with Alexander's help, he pried off a vent and lifted himself inside.

Almost immediately, the world seemed to tilt off kilter. His chest tightened. His body broke into a cold sweat. The last time he'd been trapped in a space so confined, his mother was being bludgeoned to death on the other side.

Eden hurled Tycho across the room. He slammed into the machine with a sickening crunch, then sank to the ground.

She was stronger, but only because he continued to resist, even as he attacked—apology and pain and anger a raging, swirling storm in his eyes. Eden hated it. She hated all of it. Oswin Brahm. This control he wielded. The things he could make them do. Her inability to stop it.

A soundbite shot through the static in her ear. Words

chopped into bits, impossible to understand as Morpheus made the waves of red surge brighter.

Tycho screamed an animalistic scream. His body contorted and writhed like Aurelia's.

Eden clamped her palms over her ears and shouted at Morpheus to stop. Stop! But he didn't. Not until Brahm held up his hand. "That will be enough."

The orange and red waves disappeared.

Tycho collapsed into a ball on his side, whimpering incoherently.

Eden raced to him. She shushed his apologies. She tried to help him to his feet, or at least into a position less vulnerable. But he might as well have been injected with ten doses of that wretched poison.

"Your resistance is impressive," Brahm said. "I can't help but feel almost … *proud*. How long until you break, I wonder? How long until you completely give in? It's a shame we don't have time to find out. Especially not now, knowing my not-so-dead son is in my control tower."

Eden ground her teeth, her fingers throbbing with the urge to attack, to gouge, to scratch and tear. To make Oswin Brahm pay. But even if she could get past Morpheus, Oswin Brahm would remain untouchable. He wasn't physically present.

"Thank you, Morpheus." Oswin gave him a paternal smile. "You have done exceptionally well.

Now, if you would please activate the transmission tower."

The transmission tower?

Morpheus seemed as confused by the request as she. His stony veneer cracked, revealing—for the first time—a sliver of uncertainty. "I would have to leave this room in order to do that, sir."

"Yes."

He shot a wary look at Tycho. "But—"

"You mustn't worry about me, Morpheus. So long as he remains compliant, I will be just fine." Brahm lifted his eyebrows at the device.

With a nod, Morpheus manipulated Tycho's system once more. There weren't any waves of red or orange this time. Instead, a hazy glow. Almost immediately, Tycho's shoulder relaxed beneath Eden's hand.

Morpheus pocketed the device. "They have tranquilizer," he said.

Brahm smiled indulgently. "Activate the transmission tower and not even tranquilizer will be able to stop you."

The ominous words sank through Eden like a stone. What did he mean by them?

He strolled to the door. Morpheus followed like an obedient dog. "Now that we have everything under control, how about we invite Felix to enjoy the show?"

"Yes, sir," Morpheus said. He stood on tiptoe and reached for the surveillance camera mounted above the door. Someone had stuck a round black sticker to its lens. Morpheus peeled it off.

Oswin folded his hands behind his back. "Now go. Send word to the guards at home and activate the tower quickly. I am eager to get on with it."

Morpheus bowed, then turned to the keypad. Eden readied herself—desperate to get out, desperate to warn them all, to stop Morpheus from activating anything.

As soon as he pressed his thumb to the sensor, the door slid open. Eden sprang. But Morpheus was too quick. He was too strong. He caught her by the neck and tossed her back inside as the door slid shut with a hiss of finality.

Oswin chuckled, then waved happily at the camera. "Felix," he crooned with revolting delight. "How good of you to join us. I think you will find this particularly engrossing." With another twiddle of his fingers, he turned away and strolled casually, his attention on the ceiling, as though searching for something in particular. When he reached a specific spot, he stopped and invited Tycho to join him.

Eden remained in her crouched position, watching as Tycho slowly got to his feet and dragged himself along until he stood beside his holographic *Pater*.

Her lip curled. She looked from Oswin to Tycho to the surveillance camera. Surely Asher was watching this. If only they could communicate. She cursed her broken comm when a loud, alarming noise filled the boiler room. It sounded like an industrial-sized vacuum coming to life overhead.

A small door slid open in the ceiling above Tycho. Eight steel tentacles extended from within like a writhing octopus reaching for its prey. Eden scuttled away like a crab as those tentacles attached themselves to Tycho's spine.

Oswin clapped gleefully as the tentacles lifted Tycho into the air. His limbs stretched wide. His eyes went even wider. His entire body gave one giant convulsion, like a strong electric shock. Then the tentacles returned him to the ground.

Tycho lifted his head. And what Eden saw scared her more than anything she had yet to see. His eyes were no longer his eyes. As Oswin Brahm circled his five-star general, it was as if Tycho was no longer there at all.

Stroking the air by Tycho's cheek, the Monarch whispered three hair-raising words. "Initiate the hive."

42

Violet covered her eyes, her heart punching her sternum in a violent *thud, thud, thud*. She couldn't look at the wall of monitors. Because Father was there. The bad man was there, too. Asher's father. Asher scooted away, the light brown skin on his face going a strange shade of gray. The bad man smiled a scary smile and now he was hurting Tycho with that spider-machine. It was lifting him into the air.

"Oswin Brahm is in the boiler room," Asher said into his earpiece, distracted from the fix he was running on the corrupted files. It was only twenty-three percent through. "I repeat, he's in Fredericksburg with Eden."

Violet could hear the confused responses. Oswin Brahm couldn't be in Fredericksburg. He was in Chicago. Sitting in the finest suite United Center had to offer. Lark had him in the crosshairs.

"It's a hologram," Barrett said, tapping the monitor. He'd been creeping closer and closer to the wall, making the pressure in Violet's throat swell. She wanted to yell at him to get away. Get away from Father and that bad, bad man. "In the boiler room. Look."

Asher did look, then he shook his head like he didn't understand how it was possible when suddenly, the control panel beneath his hands came to life.

He pulled away. "Whoa."

The tube behind Violet came to life, too. It awoke with a loud, suction-like sound that had her stumbling back, choking on her breath.

Barrett pointed at Eden's network.

It was lighting up like a Christmas tree.

Asher rolled his chair closer, trying to reclaim control of the panel. But it was like technology possessed. He tried shutting it down. He tried overriding the system. He usually knew how to do such things, but he only cursed as more and more lights came on in Eden's network, her Queen Bee brightest of them all.

"He activated the hive mind," Asher said.

More voices filled the comm. Static interspersed with Cassian's enraged shouts. Dvorak's insistent commands. All the while, Eden stood immobilized inside the screen. Her shoulders rose and fell like a human werewolf stuck in a beam of moonlight on the cusp of transitioning.

Asher lurched from the chair. He turned to her

network—tapping and dragging, trying to make it stop as Dvorak continued issuing commands and Cassian roared over them.

Violet plugged her ears.

Asher kept cursing—over and over as Eden's network turned into a ball of light and he pulled up three keys that would end her life. "I have to do it. I can't let him control her. I promised I wouldn't let that happen."

Violet shook her head and backed away. Eden was kind, and gentle, and patient, and good. And Asher was going to kill her. Eden bent into a crouch with her hands over her head like she knew what was coming. Asher's fingers hovered above the keys, but Barrett raised his arm—firmly but gently blocking the way, his eyes glued to the monitor.

"No one is in there to tranquilize her," Asher said.

"Just wait," Barrett replied. "She hasn't done anything yet."

All the while, Cassian kept shouting and Dvorak kept commanding and Father kept pounding. All of it, an onslaught of sound that had Violet pressing her hands over her ears, a high-pitched moan keening in her throat as she cowered into a ball like Eden. "Stop, stop, make it stop!"

Suddenly, it did.

Like a short-circuiting fuse, Eden's network burst, then went completely dark.

Eden stopped rocking.

Slowly, she came to her feet. She looked at the camera with eyes that were still her own. Asher collapsed into the chair. He spoke into the comm and Cassian stopped shouting. Dvorak stopped commanding. And Barrett was right there, crouched in front of Violet, gently grasping her wrists. "She's okay. It didn't work."

Violet breathed.

Out, then in.

Out, then in.

Eden was okay.

It didn't work.

Clutching that truth to her chest, she braved a look at the wall of monitors.

Father was gone.

The labs were empty.

The doors were open.

Guards poured inside Fort Wadsworth. An entire battalion marched through the courtyard as Eden came closer to the camera lens, her eyes wild as she shouted. Only snatches of her voice broke through the comm. But it didn't matter. Violet could read her lips.

Out! Now! Everyone get out!

It didn't take long to see why she was yelling those words. A moan scraped up Violet's throat as the unconscious soldiers—the *tranquilized* soldiers—slowly got to their feet like the walking dead.

Round them up for slaughter.

The command played like a drumbeat in Eden's mind. She could feel it throbbing in the connection she shared with Tycho, in the connection he shared with the others. An insistent pulse that roused them from a deep slumber.

They were coming awake, and the need to obey was a current. A strong undertow. Only somehow, she wasn't stuck in it. They were a single organism moving as one, and she, an errant appendage—a part of the organism, but moving of her own accord.

The hive mind wasn't working on her.

But it *was* working.

Everyone needed to get out. They needed to get out now! She turned to the camera and shouted the warning, knowing it was useless. She was shouting words at Asher, almost three hundred miles away. What could he possibly do to help the people trapped in Fredericksburg?

The steel tentacles attached to Tycho flung his body up, then released him. He soared through the room and landed in front of Eden with such force, the concrete splintered beneath his boots.

A scream tore up her throat, but she swallowed it

down and backed away. "Tycho," she pleaded. "Please, don't do this. You can fight it. You can resist."

"Oh, my dear." Oswin chuckled. "He most certainly cannot."

Tycho stood with his shoulders squared, his hands fisted, his head bent. He glared at Eden from the tops of his eyes—his cold, soulless eyes.

"But I suppose *you* can," Oswin said, his attention sweeping her body. "What a pity. I thought you'd be mine in the end."

He turned to Tycho. "She is defective. Kill her."

This time, the order wasn't a game. Morpheus wasn't playing with Tycho's network. Tycho wasn't distraught. And Oswin Brahm wasn't entertained.

Eden took another step back, her breath stuck. Frozen. Trapped, like everyone here in this facility. They were stuck with an army of super soldiers preparing to slaughter them. Her attention darted to the steel tentacles, which had slithered back into the ceiling. They'd attached themselves to Tycho. They shocked something inside him like Dr. Beverly Randall-Ransom had shocked her father's heart when he nearly died on her medical table. It seemed the tentacles had shocked Tycho, too. Awakened his other master node, the one Asher had discovered.

She took another step back.

He tracked her movement.

Those tentacles had come to life because Morpheus activated the transmission tower. She stared at the camera lens. *Through* the camera lens. She pictured Asher and Barrett and Violet on the other side, in a control tower that rose from the New York Harbor, with a large, mysterious tube running straight down its shaft.

Sharks are messing with the weapon again.

This had to be it.

Brahm had a weapon underneath the ocean floor. It generated powerful signals and transmitted those signals deep underground, all the way here, to the tower in Fredericksburg. Turning his army into a hive. Controlling them through his five-star general.

Which meant …

"Destroy it," she said, at first in a hoarse whisper. Then louder, hoping her words might get through. She stared at the camera as she communicated, all the while backing away from Tycho. Shut it down. *Shut the weapon down!* Her backside met the cool metal of the toxin machine. She could back away no further. Her abdomen tightened as Tycho took a predatory step in her direction. And then, without warning, he lunged.

He wrapped his hands around her throat and lifted her into the air. She choked and flailed, gasping for breath. Trying and failing to get oxygen into her lungs. Her eyes bulged. Her veins throbbed as she clawed at his fingers and kicked her legs.

Her boot connected hard with his groin.

He released her.

Gasping, she fell to the ground and scuttled away, around the machine, as he advanced—his movements powerful and unwavering.

Eden leapt to her feet and pulled out her gun.

Tycho knocked it from her hands.

It landed with a clatter and slid across the floor.

He grabbed her by one arm and threw her across the room. She skidded up to her feet as Tycho charged. They fought—a flurry of strikes and blocks, blows and weaves and flips. A blur of speed and motion with her on the defensive and him on the offensive, because he was undeniably stronger and faster. She couldn't beat him. She wouldn't beat him.

She screamed at Asher to shut it down. Stop the transmission! Static eviscerated his replies, making them impossible to understand. She only knew he was shouting, too. Amidst the unmistakable sound of rapid gunfire. They were engaged in a battle of their own.

Eden bobbed and parried, but not quickly enough. Tycho landed a blow to her jaw. Her head snapped back. He kicked her stomach with such force, she flew backward into a furnace, metal crunching upon impact.

Sucking in her breath, she thrust her foot straight at his ribs. Tycho caught her boot and pulled her down. She fell to the ground. He grabbed a fistful of her hair and lifted her up, then spun her around and slammed her forehead into a steel boiler.

For a second, the world went black.

Then she was twisting and kicking, pulling her hair free as she dove for the gun. Reaching, reaching as Tycho grabbed her by the ankle. Her fingers touched cool metal. She turned onto her back and pointed the gun and pulled the trigger.

He dodged the bullets.

They hit the wall and the pipes behind him, steam hissing from the holes, all while Oswin laughed a giddy, high-pitched laugh. Tycho snatched her ankle again and flung her into the hissing pipes. Her body hit with a sickening crack. She slid to the floor.

"You cannot beat my general," Oswin cooed. "Nor can you stop him."

Eden set her palms against the floor and pushed herself up.

"You can spare her for now, Tycho." With a slow, sinister smile, Oswin issued another command. "Find her parents. I want her to watch while you kill them."

No.

The word rose from the depths of her soul as her broken bones snapped back into wholeness. Oswin was right. She could not beat his general. Not unless she was willing to be beat herself. But hadn't she always been willing? From the very beginning, when she found out about the self-destruct command. She pulled a high-tech explosive from her belt. For one flash of a second, she imagined what would happen. Pulling the pin, pushing the button. She and Tycho, in the center of that explosion. She imagined her body parts and his body parts crawling toward one another in the aftermath, straight out of a horror film. Oswin Brahm was a genius, but not even *he* could make that happen. They wouldn't survive this. It would be a self-destruct function of her own making. Her own choosing.

She got all the way to her feet with the grenade in hand. "Maybe not with bullets," she shouted. "But what about this?"

Brahm's widening eyes told her she had guessed right. He didn't anticipate this. She pulled the pin, and with a great war cry, sprinted at his five-star general. Tycho whirled around, his leg swinging toward her like a baseball bat—so hard and fast, the grenade flew out of her hand upon impact. Her body catapulted in the opposite direction.

She landed hard and covered her head as the boiler room exploded.

43

At the first sound of a horrified scream, Cass kicked through a vent and dropped to the floor. The second he landed, time seemed to freeze. Like someone pulling back on the reins, dragging everything into slow, horrifying motion as the soldiers on the ground rose to their feet, joining those who were already standing. Soldiers who—up until a moment ago—had been trying to help the captives escape.

The one next to Isla—a young man named Nikos—grabbed her by the throat. Isla screamed. Cass charged. Pandemonium erupted.

A female soldier with vacant eyes and a blank expression stepped forward to block his path. She threw Cass to the ground and pinned him there with her knee on his back, her hand pressed against the side of his face, pushing his head into the floor. He grit his teeth, watching helplessly as Isla choked. As Alexander and Ruth and Dr. Norton and Jack tried to stop it from happening. The other captives, too. They swarmed the soldier, thirty against one.

He simply pulled out his gun and shot. Several prisoners fell as every cell block in the facility buzzed. Asher had set them free from their cages. They rushed out in a flurry of panic and tumult. But there was nowhere to go. They were trapped inside with thirty-one armed superhuman soldiers under Oswin Brahm's control. And Isla was purple now, flailing. Desperate for oxygen.

Huck's face swam in Cassian's mind. Those big, innocent eyes when he asked, "You're going to get my mommy, right?"

With all the strength he could muster, he rammed his elbow into the soldier's face. He turned onto his back, but she was right there, lifting her boot like she was going to stomp him dead. He rolled out of the way, up to his knees, when a deafening blast ripped through the facility. A sonic *boom* that came with an inferno of heat and fire and flying debris that had everyone ducking for cover. Cass included.

When most of it cleared, his ears rang and a smoking view of the boiler room had opened in its wake. A hologram of Oswin Brahm stood amongst the rubble. Eden and Tycho emerged from piles of wreckage. The boiler room was only half there. The other half was gone—a gaping, fiery hole where smoke billowed into the night.

A way out.

Cass was the first to move. He capitalized upon the shock. He sprinted toward Isla and the captives who'd been trying to save her. A fist swung at him as he went. He slid beneath the blow, leapt onto the soldier's back, pressed the barrel of his gun against the base of his skull, and squeezed the trigger.

Bam!

The soldier dropped.

Oswin Brahm screamed.

Cass grabbed the soldier's gun and threw it at Alexander Pruitt. He pulled Isla to her feet as she wheezed and spluttered, and together, they raced for the exit.

Violet's hands shook. They hummed with the vibration of the semi-automatic, even though she was no longer firing. Their ammo was gone. The guards were down. A topple of human dominoes along the spiral staircase. A pile of death. But where were the patients in the labs? Where was Father?

"It's done," Asher said, communicating with Cleo and Dayne. The fix he'd been running on the corrupted files was finally complete. He ran a scan for Volkova and found the specific footage for which they were searching. "Initiating download."

Meanwhile, a bloodbath unfolded in Fredericksburg. Captives dying. Soldiers murdering. They would keep on dying and murdering unless Violet and Barrett did what Eden had shouted at them to do—shut the weapon down.

"We can't shut it down without getting closer," Barrett said, ditching the gun.

He punched numbers on the keypad. Violet tried prying the doors apart. When that didn't work, she kicked the tube. She kicked it over and over. Then, with a frustrated shout, she tore the keypad off the panel, exposing wires that snapped and sparked while the tube continued to glow and hum.

"Standby to go live," Asher said.

He was about to override the New Year's Eve broadcast when a knife flew through the air.

Violet heard it before she saw it.

But Asher neither heard nor saw.

He was completely unaware. Unguarded. His back to the flying knife, about to tap the interface in front of him when the blade hit. It sank through his hand, pinning it to the panel. A scream tore up his throat as he wrenched his hand away. Another knife flew and struck him in the thigh. He stared down at the protruding weapon in wide-eyed shock.

The attacker stood in the doorway dressed in a hospital gown with long, auburn hair draped over her shoulders. Ellery Forrester. The girl who had been taken. Experimented on. A patient from the labs, with two more standing behind her.

Ellery stalked forward, straight at Asher.

He unsheathed his gun and shot.

The bullet blasted her in the shoulder. The left side of her body rocketed back from the impact, but she remained on her feet. She touched the spot where blood was seeping, then stopping. Healing.

Asher shot again. He hit her other shoulder. He fired a third time, hitting the patient to Ellery's left. The woman clutched her abdomen and dropped to the floor. Her blood didn't stop. It pooled around her in an expanding puddle of red. Ellery stared at it in fascination as the patient to her right jumped on Asher like a hyena on a lion.

The gun blasted a fourth time.

The patient slumped to the ground. Ellery grabbed Asher's chair and swung it like a club. It smacked him with a hideous crack. He collapsed with a howling moan while the override function flashed on the screen and Cleo shouted in his ear.

Ellery dropped the chair and marched forward. Barrett dove on top of her. Violet jumped in—two superhuman soldiers against one, for Ellery had obviously been activated. Together, Barrett and Violet pinned her down as Cleo's voice continued to yell from Asher's earpiece.

Asher, come in. Asher!

But he was badly injured, incapacitated on the floor, trying to give them something in his bloodied, mangled hand.

It was the magnet.

The very one that had shut Violet down for three whole months. Violet and Barrett dragged Ellery closer to Asher while she kicked and bucked. With fumbling fingers slippery with blood, he attached it to Ellery's neck. She stopped fighting. She went as limp as a rag doll.

Violet panted.

Barrett, too.

They stared at one another over the girl who was now offline. Who was now safe. Who could no longer be controlled.

"Expose him." Asher pushed the words between clenched teeth and pulled the dagger from his thigh. It clattered to the floor. Blood poured from the wound. "Start ... the override," he rasped, his eyelids sinking like they were too heavy to hold up. He was losing consciousness.

Barrett pushed himself up to move to the interface. To do what Asher instructed. This was why they'd come, after all. But before he could even get to his knees, his back bent at an unnatural angle. He fell with a frightening yelp. Like a kicked puppy. Like Kitty whenever she was hurt. Whenever *Father* hurt her.

With her breath frozen in her lungs, Violet turned slowly and beheld the man standing in the doorway. The last patient from the labs. He stared at her triumphantly, his face grotesque with scars. "He told me you would come. He promised me you would be here!"

Violet's bladder loosened. Tremors quaked through her limbs. A scream stretched wide inside her as Father lumbered toward her, holding something in his hand. A device like Eden's device. Only this wasn't Eden's device. Hers was still by the control panel.

The scream in her chest morphed into a croaking sob. She was collapsing in on herself. Shrinking smaller and smaller until she was an invisible, non-existent thing Father couldn't touch. Father couldn't hurt.

"Stay away from her!" Barrett roared, trying to get up, but twisting in pain all over again. Horrible pain. All the while, the crowd in Chicago danced and cheered. The soldiers in Fredericksburg murdered and maimed.

Asher bled out on the floor.

Barrett screamed and clutched his head.

Father's smile twisted.

And something inside Violet snapped.

A fury that overpowered her fear. A madness that unlocked her feet. With a feral cry tearing from her chest, she charged. She tackled Father to the ground. She climbed on top of him. She grabbed his head and slammed it against the floor, needing to get that device. *Barrett's* device. Father was using it to torture him. And she would not allow it.

But Father wouldn't let go, and he was laughing. Bleeding and wheezing and laughing. Violet pulled him up and rammed him into the wall so hard, a hairline fracture ran up the glass.

A tiny, crooked fissure.

Father shoved his fingers into her mouth, into her eyes. He hooked her lip with his thumb and plowed her into the opposite wall. "He made me strong." He cackled. Giddy. Gleeful. His teeth red with blood as he increased Barrett's pain. Barrett screamed and arched and writhed. Her friend. Her dearest friend. At the mercy of a man who had made her life a living hell.

Violet thrust her face forward. "He made me stronger!"

She slammed him against the tube in the center of the room, right into the exposed wires. His eyes bulged. His body spasmed. Ripples of electricity shot through him, into Violet's hands, up her arms. But she pinned him there. Kept him there. Until the device fell from his grip and the scent of burning flesh filled the room.

When she finally let go, he slid down the wall and crumpled to the floor as the doors to the tube opened.

44

Cass had gotten Isla through the anarchy into the night. They had run across the grounds and outside the gate with the Forresters and the Pruitts and Norton—frozen breath, beating hearts—as Jericho joined them outside the fence.

"We need to shut the signal down," Cass said, his eyes on the transmission tower looming over the chaos. "Can you reactivate an Atax?"

Jericho shook his head. "They don't work that way."

More people fled into the night. Through the fire and smoke, captives raced across the grounds, some toppling as bullets met their backs.

Jack held up Annette, who could barely stand on her own. "I need to get her out of here."

Cass told Isla to go with them. Run with the others. Escape into the woods. Get as far away as she could.

Alexander pulled Ruth into his arms and kissed her passionately. Then he took her face in his hands and told her to go with them.

She returned his request with a look of uncompromising ferocity so reminiscent of Eden, it was a wonder they weren't biologically related. Unlike Jack and Annette, Ruth's family was here. Her daughter was inside. She was going to stay. She was going to fight. Alexander could not convince her otherwise. Trying would be a waste of time.

They watched Jack and Annette and Isla flee into the woods. Along with anyone else lucky enough to escape.

When they were gone, Alexander reloaded his gun.

Jericho handed one of his extras to Ruth.

Cass cocked his own. "They have an Achilles heel." A chink in their armor. "You get a direct shot to the brain stem and they won't survive."

Jericho, Alexander, and Ruth nodded, and together, they raced into the smoky fray.

This might be a losing battle, but that didn't mean everyone had to lose. Not tonight. Not on his watch. Determined to save as many lives as he could, he fought beside Eden and her parents. Beside Jericho and Dvorak and Francesca and Nairobi and five others he had helped train. As a team, they ushered as many people to freedom as possible.

Through the din, Cass heard the frantic cries of a

small child—a soldier ripping a little girl from her mother's arms.

The dragon in Cassian's chest roared.

He swung himself onto a cell block, leapt onto another, then dropped onto the soldier's back with his gun already in position and pulled the trigger.

The soldier dropped.

The hysterical mother grabbed her child.

And a bullet hit Cass. It spun him around, dropped him to the ground with sharp, hot pain. A ball of fire in his shoulder that radiated down his arm like zaps of electricity.

His ears rang.

He coughed smoke from his lungs as the battle unfolded around him. Soldiers winning. Soldiers killing. Soldiers shoving captives into the center cell block. Cass pushed himself to his feet, his injured arm limp at his side. Blood dripped off his fingers and splattered to the ground as he watched Tycho force Ruth Pruitt to her knees and press the barrel of his gun against the center of her forehead. Just like Yukio had died. Just like the guards at the SafePad compound had died. Just like the Brysons had died.

Eden screamed and flailed, but she was pinned against the wall by Knox, her face streaked with tears. He was going to make her watch.

The dragon roared again.

Ruth Pruitt was going to die. She was going to be murdered in front of her daughter, just like his mother had been murdered in front of him. Unless Cass acted.

He had no margin for error.

The shot was reckless. Wild. A shot no sane man would ever take. But they had nothing to lose now. If he didn't try, Ruth would die for sure. If he did, she might die by his own bullet. With his good arm, he lifted his gun, took his aim, and fired.

Tycho's weapon flew out of his hand.

Eden used the distraction to kick off Knox. Then she tackled Tycho from behind. Her mother toppled to the ground and crawled away.

Across the facility, Dvorak shouted his name. A loud, alarmed shout. He spun just in time to look his attacker in the eye. This time, the fire wasn't a ball, but a jagged point that stole his breath. He looked down at the hilt of a knife, its blade buried in his abdomen.

Cass stumbled back, his vision blurring as he pulled the knife from his gut.

It clattered to the ground.

His knees hit the cement.

Alexander's face swam above him, his hands searching, moving, trying to staunch the flow of blood. But then Alexander was grabbed and dragged away. And all that existed was smoke and fire and gunshots and screams and an encroaching darkness Cass had no strength to fight.

Time stood still.

Violet watched the scene unfold from outside her own body like a specter floating in the sky. Asher unconscious, bleeding on the floor. The people in United Center, partying. The people in the detainment facility, dying.

Cassian, down.

Eden dragged away.

Women and children on their knees with their hands in the air.

Father, dead.

The pneumatic tube, open.

And a high-tech explosive strapped to her belt.

Shut it down.

Blow it up.

Stop the slaughter.

Rescue them all.

Memories came like a powerful wave. They hurled into her, one after the other. Every abusive word. Every painful experiment. Was all of it a necessity? Father said this was what she was made for. This was why she was born. It all came down to this one thing.

She would save the world.

Which made him right in the end. Right all along. Because here she was now, with this grenade and that tube and these innocent people she couldn't let die, and these innocent soldiers she couldn't let kill. She had to stop this. She *could* stop this. And not even her superhuman powers could put her back together when it was done.

Her destiny would be fulfilled.

She stepped inside the tube.

Barrett stood at the panel with his back to her. He punched the override button. Then he turned and his eyes found hers as she stood inside the shaft. They went round with understanding. Horrified comprehension. Perhaps her destiny was to save the world. But right then, she only wanted to save him. Barrett—this beautiful, wonderful boy who gave her safety and acceptance and love. Who filled up all the lonely, frightened space with words and stories and memories that felt like her own.

She smiled at him, hoping he would know. Hoping he would see. The little boy who always dressed up as a superhero for Halloween because that was what he wanted to be didn't have to dress up anymore. He *was* a hero. He was *her* hero.

But then Barrett did something confusing.

Unexpected.

He looked down at his belt, and he grabbed his own explosive. He pulled the pin and he threw the grenade right at her, yelling for her to catch. To squeeze.

She caught it and held the button tight, knowing if she let go, they'd both blow up and the weapon wouldn't and all those people would die. It was a distraction. The trickiest trick, because all of a sudden, he was there. Right there with her in the tube. He grabbed her around the waist and he spun her like a dancer straight out of the shaft, taking the explosive from her hand and shutting the door.

It sealed him in.

It sealed her out.

A scream tore loose from Violet's throat as Barrett set his palm against the glass, his eyes bright and fierce and filled with love.

She set her hand against the glass, too.

Palm-to-palm.

There was a second.

Only one second.

Then the tube whooshed out of sight and Barrett was gone.

45

Violet screamed.

She screamed and she screamed and she screamed, her voice ravaged as she pounded on the glass. Begging the doors to open. Open up. Let her in. Let her go. Please, please let her go.

But then a familiar voice cut through her hysteria. It filled the room like the warmest hug. "Violet?"

She stopped. She stood at attention. She looked frantically around, searching for him. But he wasn't there. His voice was coming from a speaker on the control panel. "Violet, can you hear me?"

She lurched toward the sound as the party-goers in Chicago stopped their partying, their celebration quieting into murmurs and gasps as Dayne Johnson and Cleo Ransom took over the airwaves.

Violet hit the intercom with fumbling fingers. "Barrett," she choked.

She could hear his sigh of relief. It came like a puff through the speaker as the blinking blip that was Barrett made its way down the tube—fast as lightning, traveling at mind-boggling speed. Still thirty seconds from its mark. She moaned an animalistic moan.

"Violet, I need you to listen to me."

Tears spilled down her cheeks.

"Your father doesn't get to be right. Do you hear me? You are so much more than what he gave you. Than what he told you. You were *not* born to die. That is *not* your story."

More tears spilled. She couldn't see through the blur of them.

"You were born to live, Vi."

She pressed her palm against the blinking dot that was Barrett, traveling in a tube that brought him deeper and deeper into the Earth, closer and closer to an ending that was meant to be hers.

"I've never been the hero, you know." His voice cracked. "Now look at me."

She snorted through her tears, her heart bursting and breaking. With love. With pain. So much of it, she couldn't breathe.

"I need you to do me a favor."

She nodded, like it was a sound he could hear.

"It's going to involve a lot of talking."

Her chin trembled.

"Your words can't go away again. They're too important."

The tears continued to fall—fat drops that fell off her chin and splashed onto the intercom.

"I'm gonna need you to tell my parents I love them. My brothers, too. Give my mom the tightest, biggest hug. She'll probably need more than one. Tell them our stories, Violet. We have a lot of 'em now, don't we?"

Her nodding became frantic as the tube got closer and closer.

"They're going to love you," he said. "As much as I love you."

"I love you, too," she whispered.

"Be brave, Vi. Be brave and *live*."

She sniffed.

And the blinking blip hit its mark.

Violet let loose a strangled cry as the entire panel went dark and the suction-like sound went silent. Barrett, too.

The boy with all the words. The boy who had filled up the silences. The boy who had shared his memories and his life. He was no longer talking. Because he was no longer living.

Barrett was gone.

He had saved the world.

Tycho stopped.

Every other soldier did, too.

He let go of Eden's father, his face filling first with confusion. Then with horror as he took in the surrounding scene. Fallen soldiers, fallen captives, crying children on their knees with guns aimed at their heads.

All the while, Oswin Brahm screamed. "Stop the feed! Cut it now!"

Then he disappeared. He vanished as the soldiers dropped their weapons. Eden ran to her parents—her living, breathing parents. She buried herself in their arms as they held on tight, like they might never let go. They'd done it. Somehow, Violet and Barrett and Asher had shut down the signal. Disabled the weapon. The hive mind was no more.

Cries rippled around the facility.

Sobs of relief.

Moans of lament.

She spotted Dvorak bent over Francesca—as still as death on the ground. She saw Nairobi, bent over Jericho, who was as still as Francesca. Then she saw him. Cassian. And a hole ripped open inside her chest. She sprinted to his side and dropped to her knees. She searched for the wound, trying to stop the flow of blood leaking from his side.

"Cassian," Eden said his name like a command. *Wake up. Come back to me. Right now.* She pressed her hand firmly against the wound like a tourniquet. Like she'd done before. In the back of Dr. Norton's truck, when he'd been sliced by a shard of glass by Jack Forrester in a parking garage. He'd survived then. He would survive now. Even though this was worse. So much worse. "Cassian," she said again.

He opened his eyes.

His golden irises were hazy with blood loss as her father called for bandages, for first aid. Cass set his hand over hers and gave it the weakest of squeezes.

"Stay with me. Do you understand?" It was then that she noticed another wound on his shoulder. She moved her other hand to the spot and squeezed. "Stay awake."

But his face was pale. So alarmingly pale. With a waxen, sweaty sheen.

"Is she … okay?"

Eden tried to shush him. He needed to save his energy. He needed to preserve his breath. But he refused to be shushed. "Did your mom … make it?"

Her eyes blurred with tears. "Yes," she said, pressing harder. Her mother was okay. She was alive. Eden had just hugged her. Because Cassian had saved her.

A hint of a smile crept across his face.

His eyelids drooped.

"No, Cass."

But they slid shut.

Even when she shook him.

They wouldn't open.

"Somebody help," she yelled. "Please, somebody help!"

But there were so many wounded.

They were all around.

She pressed harder as hot tears tumbled down her cheeks, creating twin paths through the grime and the grit.

She heard Lark across the comm.

The footage had been released.

Brahm had been exposed.

Her eyes were on the target.

Dvorak gave the command. "End him."

"With greatest pleasure," Lark replied.

The shot rang out in Eden's ear.

The bullet Lark had carried for thirty years finally hit its mark. A single, cold shot straight through the center of his forehead. The man who had killed untold millions of people was finally dead.

46

Monitors beeped in the dimly lit room. It wasn't located in a basement, like Dr. Norton's or Dr. Beverly Randall-Ransom's. Nor was it inside an illegal medical center that required cloaking material to stay hidden from drones. This room was on the fourth floor of a registered hospital in Richmond, Virginia, where a young man had gone into surgery and come out with a bullet-free shoulder and a bionic spleen.

Eden sat by his bedside, tracing the bold black letters on his patient identification wristband. *Cassian Gray.* Beneath, his date of birth, gender, and a barcode the nurses scanned whenever they came in to administer medicine or change his bandages. He was recovering. And he would continue to recover. Fully, according to the doctors.

Outside in the hallway, a conversation unfolded between one of those doctors and a brilliant neurosurgeon who had flown from Chicago to Richmond on her private jet to oversee not just Cassian's care, but every illegal resident from RRA-East who had sustained an injury severe enough to require medical intervention. The number was too large for one hospital. Many had been transferred to smaller clinics nearby. All of them had wristbands. Thanks to Dr. Beverly Randall-Ransom, all of them were being treated with care and humanity, Cassian Gray most especially.

The neurosurgeon's daughter—a young woman even more recognizable now than her mother—peeked into the room and shot Eden a wink. Cleo and Dayne's broadcast had sent shockwaves around the world. Over the past three days, their video had officially become the most viral in all of history.

In all, fifty-eight captives from RRA-East had perished, along with five Resistance members who had gone in to save them, Jericho and Francesca included. On Staten Island, another had been injured. And one more from their ranks had died. It was a loss that set a deep ache in Eden's bones. A loss she hadn't fully processed, and wasn't ready to talk about. The injured party suffered a concussion, a broken clavicle, a stab wound to the thigh, and an impaled hand. He'd been treated in Trenton, then released into the care of the same neurosurgeon who was currently out in the hall, chatting with Cassian's doctor.

Asher had joined them now in Richmond. He hobbled about with a cane, his left arm in a sling, his left hand in a splint. In time, he would need a second surgery. Perhaps a third, along with a significant amount of physical therapy in order to mitigate nerve damage and recover full range of motion. With Dr. Beverly Randall-Ransom on his side, Eden knew he would have nothing but the very best hand experts at his disposal. Maybe when the physical wounds were healed, Felix *Asher* Brahm would open himself up to the idea of addressing the emotional ones. If not for himself, then for Cleo, who thought that sort of thing was "romantic as hell."

Oswin Brahm was dead.

Those in his innermost circle who hadn't committed suicide were arrested and imprisoned. Their crimes had been exposed. The world had learned Brahm's dirtiest secret, and every few hours a new wave of shocking truth hit the news cycle. Not only was Oswin the mastermind behind The Attack that had killed millions, he had orchestrated the bombing at his own hotel, as well as the toxin attacks in Minneapolis, Madison, Milwaukee, Detroit, and Fresno. Authorities were treating the entirety of Fort Wadsworth like the crime scene it was, examining and preserving every morsel of evidence.

The entire world had questions. America was under a microscope, its leadership submitted to an international organization designed to step in when a country was in crisis. America was most certainly in crisis, its identity in shambles, for who were they now when the foundation they'd been laying for the past twenty-one years had turned out to be such a poisonous lie?

America the Great had fallen victim to tyranny once again. Only this time, it had come in a different disguise. A trickier disguise. There'd been no raging civil war, no left versus right. No side to join other than that of legal, upstanding citizen. Twenty-one years ago, the disguise hadn't been nearly as pleasant. There had been sides. And those sides had their own doctrine. Step away from that doctrine and you were ostracized. Stay away and you were demonized, swallowed up by the evil agenda that was *them*. It was a beast that had fed itself until everybody was shouting and nobody was listening. The country grew more and more polarized, more and more enraged until Oswin Brahm swept in with a plan to stop it all.

Tragedy would unite them.

Ad Astra per Aspera.

Salvo Impetum.

Sanctus Diem.

Through hardship to the stars.

A saving blow.

A holy day.

It was all there in his pamphlet.

Concordia—the Roman goddess of harmony and peace—would become the venue through which they would now receive their news. Division was blamed. Then division was feared. That fear silenced, and that silence oppressed. Until somehow, they'd fallen into the same trap. Only this time, tyranny came disguised as unity. This became their battle cry. Unity at all costs. Subscribe to the doctrine. Parrot the doctrine. Don't question the doctrine. Don't doubt. Don't critique. Don't talk about the problems. Don't shine light on the problems. Don't *be* one of the problems. Follow the rules and life in post-Attack America would be peachy keen.

It was an ideology so deceptive, so ingrained, it wouldn't disappear overnight. America was broken. The solutions, complex. They would not come without disagreement or dissent. But did that need to be something to fear? Were they not capable of disagreeing without treating the person they disagreed with like vermin? Like cancer? Like something less than human?

As Eden held onto Cassian's hand, she wasn't sure. She possessed superhuman strength. Superhuman speed. Superior memory and reflexes and sensory processing. But she did not possess the gift of precognition. She couldn't see the future. She could only live it out, one step at a time, one day at a time, with the rest of humanity.

A knock sounded on the door.

A nurse came in with another delivery. This time, a wrapped box that rattled in her hand as she set it on Cassian's food tray. They were a mystery, these deliveries. Neither Cassian nor Eden knew how any of them had gotten his name or his location. But somehow, the deliveries kept arriving. Bouquets of flowers. Bunches of balloons. Children's drawings. And heartfelt letters from grateful mothers. All of them from the people Cassian had saved.

After he ran back into the fray, he successfully evacuated ninety. Whether it was intentional or subconscious, almost every single one of them was a child and a mother. Eden's own, included. Cass couldn't undo his past. He couldn't change his story. He couldn't save his mom. But he had saved these.

As the nurse slipped out of the room, he awoke. His eyes opened slowly. His thumb traced an unhurried circle in the center of her palm. "Hey," he said, smiling a lazy smile.

"Hey," she said back.

He noticed the box. "What's that?"

"A new delivery." She picked it up and handed it over.

It rattled like there might be Legos inside.

Cassian sat up and took the box sheepishly. He wasn't a fan of these gifts. He was just doing what anyone would have done, he said. But it wasn't true. What he had done was uniquely Cassian. He untied the ribbon and unwrapped the paper. He lifted the lid, and with eyes that had gone a little glossy, he reached inside and pulled out a box of macaroni and cheese.

Eden brought her hand to her mouth, covering a laugh. A sob. A mixture of both as Cassian removed a hand-drawn card from inside colored with crayons. A superhero in a cape, flying through a bright blue, sunlit sky, holding on to a woman and a child.

Mommy said the hotdogs would go bad. Thank you for saving her. LOL, Huck.

A photograph slipped free.

A picture of Isla with her arm wrapped protectively around her boy, who was smiling a giant, happy, gap-toothed grin as he hugged his mother's waist.

"There's something written on the back," Eden said.

Cass flipped it over and chuckled softly.

LOL. He thinks it means 'lots of love'. Thankful forever and ever, Isla.

47

The snow fell like tiny sparkles from the sky. Violet stood outside on the balcony of her suite in Alexandria, missing Barrett so much she physically ached.

Down below, people were congregating with candles in hand. The atmosphere in Alexandria had shifted. They were no longer working toward something, but away. They had defeated the bad man. The mass slaughter of illegal residents in Fredericksburg would have only been the beginning. Together, they had stopped the dominoes from falling.

Prudence Dvorak had gone public with her story. Harlan Wallace went public with his. His granddaughter, Renata, had been removed from the catacombs in Fort Wadsworth. She was currently en route to a peaceful hill-side with family members who had gone before her.

Harlan was getting to know his great-granddaughter, a superhuman eighteen-year-old girl named Nova. Through it all, he was also doing his best to point people to a news source that told the truth.

America Underground.

Dayne was hard at work, not just telling one person's story, but the whole story. The full account in a very special edition, which included a long list of obituaries honoring everyone who had lost their lives in this secret fight against evil. Amir Kashif and Jericho and Francesca. The Resistance members who never made it out of Washington, DC. The six prisoners who never made it to Alexandria. Those who were slain in Fredericksburg. Even the Electus who had been killed while under Brahm's control—a bold, unifying move that made the two sides feel like maybe they could be one. All the way down to the final name. The best name.

Eighteen-year-old Barrett Barr.

A boy who'd been kidnapped last summer. Maligned on national news in October. And saved the world before January. But before that, he'd saved her. A hundred different ways, with a thousand different stories.

Violet turned away from the balcony and walked inside the suite to the table where she'd left the photo book. She turned to the picture that was Barrett's favorite. Violet the Green Bird and her Magical Mother.

Tears welled.

Barrett didn't want her words to go away, and yet she could feel them sinking deeper and deeper into a dark chasm of grief.

A knock sounded on the door.

She pressed her hand against her stomach and took a shaky breath. She was nervous. So very nervous. But she made herself walk forward, toward the door. Toward the sound.

With trembling fingers, she twisted the knob and opened. Barrett's eyes twinkled back at her, only they were inside a woman's face. Barrett's smile beamed at her, only it belonged to an older man. His mother and his father, dressed in coats, holding candles.

Her tears thickened.

They're going to love you, he had said.

She already loved them.

How could she not when they had made someone as beautiful as Barrett?

"Violet," his mother said with a tremulous smile. "I feel like I already know you."

She reached down deep for her voice. When she couldn't find it, she reached further still. She kept reaching and reaching until she grasped the tail end of a word. She held on tight until the word turned into four. "He told me stories," she whispered. She swallowed and kept digging. "You used to ... draw him ... a dinosaur." A silly little picture his mother would slip into his lunch box every single school day in kindergarten. "One time, on a toilet."

His mother's eyes went wide and watery. She laughed as a tear spilled.

A tear tumbled down Violet's cheek, too.

The woman took Violet's hands.

They were cold, but they were strong.

Violet's were shaking.

Give my mom the tightest, biggest hug, he had said.

So she did. Violet stepped forward and wrapped her arms tight around his mother. She tried to hug her in the same way Barrett would have hugged her. The woman hugged her back just as tightly. Her hair was soft. It smelled like vanilla and peaches. When they came apart, his father's eyes were watering.

"He told us stories, too," he said. "Hitchhiking across state lines. Evading the enemy. Finding your way through the Minnesota woods. Riding beneath a government vehicle as stowaways for twelve hours straight. Crossing that terrifying bridge. Our boy always wanted to go on grand adventures. It sounds like that's what the two of you did."

Grand adventures.

Leave it to Barrett to make it sound fun.

His father was on a roll now, talking as easily as Barrett talked, his eyes smiling like Barrett's had smiled.

"He told us you were the bravest, most amazing girl he'd ever met."

More tears fell.

Tell them our stories, Violet. We have a lot of 'em now, don't we?

They did. And she would have to follow through on her promise.

His mother handed Violet a candle, put her arm around her shoulder, and together they went outside.

People had been hard at work all day, spray painting the names of the fallen into freshly packed mounds of snow. It was a temporary memorial until they could create something more permanent.

Hand-in-hand, they walked to Barrett's mound with their candles lit and snow falling all around. Violet tilted her face up to the sky, remembering the rush of wind as she flung her arms wide and flew down the hill on a cafeteria tray beside her best friend. She could hear his whoop. She could hear his voice, too. In her ear and in her heart. Barrett Barr, a boy filled with enthusiasm and warmth and every single thing she had needed.

She honored him alongside his parents.

And when the vigil was over and his mother had yet to let go of Violet's hand, she gave it a squeeze and extended an invitation. "We're on our way to Maine. It was his favorite place to be, so we thought we'd spend some time there. I'm not sure what your plans are, but we'd absolutely love to have you join us."

Go with them to Maine?

Violet swallowed and with a shy nod, accepted the invitation.

48

FOUR MONTHS LATER

"Happy birthday to you, happy birthday to you, happy birthday dear Jameson and Graham, happy birthday to you!"

Violet sang the words in a soft, whispery voice that blended in with the others as Barrett's dad set a chocolate-frosted cake glowing with twenty-one candles on the dining table.

"This is great and all, but we're twenty-one now, Dad," Jameson said with a wink.

Barrett's dad winked back, then pulled an expensive-looking bottle of cognac and three crystal goblets from the china cupboard against the dining room wall. He poured a small amount into each, capped the cognac, and returned it to the cupboard. The three men lifted their glasses.

"To twenty-one years of life!"

"To our first sip ever of alcohol!"

Their mother scoffed good-naturedly.

The twin twenty-one-year olds insisted it was true. Then the three men clinked their glasses together with a hardy *cheers* and took their drinks. Graham coughed. Jameson clapped him on the back. Everyone laughed.

They'd stayed in Maine for a month.

Violet had talked more than she'd ever talked before, telling them every story she could think of. At first, hesitant. Unsure. But the more of them she told, the easier they came. His mother treated each one like a treasure. And then, when Violet had no more to tell, no more treasure to give, Barrett's mom treated *her* like the treasure.

When the month was through, her words weren't so hard to find anymore. The bursts of overwhelming noise had diminished to once or twice a week. And Barrett's parents invited her to come with them to Idaho. She accepted, and there discovered that when she was properly fed and cared for and loved, she shared Barrett's voracious appetite for learning. Come the end of May, she would get her GED, and after that, they would return to Maine and spend the whole summer there.

In July, they would celebrate their birthdays—Violet's and Barrett's. She hoped Eden would join them. It would be her birthday, too. Cassian would probably come with. Maybe Cleo. Asher. Maybe even Ellery.

For now, they were celebrating the twins.

His mother cut her a giant piece of cake.

Graham told a funny story about his poli-sci professor that had his dad rolling. Violet took a bite of chocolate cake and smiled at the empty chair where Barrett would have sat.

Be brave, Vi. Be brave and live.

Every day, she heard his voice.

Every day, she felt his presence.

Every day, she chose to wake up and be brave. She missed him horribly. It was an ache that hurt like crazy and probably always would. But she made a point to laugh.

To love.

To live.

For the boy who had spent his whole life doing just that.

She stood tall and proud on her pedestal with a crown on her head and a torch held high, overlooking the sun-sparkled river. The air was crisp, with a gentle breeze that brought the sweet, powdery scent of wisteria. Eden wrapped her fingers around the handrail and tipped her chin to the sky—a pale blue with cotton candy clouds—and inhaled deep into her lungs.

Breathe Paris in. It feeds the soul.

Eden chuckled softly as she recalled Barrett's horrendous impression of a Parisian accent when he quoted Victor Hugo on the train tracks late at night. She took another deep breath, relishing the memory. Relishing the fresh air.

Paris in spring.

So far, the day had been spent strolling from one Statue of Liberty to the next, enjoying the pastel pink cherry blossoms and the street markets along the way. This was the last one. Lady Liberty in front of the Eiffel Tower.

Eden wore jeans and an oversized cable-knit sweater beneath an olive green bomber jacket with a beanie and a pair of sunglasses. Cassian's jeans were darker—almost black—with a pullover and a leather jacket and a five o'clock shadow. She liked to think they didn't look like tourists. She imagined them students at the university on an afternoon walk between classes.

She wasn't in college yet. She was still finishing her senior year of high school, despite having missed the entire first half. Since she could learn a year's worth of material in a couple weeks, her long period of absence hadn't been too much trouble. It felt silly, truth be told. Going back to high school after all that had happened. But Mom insisted and Eden wanted to be a college girl, which meant high school graduation had to come first.

As for Paris, she was no longer willing to wait to see the City of Lights.

Her parents had made it happen. They allowed her to invite Cassian, which made for some interesting, sometimes amusing dynamics. Tongue-in-cheek looks exchanged between herself and Dad. Cassian Gray had never been a boyfriend, certainly not the kind who went on family trips with his girl.

It was good though, this trip. Her parents were giving them space. Mom had written up a whole itinerary. Unlike Dad, who'd been plenty of places during his time in the military, then the CIA, she had been nowhere. Today was Notre Dame and the Louvre with a flower market and Sainte Chapelle in between. Then the four of them would meet up for dinner at eight.

Cassian set his hand over hers.

"She used to face east," Eden said. "Toward the Eiffel Tower, but in 1937, they repositioned her to face west, toward her sister in New York."

As she said it, she couldn't help but hear Barrett parroting the words. When she did her research on the plane, everything she read had been in his voice. *It was a joint project, a celebration of friendship between two nations.* If he were here with them now, he'd undoubtedly be a stream of chatter. A walking, talking enthusiastic encyclopedia.

"Lady Liberty," Cassian said, peering up at her.

A piece of art celebrating freedom.

Eden felt free, like the nightmare was really over. The sinister, mysterious force out there waiting to control her was no longer. She had made it through. But not without loss. There were more ghosts now than before. It was no longer just her big brother Christopher. There was Francesca and Jericho and the biggest ghost of all—Barrett. While she missed him deeply, she didn't think her ache held a candle to Violet's.

Eden hadn't seen her since Barrett's memorial service in February. But they did write letters. She wrote Tycho letters, too. Even Ellery, whom she hadn't officially met until after the worst was over. Still, they were irrevocably connected, and there was something wonderfully therapeutic about the old-fashioned practice of letter-writing.

"Is it everything you thought it would be?" Cass asked, the sun making his eyes a vibrant gold. A striking contrast to his long, dark eyelashes and his thick, equally dark eyebrows. He had a face that never failed to make her stomach swoop.

She thought about Cassian when she first met him—a mysterious, surly, gorgeous stranger inviting her onto the back of his bike. And before then, in a coffee shop in Eagle Bend, when she bent over to pick up an old woman's fallen change. He had, too. She should have known then his heart was the same color as his eyes.

"I think we should leave early," Eden said.

He pulled his chin back in surprise. This was Paris, after all. Her dream.

"Three days seems like plenty."

"Are you homesick?" He asked it doubtfully. Eden wasn't the type. Not when she knew her parents were safe and happy, sharing a glass of wine probably at one of the cafe terraces on their way to the Louvre. Besides, she'd never been homesick for a place. She'd only ever been homesick for people.

"I think we should go to Marseille." She turned to face him, then, with her hip leaning against the balustrade, ankle crossed casually over ankle.

He mirrored her posture and tipped her sunglasses so he could get a proper look at her eyes. "You want to go to Marseille?"

Eden nodded. "Tomorrow."

"Don't you think you should consult your parents first?"

"My dad already bought the train tickets. My mom really wants to see the Basilique Notre-Dame de la Garde."

And Eden wanted to walk with Cassian in Le Panier, stroll hand-in-hand with him along the harbor. Tread the same paths his mother had once trod, when she was there covering a decades old conflict that was no more. Cass had told Eden about it, opening up a little more each day. Sharing these places his mother had shared with him in pictures and descriptions, when they were living together in a cramped one-bedroom apartment. The more he shared these memories—the more he recalled her life—the less consumed he seemed to be with her death.

He looked at her with a furrowed brow, not in confusion. But surprise. Like he was glimpsing some facet of her he hadn't seen before, and he liked this facet. Her stomach dipped again. She loved when Cassian looked at her like this. He leaned closer with his hand on her hip, his thumb moving in a way that made her abdomen tight, her breath flutter.

"I was thinking about what you shared with me in Alexandria," she said, "after we buried Aurelia. How your mom doesn't have a gravestone." Eden ran her teeth over her bottom lip, taking care with his sadness. "I was thinking we could go for a hike on *Ile d'If* and make her one of those cairns."

A stack of small stones, built in her honor.

Cassian's mouth twisted slightly to the side. He glanced out at the water again, then up at Lady Liberty and the Eiffel Tower beyond, as if deep in thought. When his gaze returned to hers, his hand slid to the small of her back. He pulled her to his chest. He brushed his lips against her temple. He kissed her ear. The tip of her nose. Then he swept her hair from the nape of her neck and kissed the curve of her throat.

Eden's toes curled.

Her eyes might have rolled a little, too.

"I would like that," he whispered, his voice a deep hum against her skin.

Man, she loved him.

He pulled his lips away and smiled down at her a little wickedly, like he knew exactly what he was doing. With her skin flushed, she turned back to the balustrade to catch her breath. She set her elbows on top of it and leaned over the edge, looking down at her reflection in the water.

Across the Atlantic, America's identity was still in flux. A country trying to heal. A country trying to find itself. Meanwhile, most days, her own identity was sure and strong.

My name is Eden Pruitt, she thought. Recalling the words she had spoken to herself inside the Eagle Bend police department when her identity was unraveling.

I live at 3235 West Buckle Lane.

My parents are Ruth and Alexander Pruitt.

She had her father's eyes.

It was an impossibility.

But it was true, too.

A Parisian flight attendant had just said so three days ago when she handed them both a bag of pretzels.

Her reflection rippled with the breeze.

On the rare occasion her identity wobbled or slipped,

she had a mantra. Not the one from the police department, but the one her father had whispered when she was desperate and in pain and spinning out of control with a gun pointed at her mother.

Her name was Eden Pruitt. She was his and she was loved.

Cassian leaned over the balustrade, too, his reflection joining her own. And his mother's whispered words swirled in the breeze with her father's.

Voila. Tout au mieux.

Maybe not yet, but they were certainly on their way.

49

SUMMER

Tycho stood on the beach listening to the waves as a canopy of stars twinkled overhead. Inside the beach house behind him, a birthday dinner unfolded. A crowd of travelers toasted to Violet Winter, Barrett Barr, Eden Pruitt, and Ellery Forrester, four of the original six.

Except Ellery wasn't with them.

She sat several paces ahead, scooping up handfuls of sand and letting it slide through her fingers. Moonlight reflected off her auburn hair as foamy waves raced up to meet her toes. He wondered why she was out here when she could be in there, celebrating. She was an official member of the group, after all.

Unlike himself.

He still couldn't figure out why he'd come. He didn't have to accept Eden's invitation. The moment he arrived, he wished he hadn't. He didn't belong. He wasn't part of the original six. But he didn't feel part of the Electus anymore either. He didn't know how to connect with his brothers and sisters like he once had, before he was kidnapped by the Resistance. Before his entire identity was yanked out from beneath him. Even Knox seemed to march to a different beat than he.

He was trying with Prudence Dvorak, the mother he was poisoned to hate. Just last month, they'd traveled together to Colorado to visit Nova and her grandfather, a wealthy old man named Harlan Wallace. There had been some nice moments. But mostly, it was awkward.

Another wave raced up the sand. He closed his eyes and inhaled the briny air, remembering all the times he'd swam in this same ocean with Aurelia. He felt like a man missing a vital piece of his soul. Now that Pater was dead, he didn't know what to do with himself. He had no one to direct his anger at any longer. He was lost at sea, impossibly adrift. Missing Aurelia more and more each day.

The breeze ruffled Ellery's hair. He wondered what she was thinking. Subject 005—a girl with shadows under her eyes. It had been strange meeting her here. Their first encounter had taken place in Fort Wadsworth, when she'd been locked up against her will.

He approached quietly. Still, she heard him coming. Of course she heard. She turned and looked at him—a quick, unimpressed up and down glance before turning back to the ocean. "Are you lost?" she asked.

"A little," he admitted. He sat down beside her and corrected the lie. "A lot."

She huffed like she knew the feeling all too well. "I guess I'm not alone, then."

"You're lost, too?"

"Horribly."

He quirked his eyebrow.

"Do you know what it feels like to be lied to your whole life?"

"A little bit," he said with a definite note of satire. She'd just described his entire existence.

"My parents pretended to be my biological parents, but they aren't my biological parents. I had to sneak around to find the truth. And even then, my dad still fought to keep me in the dark. I was so angry. So positive I knew what I wanted."

"Which was?"

"To be activated. To be who I was meant to be. Then I was." She wrapped her arms around her shins and shivered. "Against my will."

Tycho frowned. Pater had subjected her to *cleansing*. Which was, of course, pure and utter abuse.

Ellery hugged her legs tight. "Seven months later, and I still feel disoriented."

So did he.

She let go of her legs and turned to face him. "Like … how am I supposed to know what's true anymore? My identity was in shambles when I was taken. Then that man—" Her expression soured, like someone sucking on a wedge of lemon. "He totally messed with my brain."

Now it was Tycho's turn to huff. He resonated with her words more than she knew. He scratched his head, then shifted his body so he was facing her, too. "It's baffling how fast we can learn."

She bobbed her head in that way that said *keep going. Tell me something profound.*

"We could pick a practice—any practice that strikes our fancy—and become experts within a week."

Her head bobbing continued.

"And yet, I think it will probably take a lifetime to untangle the lies I've been told." He shrugged. "I guess there's no superhuman shortcut to *un*learning."

Her mouth opened ever so slightly, like he *had* said something profound. She seemed to chew on his words. In the end, he suspected she liked their flavor. She set her chin on her knee and quirked her eyebrow at him. "What made you see the truth?"

His first inclination was to say Aurelia. Witnessing her death had done it. But then he stopped himself, because it hadn't started with Aurelia. Not really. The foundation of lies had been cracked before that, by a girl who treated him with kindness when everyone else had treated him like a leper. She'd given him a pillow and a bedroll, and she didn't laugh at the foolishness he believed.

He shared this with Ellery.

She seemed to like its flavor, too.

Tycho felt himself relax, the muscles in his chest unwind as the ocean whispered its nighttime lullaby. He didn't mind being out here with Ellery Forrester. Subject 005. A girl who seemed to hear the same drumbeat he did.

Sitting with her on this beach—someone who'd been wounded like him, who felt lost like him, was trying to find her way like him—made him feel a little less alone.

And for now, that was enough.

THANK YOU FOR READING!

IF YOU'RE READY FOR A NEW ADVENTURE,
CHECK OUT ...

THE CONTEST
A ROMANTIC FANTASY ADVENTURE

THE CONTEST
a novel
by Christy-award winning author
K.E. GANSHERT

ABOUT THE AUTHOR

K.E. Ganshert graduated from the University of Wisconsin in Madison with a degree in education. She worked as a fifth grade teacher for several years before staying home to write full time. Now she's an award-winning author published in two genres: contemporary fiction of the inspirational variety and young adult fiction of the fantastical variety. She is currently pursuing the latter.

Shop direct from K.E. Ganshert at
K.E. Ganshert Books

Stay in the know! Join K.E. Ganshert's email list and
receive 20% off your first order!

Made in the USA
Middletown, DE
01 September 2023

37753883R10257